HACK LIKE ME

Harold Fiske

WITH FILES FROM JOHN STINCHCOMBE

VIKING

VIKING

Published by the Penguin Group

Penguin Books Canada Ltd, 10 Alcorn Avenue, Toronto, Ontario,
Canada M4V 3B2
Penguin Books Ltd, 27 Wrights Lane, London W8 5TZ, England
Penguin Putnam Inc., 375 Hudson Street, New York, New York 10014, U.S.A.
Penguin Books Australia Ltd, Ringwood, Victoria, Australia
Penguin Books (NZ) Ltd, cnr Rosedale and Airborne Roads, Albany,
Auckland 1310, New Zealand

Penguin Books Ltd, Registered Offices: Harmondsworth, Middlesex, England

First published 1999

1   3   5   7   9   10   8   6   4   2

Printed and bound in Canada on acid-free paper ∞

CANADIAN CATALOGUING IN PUBLICATION DATA

Fiske, Harold 1951– .
Hack like me

ISBN 0-670-88785-4

1. Canadian wit and humor (English).*   I. Title.

PS8561.I84H32 1999   C818'.5402   C99-931269-3
PR9199.3.F5365H32 1999

Visit Penguin Canada's Website at **www.penguin.ca**

TABLE OF CONTENTS

FOREWORD

COMING TO TERMS WITH THE F-WORD

FOR THE past decade and a half, I've been hosting a Saturday morning radio show called *Basic Black* on the Canadian Broadcasting Corporation airwaves. It's a show that specializes in finding weird people in bizarre situations. I've talked to a transvestite calf-roper, a motorcycle-riding nun, a guy who spent three weeks perched on a flagpole and a woman who knits testicle warmers for prairie livestock.

I'm used to mixing it up with eccentric folks every Saturday morning, but I still develop a nervous tic in my left eye when my producer comes on the talkback and shrieks: "Fiske's up next—he's coming in now!"

Harold Fiske. You know what happens when you try to spell-check "Fiske" in a computer? It tells you there's no such word. Spellcheck suggests replacing it with "fiasco."

Who says computers are dumb?

Over the past fifteen years Harold Fiske has introduced me to a gun-toting tabloid editor, the reincarnation of Elvis, the discoverer of Mozart's skull, a pod of telepathic dolphins, and more of his twisted past lives than I care to remember.

When I hear the thunder of his size twelves outside the studio, I feel like a Christian in the coliseum. I have no idea what's going to happen next. But hey, I get paid big bucks to face Harold.

You're about to open his book voluntarily. What's your excuse?

Oh well . . . you can't say you weren't warned.

Arthur Black
Vancouver, B.C., October 1999

HACK LIKE ME

CHAPTER ONE

HACK LIKE ME

Portrait of the author as a young hack. Harold
at his desk at the *National Examiner* in July, 1980.

1. FISKE: THE FORMATIVE YEARS

Harold's salad days at the *National Examiner* and how he got to be such a big-time radio star.

PEOPLE I MEET never tire of asking me a couple of basic questions: "Harold Fiske," they say, "have you always been a decrepit, dishevelled and broken-down hack? Is no story too sacred for you to trivialize?" To which I always reply, "Enough with the questions already! I'm the journalist and I ask the questions around here!"

But now I guess I have to answer those questions, mostly because I'm now such a big radio celeb and people want to know more about the guy behind the voice on the airwaves. Fair enough, although I realize it's only a matter of time before you all turn on me. I warn you, however, my phone number's unlisted and I'm armed to the teeth.

I've been on CBC Radio's *Basic Black* show almost as long as it's been on the air—since 1984. As I'm writing this I realize I've done more than 225 items for the show, and heck, that's a rich mine of material to rehash and repackage into a book—with minimal work, too. The rehash-for-print is a fine tradition in Canadian broadcasting and I figure if Peter Gzowski, Stuart McLean and heck, even my *Basic Black* boss, Arthur Black, can do it, then why not me, too?

My first appearance on *Basic Black* grew from a sense of personal outrage and violation that I experienced when I first listened to the show back in 1984. As was my custom in those days, I was watching Saturday morning cartoons on TV when, during a commercial, I went to the kitchen to mix myself a refill of rye and cream soda, my favourite eye-opener.

My first wife was listening to the radio, and to my amazement, a CBC personality whose name I've long forgotten came on and started a commentary about supermarket tabloids. Weren't they just *too* wacky for words? And just who *were* the people who made up the stories that went into them? How could anybody read these trashy papers, much less buy them? And on and on it went.

The big weakness of her commentary was that none of these questions actually got answered. To paraphrase Anton Chekhov, when you ask an idiotic question in the first paragraph, you've got to lob back an equally stupid answer before the story ends. The second problem with her item was that she undoubtedly got *paid* for it. It's not that I object to people being paid for drivel (Lord knows, I've sold enough drivel to fill a ten-gallon drool cup), but that money should've been *mine*. I'm the one who knows about the tabloid newspaper world—I could've done a much better job than she did. Why couldn't they call *me* to do that?

In short order, the end of the show came up with the name of the big boss in the credits: John Disney. The following Monday I cabbed it down to the CBC's down-at-the-heels Jarvis Street radio studios and weaseled my way past security. I followed the signs through hallways strewn with insect parts and pigeon feces and eventually made my way to Radio Variety on the third floor. Disney, his name on the door, was in his office.

I launched straight into my rant about the abomination that had polluted the airwaves the previous Saturday, but instead of trying to find a weapon, Disney actually listened politely and wanted to know more. He also noticed I was carrying a fat red scrapbook.

It contained clippings from four years of tabloid toil, including such personal triumphs as "Junkyard Dog Digs Up Mom's Head," "Three Psychics Hunt Down FBI's Ten Most Wanted," and the unforgettable "UFO Base Under Lake Ontario."

Disney invited me to appear as an unpaid guest on the show the following Saturday. Guest-schmest, I told him—you stumped up for little Miss Pointy-Head Know-Nothing last time, you should pay for the *real* thing next time.

My winning ways must have impressed him, and he agreed to cut me a small cheque, so the next Saturday morning I was shoehorned into a vile telephone-booth-sized room that stank of sweat and stale cigarettes. If you've ever visited somebody in prison—hell, *been* in prison—you'll have an idea of what that radio studio was like.

Arthur Black, it turned out, wasn't even in Toronto at the time, but came over the land line from somewhere called Thunder Bay; I listened to him through a pair of greasy earphones.

That first item I did basically set up who I was and why I mattered. I gave a capsule history of how I came to work for the Globe tabloid newspaper chain and how I rose to the dizzying heights of news editor at the *National Examiner*, "America's Brightest Weekly," even though at the time it was entirely produced in Montreal, Quebec.

My story started back in 1978, the year the *Montreal Star* had a long, long strike—it lasted the better part of a year. When that strike ended and the paper was inking its back-to-work protocols, management realized that most of the *Star*'s editorial staff had gone and gotten jobs elsewhere—there were kids to feed, mortgages to pay.

The *Star* needed to staff up fast, so its editors raided one of the biggest employers of English-language journalists in town—the Globe Newspaper Group, publishers of supermarket tabloids like the *Globe* (it was called *Midnight* back then), the *National Examiner* and something called the *National Spotlite* (don't ask!).

The *Star*'s recruitment efforts were very successful. They matched the tabs' four-day work week and wages, and many Globe people were young and unaccountably greedy for journalistic respectability.

The *National Examiner* was the fourth largest supermarket tabloid in North America, with a circulation of close to two million, and when all the dust settled, it ended up with some serious personnel problems. The paper was so desperate for staff that its senior assignment desk editor had, just three weeks earlier, been the police-and-fire reporter at a rural weekly out of Elora, Ontario. This was an old buddy of mine, Ian, whom I met by chance in a bar in Old Montreal while all this raiding and recruiting was going on.

I hadn't seen Ian in ten years and, catching up, I told him I was an out-of-work journalist; my last job had been with the Ottawa *Citizen*. True enough—I *had* worked at the *Citizen* for about three months in 1975, as the guy who changes the paper rolls on the wire service machines. I didn't mention I'd been fired over some silly misunderstanding about taxi chits, and hadn't worked since.

The next day I got a frenzied phone call from Ian, asking me in for a try-out at the *National Examiner*. The try-out was completely bizarre. A copy editor gave me a pile of tabloids and told me to read through them and get the hang of the style. Then she gave me a clipping from the *Minneapolis Star-Tribune* and told me to rewrite it into a tabloid story.

The clipping, from the paper's cooking pages, was a recipe for some Mexican soup made with hot peppers—and buried down in paragraph 37 was something about Mexicans believing this was a good hangover cure.

With an instinct I can only describe as spinal, I sat down immediately and banged out a lead—something about docs discovering a miracle Mexican hangover cure. "Tequila-drinking Mexicans," I wrote, warming to my theme, "are known to medical science as the world's worst alcoholics, but thanks to an all-natural, just-discovered hangover cure, they can lead normal lives once again." Then I more or less listed the recipe as it had run in the original (I left out the peppers though—they give me gas).

I was hired immediately and what's more, the try-out piece was accepted for publication, with a $75 freelance fee paid on the spot out of petty cash. It went immediately into that week's paper—they were *really* hard up for material. My try-out was on a Wednesday and I told them I could start the following Monday, but they said forget that and shoved me towards an old Underwood manual typewriter. My very first staff-written piece, finished later that very day, was "Disco Dancing Can Kill or Cripple, Docs Say" (hey, it was the seventies).

I stayed at the *Examiner* off and on for the next four years, sometimes quitting in a huff, sometimes being ignominiously fired over some minor misunderstanding, like the time I insulted my supervisor in front of the whole newsroom or got caught smuggling cheap American cigarettes using the company's mailbox, just over the border in Rouse's Point, New York. But I always came crawling back to my dirty, stamped metal desk at 1440 Ste-Catherine St. West, usually with a promotion or a raise in pay.

My try-out was prophetic. That miracle-hangover-cure story led to my being assigned to the medical-science beat, which consisted of other miracle cures plus "courageous cripples" and the biggie: arthritis. The *Examiner*'s readers tended to be older folks, and they ate that stuff up. I also branched off into UFOs (it's "science," okay?) and, later, ghosts and psychics.

I kept detailed files of all the stories I'd written for the *Examiner*, files which were to stand me in good stead later when I started on *Basic Black*—I was able to recycle much of the material I'd already used once in the tabs, and now I'm able to re-purpose it yet another time for this book. That's one thing I've learned: don't throw stuff out—you never know when you'll be able to double—hey, triple—dip.

THE FIRST couple of years on *Basic Black,* the pieces I did were usually straight rehashes of earlier tab stories, generally based on beats I'd had at the *National Examiner*. I'd tell the folks at home about the stories I'd already written—stuff about oddball animals, Elvis, face-of-Christ sightings, or UFO abductions. We did funny follow-ups for both "Three

Psychics Hunt Down FBI's Ten Most Wanted" and "UFO Base Under Lake Ontario." But "Junkyard Dog Digs Up Mom's Head," never made the cut—it was just too weird for *Basic Black*.

"Remember, Harold," John Disney told me when I offered a genteel protest about this censorship, "it's a Saturday morning show when kids are listening. If you want excitement, go to Peru and join the Shining Path. You want to stay on the air, forget about that junkyard-dog-mom's-head thing."

Well put, I thought.

THE GUYS who worked at the tabs tended to be young journalists on the way up (like me) or broken-down old farts on the way out. The older guys often tended to be burnt-out alcoholics.

Ironically enough, about six months after I'd started working at the *National Examiner,* the *Montreal Star* went belly-up and all the ex-tab hacks who'd "gone over to the dark side" (*i.e.,* back to straight journalism) tried to get their old jobs back. Fat chance. Six months in a *real* newsroom is enough to ruin any talented writer—those guys were incapable of ever writing anything decent again.

They'd picked up terms like "narrative tension" (whazzat?) and spelt the first paragraph in a news story—the lead—as "lede." Their newly acquired conventional prose style had lost its adjectival snap. Their sentences and paragraphs would goosestep through a story like an army invading Poland. Good riddance, I say. Many of these folks now hold top positions in the Canadian media.

HOW COME we had a big tabloid newspaper industry in Canada in the 1970s? To answer that, you have to go back to the 1960s, when the legendary Joe Azaria started *Midnight*. It specialized in local crime, sex and what are known in the trade as "dead baby soup" stories.

It's rumoured Azaria started *Midnight* after he was treated like crap during a job interview with the *Montreal Star*. As a young grad from Sir George Williams University, he was so upset by the paper's refusal to hire him that he started his own paper.

After a decade of running from obscenity charges and distributing the rag from the trunks of taxicabs, he sold out in the mid-seventies, to his accountants, the Rosenbloom brothers. Azaria retired to Costa Rica, where he reportedly lives like a feudal prince to this day.

It was the Rosenblooms who realized that the future of the tabloid newspaper was at the supermarket checkout counter, where it can be impulse-bought while you're waiting to pay for your groceries. America's biggest tabloid, the *National Enquirer,* had already figured out this marketing strategy and recreated itself, abandoning sex and gore, and focusing on celebrities and the bizarre. The change to a gentler format resulted in massive sales, making the *Enquirer* the largest circulating paper in North America, selling about five million copies a week.

The Globe tabloids followed in the *Enquirer*'s footsteps a few years before I came aboard, and by the late seventies, they were the foundation of a multimillion-dollar business employing scores of editors and journalists in Montreal.

At the *National Examiner* (and that's *not* the *National Enquirer,* although we probably sold hundreds of papers to people who confused the names), we wrote as "American" journalists, even though we were sitting at desks in Montreal. Why? Because 95 percent of the circulation was in the U.S. On the rare occasion we did run a Canadian story, events took place "up there in Canada." We used American spellings and speech style for all our stuff.

We were assisted in this misrepresentation by the fact that we all had phone numbers in New York City—calls were automatically forwarded (and this was very sophisticated technology in 1978) from Globe's mini-offices on 42nd Street. This sometimes had wacky consequences, like the time the *National Enquirer* came on a raiding mission. They'd hired a New York headhunter to quietly approach four *National Examiner* writers (including me), and we agreed to go down to Lantana, Florida for a six-week tryout (starting at US$1,200 a week—big cash in the late seventies, but chickenfeed today).

Screw the *National Examiner*, we told each other in the bar that night—this is real money, this is Florida calling! This is the major leagues! We even planned the trip down to the last detail: we'd get a drive-away car, a white Cadillac, and take nothing with us but a change of underpants and a few cases of Thunderbird wine, which we'd pick up in Plattsburgh, just over the border. Then we'd point that fishtailing sucker south on I-87 and say goodbye to Montreal winters forever— hello Florida, and six weeks of living in a cheap Palm Beach motel!

When the *Enquirer*'s headhunter called and told us to come on over and sign the contracts, we told him we'd be there the next day, because we had to drive down to New York from Montreal. "Wait a minute," he said. "You're not over on 42nd Street?" It turned out he'd fallen for the phone gag and actually thought we worked locally at the New York office. Since he was able to dial us up with a local call, there was nothing to indicate we were three hundred miles north. The last thing he wanted to deal with was Canadians and their immigration problems. Just like that, the deal was off. Bye-bye, guys.

AROUND 1981, the Newspaper Guild suddenly realized there was a huge number of journalists at the Globe group who didn't enjoy the benefits of union membership, so they came over to our office and organized. Their drive was very successful—the Guild managed to sign up about 82 percent of the bargaining unit over one weekend.

Why so successful? The writers and editors weren't unhappy about what they were paid (they did slightly better—sometimes a lot better— than at the local dailies), but job security was lousy and everybody was mad at the company about their friends being victimized by high-handed firings.

The Globe group was very capricious about dismissals. It would throw editors and writers out with the trash on a moment's notice. The big thing was to make it through a Thursday. The paper had a four-day week and that was the last working day. Firings would always happen at 5:45 P.M. (the place shut down at 6:00), and things started getting tense in the newsroom at about 4:30. Once the week was over and we'd survived, the relief was palpable, and we'd all head to the bar and drink our faces off, mostly because we were celebrating still having a job.

The company responded to the certification a couple of months later by firing *everybody* and moving lock, stock and barrel to Boca Raton, Florida (a "right-to-work" state), where the company continues to do business to this day.

The day that everyone got fired started normally enough. Then after lunch, Madge, the lady who usually handed out the paycheques, came around and gave everybody a pink slip and a cheque for wages and vacation pay. And the next thing we knew, all these professional wrestlers showed up—muscle hired to herd everyone out onto the street.

The closure killed about seventy journalism jobs in Montreal and it got a two-inch story in the Montreal *Gazette* the next day. Local CBC-TV covered the closure but only because an ex-tab hack worked there and persuaded his producer it was an important local business story (which it was). That was the end of the Montreal English tabloid industry—and nobody much cared except those who'd worked there.

Most of the people who got sacked have gone on to other journalism jobs, and a lot of them are well-known public figures so I won't "out" them here. It seems I'm the only one who kept doing tab stories, even if it's just on the radio every few weeks.

And every few weeks is just fine with me. Any more than that and things begin to pall. Tab reporters find the first six months of their jobs are heavenly—they can't believe their good luck in getting such an interesting and funny job. For the next six months it's just a job, and after that, the ridiculousness of it all begins to dawn on you. Sane writers begin to wonder if they were really placed on this earth to write stories on Jackie Kennedy Onassis's menopause—I'm dating myself, I know. We called these awful realizations "inanity attacks."

WHILE I hadn't intended to rehash my *Examiner* stuff indefinitely, *Basic Black* went on far too long—year after year. As a veteran of the tabs, I expected to be fired every week—I couldn't understand why they kept having me back, so I eventually ran out of material I could rejig for the show.

"Fiske, you're slicing your baloney pretty thin," said executive producer John Disney. "Time for you to go out and actually do some work."

That's when I started chasing down new and fresh tab stories for *Basic Black,* using exactly the same skills and tricks I did at the *National Examiner.* The idea was, I would get assigned a story by the producers, or find one myself, and go out and do it for the radio, although in tabloid style.

Not everything in the tabloid world transfers easily to the radio. Radio is a medium that doesn't use pictures, but the tabloids are very picture-oriented. That was one key rule for all stories: "Get pix." A story would be killed if there wasn't a good visual, so if there were no pictures you went and got some. The local police sketch artist was a good person to start with and most tabs have freelance illustrators available for "artist's conceptions."

Even for *Basic Black* radio stuff I still try to get pictures for every story I do—you never know when you'll be able to rehash the story for another medium, and they'll turn into cash-flow.

II. EAT *ALL* THE SEAFOOD FIRST

Harold proves you can survive, and thrive,
without ever having to pay for a meal, thanks
to press parties, receptions and freebies.

THE REPORTER'S craft should not be viewed as mere information-
gathering, but also as an opportunity for personal enrichment.
This doesn't mean taking cash payments from sources for doing the
stories they want—only public relations people are lucky enough to get
those kinds of perks. But it *can* include a host of free samples, food,
books, junkets, admissions, entertainment and gifts.

Always say yes when offered free food and drink while on a story—
and for heaven's sake, don't ruin things by actually writing something
after you get the free stuff. The trick is to get on public relations agents'
mailing lists for invites to movie screenings, book launches, receptions
and other gala parties. If you have *any* influence at a publication, even
if you're a freelance ad salesperson for *Drywaller's Quarterly*, don't be
afraid to abuse your power. And once you're at a media event, suck up
shamelessly.

A few years back, as a controlled experiment for *Basic Black*, I tried
to see if I, as a laboratory rat, could survive for a week solid on *nothing*
but PR media-event food. I ate only what I could scavenge at press parties, and even though I'm not exactly on anybody's A-list, I managed to
pull it off. I wheedled my way into three or four affairs a day and dined
magnificently on finger food for a solid week.

But there was a downside. I had to endure inane banter from the other cheap media hounds who show up at these functions like a pack of ravening dogs fighting over a bone. And the folks hoovering down the buffet are never the ones actually writing about it—those guys rarely eat anything, or even show up, for that matter. They'll do it all on the phone the day before—if you really have to work, why leave the office?

Plus, you have to be willing to turn your liver into a football, to clog up your arteries with fat—the food at these affairs is mostly cheese-based cuisine or fatty nitrogen-laden sliced meat. After a week of these events, my big toe swelled up with gout and my doctor put me on some nauseating drug to cure it. (While it's still not a healthy diet, things are better these days thanks to those little trays of crudités—bits of cucumber, cauliflower—so there's enough roughage creeping into the buffets to keep you regular.)

One reception had an all-organic, mostly vegetarian food tray with sprigs of basil arranged around it—all very healthy. The only thing was, there wasn't enough of it. I mean, I'm a growing boy. I need handfuls of these things.

And one party cut me off after one miserable little shrimp and one minuscule prosciutto-and-melon-ball thingy. Seconds? Forget it. I ended up scarfing down the toothpicks. At least that way I worked a little fibre into my diet.

If any of this sounds the least bit palatable, the good news is that you don't have to be a journalist to hop onto this gravy train. Go down to one of those insta-print places and have a fake press card made up. Flash it as you go in—they never turn the press away at these things.

And once you've conned your way into the event, you'll need these four simple survival tips:

- Arrive fashionably late. Once the party's started, any PR flack who could throw you out will be too busy to notice you. Also, that way they won't get a chance to bug you with "suggestions" on how to write your story which, of course, you have no intention of doing anyway.

- Bail out when the speeches start. When you hear the polite applause and somebody walks up to a podium, that's your cue to head for the door. Don't worry about being noisy or offending people; you won't be going back there again anyway.

- Spend *all* your time at the buffet—it's amazing how quickly food disappears at these affairs.

- Memorize the media freeloaders' mantra: *Eat the seafood first.* It's always the most expensive stuff on the table, plus with seafood, you want to get to it early, before anyone else eats it all, or before it starts to go bad.

III: TOO HOT TO HANDLE

Finally revealed! The meaty stories the tabloids and the oh-so-holy CBC just wouldn't let Harold tell.

I T'S NOT TRUE that tabs will print anything—I personally saw several stories the *National Examiner* wouldn't touch, not for reasons of good taste, but because the writers feared for their personal safety.

A good example was a story headlined on one cover proof: "Elvis Was Gay." We thought we'd gotten a hot story and we'd set up the header in 288-point type. It was ready to go to the printer and we figured we'd sell millions of copies.

Just to give a little background on this before you Elvis fans go into shock, Elvis was *not* gay . . . as far as we know. Basically, what we had was a Memphis hairdresser who claimed he'd had a long-time homo-sexual relationship with Elvis. The King had supposedly given him gifts, Cadillacs, a hair salon. When the publisher read that, he had a fit and killed the story.

Now, Elvis sold newspapers like nobody else, but our readers wanted *nice* stories about Elvis. You've got to understand who the tabs are written for. When I joined the *National Examiner* I was told to imagine I was writing my stories for a fifty- or sixty-year-old woman in Mobile, Alabama who was sitting in a laundromat watching her dryer spin. And boy, could those gals be mean and vicious.

The publisher was still smarting from a story we'd already run called "Elvis Hated His Father." We got a ton of hate mail over that one, including a cardboard box full of death threats. He wasn't going down that dark alley again. "Elvis Was Gay" never saw the light of day.

IN "Dolly Parton Turns Commie" we tried to argue that because country-and-western star Dolly had co-starred in *Nine to Five* with "Hanoi Jane" Fonda, that meant she had "gone Commie." We claimed she had contacts with some socialist groups and, in fact, we interviewed some socialists who admitted they'd seen the movie—and liked it. Ironclad proof! The editor nixed that one. "Too un-American."

I'VE ALREADY said that stories without pictures often didn't make it into the paper, so when we got a story with the working title "A Hay Baler Ate My Legs," we did our work too well.

What had happened was, a farmer in the midwest somewhere had fallen into a hay baler and the thing had chewed off his legs, "inch by agonizing inch," while he screamed to high heaven.

We called up a local photographer for the rural weekly paper in the guy's area and we told him to shoot pictures in *exactly* the following order: "First take pictures of the farmer inside his house in his wheel-chair, and showing the stumps of his legs. Then take him out to the yard and shoot him next to the baler, pointing at it and looking angry. Then put him back into the hay baler that ate his legs, to 'reconstruct' the scene." The pix had to be shot in *exactly* that order in case the guy got mad and threw the photog off his land—at least we'd have something in the can.

But the farmer didn't mind the reconstruction shots a bit. He cheerfully jumped out of his wheelchair and walked on his hands back up onto the baler and popped himself back in the hopper. Then he started waving his arms around and pretending to be in agony. We thought it was great stuff but the editor, John Vader, killed the whole story. "Too weird," he muttered, after taking one look at the pix.

"MR. LUCKY," somewhere in Arkansas, won a contest and got to walk into the local bank's vault where they'd placed a huge pile o' cash, and he could keep all he could carry out in one double armful. He ended up getting about $12,000. I wrote the story and we had great pix of him coming out with the armload o' dough, but the story never ran because he couldn't keep his mouth shut.

When I asked him how he felt he said, "I ain't had so much fun since the hogs ate my baby brother and made me the baby again." The comment was enough to get the story killed. I argued it was just a quaint local expression, but the editor wanted no part of the whole weird Faulkneresque subtext.

SOMETIMES there were entire beats where even hacks like me feared to tread—take local cults, for example. After the Jim Jones Jonestown Kool-Aid cult mass murder-suicide thing in Guyana, strange cults became the hot tabloid flavour-of-the-month, but we had standing orders not to cover cults, at least not locally or within driving distance of Montreal. The ones in California were okay.

Our troubles started when we did a Jonestown-style treatment of a local group called The Apostles of Infinite Love, which was located in the Laurentians just north of Montreal. We'd interviewed some local guy who claimed they'd kidnapped his wife and kids and we never bothered to get the group's side of it, so they became the apostles of infinite anger.

It turned out they were a strange little Catholic splinter group led by a guy who called himself Pope Grégoire. There were also female adherents who dressed up as nuns, in full habit.

About three weeks after our story ran, my buddy Ian, who'd set me up with my tabloid job, got a buzz from Peggy, the Globe receptionist. "Ian, you better get out here," she told him.

Ian, who'd stupidly put his real name on the story, went to the front foyer and was immediately confronted by three nuns dressed in long dark robes. One of them said menacingly, "Ian? We have something for you," then reached slowly into her habit and pulled out a dark cylindrical object.

At that point, Ian freaked out and grabbed the nun and threw her up against the wall, then started patting her down to see what kind of lethal weapon she was packing.

It turned out the nuns wanted to give him a scroll they'd made using ornate calligraphy. It demanded a retraction and an apology from the paper.

You can imagine the stink over this. And even though the cops were called, the nuns wouldn't leave. In fact, we couldn't get rid of them for three weeks and we had to come in the fire escape door the whole time.

When they finally ended their occupation, we were forbidden to cover local cult stories and the free-and-easy days at the *Examiner* were gone forever.

The company installed a brand-new, state-of-the-art electronic security system in the front entrance lobby. It was so complex that it was a total pain in the ass, so we just came and went by the fire escape from then on.

BACK IN the early eighties, I wrote a *National Examiner* story, "Hairdresser to the Dead," about a Canadian lady who lived in Hollywood, Florida—Noella Papagno. Noella's aim in life was to make sure that deceased persons were adequately coiffed when they went on to their next lives. And she'd written a book she was anxious to flog, *Desairology: Hairdressing for Decedents.*

Originally from Montreal, she was a wonderful interview on the phone. She told me all about what she did and sent me before-and-after pictures of dead ladies with very nice hair-dos indeed. (See for yourself at the start of Chapter Six.) But when I filed the story, the editor just said; "Forget it. We don't put pictures of dead people in our newspaper." Then he killed the whole story—and he was the one who'd assigned it in the first place.

The really sad part was that sweet Noella called me up a few months later and said, "What happened to the story? The book's failing. Nobody wants to buy it. I've had dozens of interviews with the press but nobody's printed a thing about my book. I can't understand it."

I always remembered her story and made it my personal mission to get word of Noella and her book to the masses.

I finally succeeded in March 1987, when I got to host *Basic Black* while Arthur went on vacation. I got to line up the guests to be interviewed and Noella was my first pick.

I asked her where her coined word, "desairology," came from and she told me *d-e-s* came from "deceased," *a-i-r* from "hair" and the suffix *-ology* meant a branch of learning. And that pretty much sums up what the book is about. She told me she got started in her fascinating line of work after she graduated from hairdressing school at the age of seventeen.

The lady who ran the beauty parlour where she worked sent her across the street "to fix the dead lady's hair," something she'd never learned in beauty school. Noella realized that, even though hairdressing for decedents had existed as a subdiscipline of cosmetology for the past fifty years, "hairdressers always feel threatened when they have to do it."

Noella realized that "promoting understanding" was the only way to dispel the terror most stylists feel when creating a 'do for the dead. Education was the key, she thought, teaching hairdressers to "disassociate their feelings about dead bodies" and focus on the creative elements of doing hair. She thought that would be easy, because "hairdressers love their work," whether the customer's alive or dead.

Hairdressers come to the funeral home with a lot of preconceived notions about what's involved with hair-styling for the dead so her book, she hopes, will "dispel ignorance on the subject."

It's not just hairdressers who are ignorant when it comes to styling for the dead, but the consumer actually paying for the service, says Noella. Some funeral directors charge as much as $150 to have the decedent's hair done. Sometimes the funeral home marks up the hairdresser's fee and sometimes it's the stylist herself who charges such outrageous prices. Hairdressing the dead creates "a situation ripe for abuse," Noella agreed. She thinks $40 is a fair price for a hairdresser to charge when she has to leave the shop and go to a funeral home.

Noella even advises putting a clause in your will so the decedent's regular hairdresser can come by and do her client's hair one last time. Not only will the price be reasonable, but a decedent's longtime hairdresser will know what the dearly departed would have chosen as a hairstyle for her final public appearance.

But one question burned in my brain as I pressed on through my interview with Noella—and finally, I tentatively asked her. "Does your hair continue to grow after you pass on?"

"It depends," said Noella, taking the question in her stride. "Maybe if a person dies and is buried within twenty-four hours, and isn't embalmed, then it might just continue growing for a little bit. But otherwise, really, it doesn't, because, like grass, you need water to feed the grass and the same thing with hair. You need a good active nutrient system or it does not grow. You don't have that if you're dead."

NOW, even though *Basic Black* ran a story the tabs wouldn't print, the show's producers, and even Arthur himself, have scotched items that the public deserves to hear. The ugly spectre of editorial interference, and in fact outright censorship, has reared its head at times:

> **Arthur:** Well, as promised, *Basic Black's* guru of the gutter press, Harold Fiske, is with us again. Harold, you're looking more smug and self-satisfied than usual—like the cat who ate the canary. What gives?
>
> **Fiske:** Arthur, I bring news of some cutting-edge research that's being done at the University of Wisconsin's Foundation for Health Research and Education in Madison—the groundbreaking work of Dr. James W. Jefferson and his colleagues, who are exploring a facet of human behaviour that touches millions of us and yet about which little is known . . . the disorder called "rhinotillexomania."
>
> **Arthur:** I don't doubt the research is groundbreaking, Harold, considering I've never even heard of rhinotillexomania. What is that?
>
> **Fiske:** How about we let Dr. Jefferson tell us. I've got him on tape:
>
> **Dr. Jefferson:** Rhino, meaning pertaining to the nose; tillexo-, meaning to pick at; and mania, something done in excess.
>
> **Fiske:** In other words, excessive nose-picking. Okay, Dr. Jefferson, what does your study of nose-picking tell us about our humanity and, indeed, the human psyche?

Before the vast radio audience could listen to Dr. Jefferson's wise words, Arthur angrily interrupted my interview and signalled the technician to stop the tape.

As millions of listeners sat stunned by his high-handed gesture of censorship, Arthur bellowed at me from across the country (he was in the Vancouver studio, I in Toronto); "That's enough, Harold! That makes three times you've tried to get that supposedly scientific study of nose-picking on this show," he raved. "I said no in 1995. I said no last year. What part of 'no' don't you understand? It ain't going on—not now—not ever!"

Arthur's reaction was, of course, a classic study in hypocrisy. Two weeks earlier he'd had a woman on talking about the history of mucus, phlegm and burping, and that was just fine. And then there's his legendary interview with "Mister Methane," the British entertainer who makes music by passing gas. That one not only got the CBC seal of approval, it was repeated—twice!—as a *Basic Black* "classic." But a serious and genuine study on nose-picking, by a respected scientist? Forget it.

As a courtesy I called Dr. Jefferson back later and explained how Arthur had killed the interview. His reaction was immediate and succinct: "Obviously a closet nose-picker," he said.

CHAPTER TWO

INDIANA FISKE

The man who was reincarnated nine, count 'em, nine times!

I ADMIT IT.

I've been "shovelling it" most of my life—it's what I do for a living. If you haven't figured that out by now, then you haven't been paying attention. Your average wussy pack of reporters is afraid to get their hands (not to mention their Armani duds) dirty. They're too chicken to go rooting through dumpsters and generally mucking around with the kind of material the tabs wallow in.

Me? Hell, I'm knee-deep in dirt and I shovel it with pride. Me *and* Harrison Ford both. Let's face it, Indiana Jones and I have a lot in common (aside from an uncanny physical resemblance and a penchant for bullwhips). We are, in fact, brother archaeologists travelling the globe in search of buried treasure. He's got his Holy Grail and his Lost Ark, but I've got my own treasure trove of archaeological sites that I've looted and sacked.

I: WHERE'S THE MEAT?

Archaeologist Confirms:
MAN-EATER BAD TO THE BONE

or maybe . . .

Scientist unearths terrible truth:
COLORADO CANNIBAL CARVED UP CLIENTS

or better yet . . .

Forensics find filleted five:
DENVER MEAT PACKER MUNCHES MATES!

THESE DAYS I do most of my tabloid work on the radio, and I confess that, on occasion, I do miss the glorious ink-stained reality of actually seeing my stories in print. So, for old time's sake, I still like to work up a snappy in-your-face headline for all my radio items.

This time it was a piece of cake. Those inspired little tab-worthy nuggets seen above flowed out of me like poop from a goose while I was in Denver digging up some dirt on the famous "Colorado Cannibal." I say famous because, although he may not be a household name in the rest of the world, Alferd (yes, I spelled it right) Packer is a really big deal in Denver.

Dozens of learned historical tomes have been written about Alferd "Meat" Packer, and songs have been sung about his grisly deeds.

In fact, he's so infamous that a local university even named its cafeteria after the guy. I'd like to meet the genius who thought *that* one up. He really hit the PR mother lode. Linking cafeteria cuisine and cannibalism has turned the place into a must-see stop on the Denver tour bus circuit (I recommend the ribs). But, as you're about to see, the University of Colorado cafeteria wasn't the first business to make a killing riding the coattails of the Colorado Cannibal.

Alferd Packer's saga started in Utah. It was back in the late fall of 1874 and a bunch of city slickers were getting a stake together. These five greenhorns were planning on prospecting for gold in the Colorado Rockies and they needed a guide. That's how they ran into our boy Packer.

Alferd Packer was a petty thief and a pretty good liar and he convinced these would-be miners that he knew the Rocky Mountains like the back of his hand. He offered to lead the suckers down the Mormon Trail, through a mountain pass, on into the Colorado goldfields and, from there, straight into prospector paradise. The rubes bought Packer's story hook, line and sinker.

They set out and before too long they met a famous local Indian chief who warned, "Whatever you do, don't go through that mountain pass, because it's going to snow and you'll be stuck in there all winter."

Now remember, Packer was a phony. He was no more a mountain guide than *I* am, and the old Indian could see that these fellas were in a mess of trouble. They didn't have enough equipment or food or winter clothing or anything, but there was no talking to guys with gold fever. They ignored the warning and forged ahead with Packer leading the way into that mountain pass. Sure enough, before the day was out—*kablooey!*—they got coldcocked by the worst winter storm in Colorado history.

Bear with me a bit while I put Alferd and his prospecting pals on hold. I want to introduce you to Thomas Noel. He's a professor of history at the University of Colorado in Denver. He's known locally as "Doctor Colorado" because this guy knows more about Colorado than the Pope knows about Poland. I looked him up when I was down in Denver and I got him to pick up the sad saga of Alferd Packer where I left off.

"Alferd Packer," Professor Noel told me, "emerged from the wilderness all alone with a tale of woe. How first off his expedition was snowed in. How they had a run-in with Indians and how they had all kinds of problems. Packer claimed that his party was facing starvation and that all the other prospectors had died and that he was the only one who had been spared.

"But," Noel continued, "people looked at Packer and you know how a man looks when he's well fed, when he's eaten a lot of beef? He looks kind of bloated, with a happy look. That was Packer. Here was a man who was supposedly starving but the first thing he asked for when he came out of that mountain pass was not food but *whisky*! On top of that, Packer was broke when he went in there but he came out with a lot of money.

"It wasn't until that spring when things began to thaw that people got up into the mountains and found bits of the flesh and bones of those prospectors. They got suspicious and started questioning Packer again. There was a kind of shifty uneasy look and feel to the man, and he started changing his story.

"Under pressure he finally admitted that he *had* eaten *one* of the victims. But he claimed that the prospectors had killed each other, and he had come back and found this grisly scene. At that point, starving, he'd had his . . . well, his supper.

"Well, Packer," said Noel, "was tried in Hinsdale County where this alleged crime was committed, and as the judge (a strong Democrat in the county) put it, 'Packer, you man-eating son-of-a-bitch, I sentence you to hang! There were only seven Democrats in Hinsdale county and you ate five of them!'" According to the professor, "That judge wanted to jerk Packer to Jesus right on the spot."

But Packer *didn't* hang. Remember, Professor Noel said that the Colorado Cannibal was sentenced by a *Democratic* judge. Packer appealed his case and, lucky for him, the appeal court was made up of Republican judges who commuted the death sentence to forty years in the slammer. But Packer did even better than that. He actually got out in 1901 after serving just seventeen years—and it was all thanks to the *Denver Post*.

Back then, the *Post* was having a big circulation crisis. It was just a small-to-middling rag, a far cry from the big-city publication it is today. So they were desperate to sell more papers, and we all know nothing sells papers like an innocent man railroaded into doing hard time. So the *Post* took up Alferd Packer's cause. They started an all-out campaign to free the "innocent and wrongly incarcerated" Colorado Cannibal.

Right from the beginning, the prosecution's case had been that, when that winter blizzard hit, the prospectors were trapped in the mountain pass with next to no food, and Packer had decided to kill the other five men in cold blood. He killed them for their money and for the meat on their bones to keep himself alive.

But the *Denver Post* said that was all a pack of lies. They were partial to the latest version of the story that Packer was spinning. He had finally admitted that, yes, he *did* kill one of the prospectors. But that was in self-defence because that guy had already done in the other four prospectors and then had tried to kill Packer, too. And Packer *did* admit to cannibalizing the remains, but only as a last resort, when at the point of starvation, and even then, he ate "just enough to barely keep alive."

The *Post* campaign was a huge success. They sold a ton of papers and they got Packer a new trial. He was acquitted and released in 1901. He died seven years later.

Was justice done? Was the Colorado Cannibal in fact innocent? Was Alferd "Meat" Packer really just a victim of circumstance and a cannibal not out of choice, but out of necessity?

That was left to the archaeologists to decide. Back in the summer of 1989, a crack team of forensic bone experts dug up the remains of Alferd Packer's alleged victims. They found what little was left of the bodies all buried in the same town but not, as you might expect, in some anonymous mass grave. No, they were respectfully laid out side by side in a string of five adjacent plots, all nicely marked so that individual identification was not an issue.

The scientific team that unearthed the Colorado Cannibal's victims was led by James Starrs, a professor of law and forensic science at George Washington University in Washington, D.C. He told me some of the naked truths his research had uncovered about the Colorado Cannibal.

"Alferd Packer," he said, "did two things that we do not condone in our society. One: he murdered those [five] men. Two: he cannibalized them from top to bottom and stem to stern."

According to Starrs, Packer's story about how he only killed one of the prospectors and how he only did that in self-defence was "at least hogwash, or worse. Packer claimed that he was being attacked and that he was defending himself, when in fact, Shannon Wilson Bell (the one Packer said was attacking him) had defensive wounds all over his left arm."

But that wasn't the half of it. "In addition," Starrs went on, "Bell had five hatchet wounds to his head. Those blows could hardly have been inflicted by Packer if he were defending himself *against* Bell. Obviously, the reverse is true."

Obviously? Starrs's conclusions weren't so obvious to me. Who's to say those prospectors weren't mauled by some grizzly bear then gnawed by a pack of hungry wolves? I mean, how much can anybody know for sure by looking at scratches on old bones that have been lying around rotting in a grave for over a hundred years?

To hear Professor Starrs tell it, a hell of a lot. "We were very lucky," he told me. "We found the bones in beautifully well-preserved condition. They were 115 years in the ground and it was as if they had been buried yesterday. They were eminently analyzable."

What Starrs's eminently analyzable bones categorically revealed was not the savage attack of some ravenous beast of prey, but rather the meticulous systematic butchery of the human hand. "We found nicks aplenty," Starrs explained. "More than three hundred knife marks following the curvature of the bone, indicating a concerted effort to de-flesh, to cannibalize. There was no dismemberment. Just de-fleshing.

"When Packer emerged some two months after the killings, I'm sure that if a blood test could have been taken he would have had a very high cholesterol level. We found that all the bodies had all the meat taken off. Packer ate human flesh fillets three times a day."

Which, it turns out, is the main reason the bones were in such great shape when Starrs disinterred them. By stripping the carcasses of every edible ounce of human flesh, Packer had cut down both the available meat for animals to fight over and the opportunity for the bodies to putrefy. What Packer left behind wouldn't draw flies, let alone be torn apart by scavengers. The pristine condition of those tell-tale skeletons from Alferd Packer's closet didn't leave much to the imagination.

Packer's five victims were pointing their bony fingers right at the Colorado Cannibal. And curiously, his chief accuser, the most prominent of the five suckers he snacked on, turned out to be a Canadian.

"His name," Starrs told me, "was Israel Swan. He was born in Upper Canada, which I take it is now the province of Ontario. Swan was probably the most prominent member of the five that were killed. One, because at fifty-eight, he was the oldest; and two, because he was the wealthiest—he probably had three hundred dollars or more on his person at the time.

"He was the *only* person of the five for whom Alferd Packer was convicted of murder. The prosecutor chose to prosecute the killing of Israel Swan because it was the most brutal of all."

How brutal? Remember Packer whining about how the only killing he did was in self-defence? Well, that story was a bit of a stretch in the case of Israel Swan. According to Professor Starrs, Swan died in his sleep. "They found that the blanket he had been lying under, trying to keep warm, was imbedded by reason of a hatchet blow *right into his skull!*"

Professor Starrs had, of course, figured this stuff out through sound, careful, objective scientific methodology. Still, for all his detached scientific objectivity, I could hear an awful lot of naked disgust in the man's voice. So I asked him if he'd learned enough about Packer to paint me a psychological profile of the Colorado Cannibal.

"I would say this. If Packer walked into my office I'd want to have the Royal Canadian Mounted Police around—in large numbers. He's not the kind of person to take home to mother, or father—or even your worst enemy."

That was good enough for me. Starrs and his crack team of forensic archaeologists had put the final nail in Alferd Packer's coffin. The mad man-eater was one mean piece of work. Packer made Hannibal Lecter look like a vegetarian and the *Denver Post* like a shameless rag that would sell its soul to flog a few papers.

And me? I was having a field day blue-skying tabloid variations on Packer's story. How about . . .

**CANNIBAL IN KITCHEN
COOKS UP MIRACLE PROTEIN DIET!**

II: HAPPY AS A PIG IN . . .

FORGET INDIANA JONES—meet "Illinois" Lang. Illinois is the *nom de guerre* of amateur archaeologist Don Lang, who lives with his folks in the quaint little town of Forest, Illinois, just outside of Peoria. Now, Illinois Lang doesn't fly off to exotic locations so he can go digging around in crumbling Mayan temples or Egyptian tombs looking for buried treasure.

Oh, he's looking for loot all right, but Illinois Lang's idea of a treasure hunt is to stick close to home. Most of his digging is restricted to a modest area within a hundred-mile radius right around Peoria. And the ruins that he digs up are like nothing Indiana Jones ever imagined.

Illinois belongs to a club called the National Privy Diggers' Association. Don't laugh. The NPDA is no joke. Its membership is a proud and serious band of dedicated hobbyists who get a real hoot out of digging up old outhouses.

Illinois Lang likes to wax eloquent about his odd little hobby. "It's real exciting. To me there is nothing greater than the feeling of digging a privy, and knowing that *you're the first one to touch that thing in a hundred and fifty years!*"

Not that there's a whole lot of folks lining up for the privilege. Mind you, membership in the NPDA could mushroom once word gets out about the healthy cash flow in privy digging. You heard right. There's money in that old three-holer out back.

Example? Illinois told me about the latest treasure he's hauled out of one of his odiferous digs. "Just the other day I dug up a cobalt blue quartz soda bottle from 1875. Then I turned around and sold it to a guy over in Chicago for $650."

Well, I figured a nice piece of change like that was nothing to sniff at, but what the heck was an antique bottle worth $650 doing floating around in an old crapper? Illinois explained that "they didn't have garbage pick-up back in the 1800s and you find all kinds of bottles, crocks and jugs in old outhouses. See, back then, what was a pop bottle or a whisky crock worth? The old man would be out in the privy drinking some whisky and he wouldn't want the wife to know about it so he'd just drop it down the old shooter there and get rid of the evidence."

But old whisky crocks and soda bottles are small potatoes compared to some of the outhouse artifacts Illinois has unearthed. "Heck, one day I dug up a Doctor J. Hoffstedder Stomach Bitters bottle. In the Civil War, Doctor J. Hoffstedder had a contract with certain Confederate regiments that they would drink this stuff and it would give them courage before they went into battle. And what his stomach bitters turned out to be was about 80-proof alcohol. So when they went into battle they were half-bombed."

But outside of Civil War trinkets, Illinois Lang gets his biggest kick from unearthing a much more innocent brand of salvage. "Doll heads," he told me. "The old porcelain type that are as big as your fist. They've still got the hand-painting on them and the pink cheeks and all that. They're just beautiful."

Actually, I thought P-U-tiful might be more like it. I mean *pink* cheeks? That didn't sound too likely when you figure those doll heads have been floating around for a hundred years in human waste. On top of that I wondered if Illinois wasn't just a little bit scared about picking up some festering disease every time he picked up one of his treasures?

"Oh, no!" he said. "That stuff all dissolved years and years ago. It's just all turned to earth, and I mean really good rich soil. In fact, the difference in the feel of the ground is how come you can tell when you've found an old privy site, because good rich soil like that's so soft."

Illinois explained that the ground where an outhouse once stood is always squishier than the rest of the yard. There's no clay or rocks or any of that kind of stuff, so it's not hard to dig through. And even though your great-grandfather's outhouse may have been torn down or moved or turned into a tool shed, or even have vanished completely, the experienced foot of somebody like Illinois Lang can feel where it once proudly served the call of nature.

By the way, Illinois told me his foolproof trade secret to sniffing out a deserted crapper. "If you're questioning it, if you get down about four or five foot and you're not sure you're on the right track the trick is if you see any tomato seeds. That right there tells you one hundred percent that you hit privy dirt."

The way Illinois sees it, most people eat tomatoes and tomato seeds never dissolve. I mean never! Not in your stomach, not in your intestines, and not even in the privy pit once you've done your business. So tomato seeds are a sure-fire sign to keep digging. But just how far you have to dig might surprise you.

"As far as the average depth," Lang said "they can be anywhere from four foot deep to down about a twenty-footer." Twenty feet sounded ridiculous to me, but Illinois said "no, not really. That way you only ever had to dig a new hole every ten or fifteen years"—depending, of course, on how big your family happened to be.

Now I always associate privies with roughing it out in the country—on farms or at the cottage. So I just assumed that Illinois found his digs by driving around the boondocks and poking around old farms. It turns out I was way off base.

In the golden age of outhouses, before indoor plumbing, the vast majority of privies were actually dug inside the city limits. Your average city crapper was in the backyard, straight out from the rear door of the house, usually no more than three feet in from the back alley. In other words, close enough so you didn't have to take a really long walk in the middle of the winter but far enough away to cut down on the stink and the flies when the contents started to bake in the dog days of summer.

What that all adds up to is easy pickings for Illinois. Every old house in every old section of every old town is a potential gold-mine to a member in good standing of the NPDA. "There's been times," Lang said "where I dug out forty bottles out of one privy."

Mind you, it's not *always* smooth sailing. Illinois told me that he's actually had fights with the people who own the land he's digging on. First they give him permission to excavate. But once they get a load of all the cool stuff he's hauling out of their old crappers, they say, "Hey, I think I'll keep those for myself. Gimme, gimme!" They figure it's their land so it's their loot, and there's not a thing he can do about it.

Still, he's philosophical about losing the odd nice bottle or crock that way. He's learned to take those setbacks in stride. After all, a lot worse has happened to some of his privy-digging peers. "I'll tell you, there is hazards to it," he said. "I know of one gal, her husband had dug out a bottle. He handed it up to her and it still had a partial piece of the cork and some stuff inside. Well, when she was looking at the bottle the contents spilled on her hands and she got deathly sick and was taken into hospital. They found out it was a poison bottle and it contained strychnine and it was absorbed through her skin, and it just about killed her.

"There's another thing you have to watch out for. If you've got a twenty-footer and you go down that deep, you have to try to brace it up with two-by-fours and such. That's because you get down there and the walls will start caving in on you. There have been people digging up these old things and the dirt caved in and killed them. They always say—and it's real good advice—they say, *'Never dig a privy alone!'*"

But Illinois goes against the conventional wisdom. He works solo although he says it's not by choice. He'd love a partner, but it so happens that Lang is the only card-carrying member of the National Privy Diggers' Association in his neck of the woods.

Well, I got to thinking that if Illinois needed a partner I just might be his man. I was being really coy and subtle about it but all through our little chat I was hinting around that I wouldn't mind hopping into the outhouse with him and getting in on the action.

But Illinois didn't take the bait. The truth is, I really don't think he was all that interested in a two-man operation. Too bad. I'd have been a natural. Like I said before, I've been shovelling the poop most of my life.

III: THE REINCARNATION RAG

I call it Astral Archaeology.

A ND IT'S JUST like what Indiana Jones (or for that matter Illinois Lang) does. Except that the sites a skilled astral archaeologist explores are the caverns of the mind.

The astral archaeologist brushes aside the cobwebs that cloud your memory. He carefully sifts through the countless layers of day-to-day dust and debris that conceal the treasure buried in your subconscious. I'm talking *reincarnation* here, people—and at the tabs reincarnation always spells big bucks!

I used to think that the readers of papers like the *National Examiner*—many of whom were fundamentalist Christians—would find a big conflict of interest between the doctrine of reincarnation (coming back for another go-round at life on earth) and their own Christian beliefs (which presuppose going on to a nicer place than this earth). But not a bit of it! They lapped this stuff up.

Like most of the other news in the *National Examiner,* we stole our reincarnation pieces from elsewhere. One memorable "heist" involved a story we lifted from a rather unlikely source—the *Wall Street Journal.*

The *Journal* ran a feature on an entrepreneur in Kingfisher, Oklahoma, named Ernie Shafenberg. Ernie's a wealthy businessman who's amassed a fortune by running a camp for reincarnates. People who want to explore their past lives flock to his camp and Ernie regresses them at US$600 a pop.

Now I will admit that at first I thought the whole thing sounded like a pretty slick scam, but it turns out Ernie's got impeccable credentials for running his reincarnation ranch. Ernie Shafenberg has lived *nine* times before, so he knows whereof he speaks. And the amazing thing is, most of Ernie's past lives correspond to American historical milestones.

For example, he came over on the boat with Columbus. He fought side by side with George Washington. He died defending the Alamo. The list goes on and on. This, of course, has given Ernie a unique bird's-eye view of some of the formative moments in U.S. history.

Now I can hear you sceptics whining about how this all sounds too good to be true. How come guys like Ernie Shafenberg never remember having past lives where they were no-account nonentities—chicken thieves or winos or lepers? Well, although he's proud to have served alongside the great men who set the course of a nation, Ernie is quick to point out that he himself was never a recognizable VIP-type historical figure in any of his previous incarnations. He was always just a regular Joe and that *does* go against the grain of most reincarnation claims.

Speaking of which, what about those reincarnation clichés? How come so many people used to be Cleopatra or Napoleon or Genghis Khan?

Well, think about it. Those guys, along with most of the other great figures of history, were not famous by accident. They were all complex, multi-faceted individuals.

The common wisdom among reincarnation scholars is that each glorious facet of an intricate personality, such as Cleopatra's, for instance, can splinter off and, in turn, be reincarnated as a different person. So hundreds or even thousands of people can be reincarnated from one basic personality lump in the ether of time.

Anyway, writing about people like Ernie Shafenberg got me wondering what kind of long-forgotten lives might be kicking around inside Harold Fiske's closet. It would be a hoot to get the poop on which famous movers and shakers I'd been before, and to find out how they helped make me what I am today.

According to reincarnation theory, each of our past lives is a training ground of sorts, where we get to test drive our psyches and experiment with the virtues and foibles of our existence. It's sort of like going to school. Every time you die you either pass or flunk, so in your next life you either graduate to bigger and better things or you repeat the grade until you get it right. Put together, all your past lives add up to your spiritual DNA—a kind of secret code to your current predicament. Regression therapy helps you decipher that code and find out what makes you tick in the here and now.

Well, here and now in my case happened to be 1988. I was in Toronto and another ugly Canadian winter was giving way to spring. I figured what better time to explore *my* reincarnations than the very season of rebirth itself, so I went to a regression therapist by the name of Russell H. Simmons. Why'd I pick him? Simmons is well regarded as a top expert in the field and, more importantly, he agreed to do it for free. No way was I going to fork over US$600 just to find out what makes *me* tick.

When I got to his office, Simmons said he was going to hypnotize me. He sat me down and played this soothing tape of waves ebbing and flowing and gently breaking on the sand, and he talked to me in a calm, restful voice and pretty soon I went under.

Now, just to be safe, I had a tape rolling on the whole session and that's how come I'm sure that I'm not making this stuff up. Every word of what I'm about to write is absolutely the truth as I spoke it then.

By the way, it's too bad you can't hear that tape because the voice that came out of my mouth was really spooky. See, when you're hypnotized your vocal cords tend to relax, so my voice was much slower and more halting than usual—but it was higher pitched, too. It almost sounded mechanical. Imagine Robby the Robot's batteries running low after he'd inhaled some helium and you'll get the idea. Very weird!

Anyway, once I was hypnotized, Simmons said, "I want you to tell me about your past life," and instantly I had an amazing vision: I told him that I saw myself wearing a black cowl-like cap, a green tunic and thigh-high boots, and that I was sitting on a horse in the middle of a wretched-looking field of roughly ploughed muck. I rode through the muck to a muddy makeshift road that led to a big, square, blocky-looking castle—it was really just a big stone cube—with a huge door on it. That was where I lived.

Now all through my session, whenever I ran out of steam, Simmons would gently nudge me on with questions and I would just spew out more of these visions.

My name, I found out, was Guillehomme de Portiers—a name that meant nothing to me at the time and which, I've since determined, has no connection to any branch of the Fiske family tree. I was a boy, twelve years old, living in Normandy. The year was 957.

Inside the castle I saw my mother. She was wearing a brown dress, and had served a great feast around a huge wooden table. There were dogs everywhere, and people flinging bones around. There was straw on the floor, and the whole place stank.

Interestingly enough, my father was nowhere to be seen. He was off on the Crusades. He'd gone to liberate the Holy Lands from the infidels and, although that was supposed to be a great and glorious cause, I just remember that I, little Guillehomme, hated my father for deserting us.

Anyway, I remember I wasn't hungry, or maybe I was sick, but I left the feast early and went to bed. This part was interesting—my tenth-century Sealy Posturepedic turned out to be a sack on the floor. It was a sort of a sleeping bag-type thing. Pieces of leather, odds and ends that the local shoemaker chucked out, had been cut up and stuffed into this bag. That's where I tossed and turned during my lonely, fatherless, formative years.

At this point Russell, my regression therapist, got me to flash ahead to when I was sixteen. This time I saw a band of armed men coming up the muddy path to our castle. They all had beards and sort of looked like Vikings and they were really scary. I called to my mother. She saw them and screamed, and we ran inside, locked and barred our door and huddled together with our servants. But these men splashed some kind of flammable liquid goop on the door, set it on fire and eventually burned their way in.

The Vikings killed all the servants, but my mother and I were able to sneak away and hide in a secret room under a moving stone in the castle's chapel. We stayed there for three days until we ran out of water.

By then it was either die of thirst or face the invaders, so we came out of hiding. The Vikings were right in the chapel, drinking and partying like a horde of pagan louts. When they saw us they just laughed and laughed. They kept on laughing while one really ugly guy with a red beard drew his broadsword and ran me through. And that, as they say, was that.

Actually, that's not quite true. There were more visions about how I moved on to a spiritual plane of existence and met up with all sorts of wise ethereal beings, but I won't get into it here because that stuff's really boring compared to seeing yourself disembowelled by a Viking.

That part, about getting killed, really blew me away. Later on, listening to the tapes again, I was still so shaken up by it that I decided I just had to share my past life and death with the world.

I played the tape for the *Basic Black* people at the CBC and as usual they were sceptical namby-pambies. "Okay, Harold, here's the deal," said my then-producer, John Disney. "The only way that crap ever goes on the airwaves is if you'll let us call in a real certified Middle Ages expert to check out your story and say what he thinks on the show."

Hey, no problem, I said. Go right ahead. Guillehomme and I have nothing to hide. We *know* what we saw. So the brass at *Basic Black* asked Professor Steven Muhlberger, a professor of medieval history at the University of Toronto, to study my reincarnation tape. Then Professor Muhlberger (with his vast knowledge of tenth-century Normandy) joined Arthur Black and me *live on the air!* (He was there to pass judgment on my story, to scrutinize it under the hard light of historical accuracy.)

Muhlberger: The first thing is that it comes off as generic Middle Ages—sort of MIDDLE AGES in big letters with a universal pricing code. It's what a lot of us might know about the Middle Ages without thinking about it too hard. It's got only a few real specific details in it that could be checked. Some of them are reasonable, but others ring false.

Fiske: What do you mean, "ring false!?" Let's have some examples.

Muhlberger: Well, the big one is the fact that your past self Guillehomme has a father gone off on the Crusades. Now you're supposedly living around 957, but the Crusades didn't begin until 1095. This is a little bit like having President Andrew Jackson watching the first moon landing on TV.

Arthur: In other words, what is Stonewall Jackson doing with a package of Frito's corn chips?

Muhlberger: Yes, that's right. Another thing is that tenth-century Normandy was a very rough place. Compare it to drug wars in Colombia. It's remarkable that this young boy is hanging around with his mother and no protective male figure and no armed followers and nobody bothers them for a very long time. Eventually somebody comes along and kills them, but by any reasonable standard they should have jumped in and killed them within weeks of the old man disappearing, not four years down the line.

Arthur: [*giggling, clearly enjoying this*] Professor, it sounds like you're very politely shooting Harold's regression experience full of holes.

Muhlberger: Well, there are several inconsistencies. It really reminds me of 1940s historical movies. It's bright. It looks good, but if you sit down and look at it closely, it's kind of what any intelligent person might know in the back of their mind about the Middle Ages. And it does seem that people usually regress to periods that they already know about. Unless they're from Sri Lanka themselves they never show up in the tenth century in Sri Lanka, and if regression is a soul migration type of experience, I don't see why it should be tied down to any particular geography.

I was getting a little ticked at these guys sneering at me. Arthur and the professor were having a good old time poking holes in what to me had been a profound and deeply moving experience. Even worse, they were laughing at me.

And I was hurt by the unspoken implication that I was making all this stuff up. The visions I'd relived through regressive hypnotherapy were damn real to me, not just stuff I'd picked up from old movies. For example, what about Guillehomme's weird bed. I know I didn't get *that* out of *Prince Valiant* or *Robin Hood*.

Muhlberger: Yeah. [*laughing*] This bed is made out of a bag full of leather scraps.

Fiske: What's wrong with that? I mean, it could have been like that.

Muhlberger: Sure, it *could* have been, but if you had any choice you wouldn't pick leather scraps to sleep on would you? I don't think people in tenth-century Normandy would, especially if they were rich like Guillehomme. If they were rich they had a feather bed or a goosedown-filled bag or something. But leather scraps? That's something you pull out and sleep on in the shed when you've worked yourself into complete exhaustion. But this guy's rich.

Fiske: [*clearly dejected*] Gee, I kind of liked that touch. It seemed to add a note of authenticity.

Muhlberger: [*really laughing now*] Yeah, that one killed me!

Okay, so I got slammed pretty good in front of countless millions of listeners, but I took my lumps like a man, thanked the professor for his trouble and filed away his comments and his tips for future reference. In my *next* past life, I'd be ready!

IV: GOING BACK WITH BLACK

My three past lives with Arthur Black.

IT TOOK A while, but six years later I finally got my chance, and Arthur Black got his comeuppance. I was sitting in our CBC studio across the table from Arthur. I had just returned from my annual pilgrimage to the Mystics, Seers and Psychics Fair at the Canadian National Exhibition grounds in Toronto.

The fair had been jammed to the rafters with mystic merchants hawking their wares. And I had great tape on everything from your traditional turbaned crystal-ball gazers to the very latest in high-tech seerage—the fortune-telling Fingerprint Graph-o-plot Analyzer, a machine that cuts out the mystic middleman and actually reads your palm electronically.

As I am wont to do on these occasions, I dove into the deep end and bathed myself in a psychic sea of free readings. However, as complex and admittedly fascinating as these readings were, I was skimming over this stuff pretty fast on the radio show because I had bigger fish to fry.

I introduced Arthur to a groundbreaking psychic named Helen Massingham. She works out of Toronto and had a humble little booth tucked away in an obscure corner of the fair. No flash, no hype, no neon. But something about her unprepossessing little set-up seemed to be calling out to me. It, or to be more precise, *she* was irresistible.

We started to talk. Helen explained that her special gift was past-life regression. Bingo! I told her about my humiliating experience on live radio and about how my close personal friend and colleague Arthur Black was a sneering disbeliever.

Helen said that *he* should try it. If Arthur got a look at *his* past lives he might change his mind. Fat chance of that, I told her. Arthur Black wouldn't be caught dead—well, maybe dead—at a psychic fair. According to Helen that was no problem because we didn't actually need Arthur to be there physically in order to explore his previous lives.

It turns out that many of the key people in your life aren't there by accident. Remember? Reincarnation is like going to school. Each life is another grade, another chance to graduate and grow up and move along to something better. It's the same way with our primal relationships. We keep working at them, life after life, until we get them right.

Helen wasn't offering any guarantees, but Arthur *could* be one of my primal people. That made sense because we *are* pretty close, almost like brothers. After all, he does treat me like the black sheep of the family and, let's face it, we sure as hell fight like brothers. The *Basic Black* production bible even goes so far as to define my role on the show as "the older brother who takes Arthur places and shows him things he normally wouldn't go near on his own." (And believe me, there *is* such a document. This is government-funded radio after all, run by gangs of bone-idle civil servants who have nothing better to do than sit around writing idiotic character summaries of all the on-air folks for some stupid sub-assistant deputy minister who never even listens to the show.)

Anyway, the more I thought about it, the more I was convinced that Arthur would turn up in at least *one* of my past incarnations. So I went for it. For the second time in my life I agreed to let an astral archaeologist dig through the murky ruins of my past lives. Only this time, with a little luck, the skeletons we'd be unearthing would be rattling around in *Arthur's* closet.

Naturally, I got it all on tape and let it rip on *Basic Black.* Countless millions of Canadians heard Helen Massingham tell me to empty my head of any and all miscellaneous clutter, to create a *tabula rasa.* Next, she instructed me to concentrate, to focus all my mental powers just on Arthur's name. Naturally, my mind went Black.

Then she put me under. She sent me floating off in a trancelike quest for any common ground where Arthur's past lives might have converged with mine. There turned out to be at least three such lives!

The first one was around AD 1200. I was a thirteen-year-old scullery maid. I got abducted by a Mongol chieftain who had *really* bad BO. He worked me to a frazzle, used me, abused me, then tossed me aside and left me to die on a dungheap. The only good thing about that was that *it* smelled better than he did!

The second life happened about three hundred years later in London, England. This time it was about 1530 and I was mugged and murdered by a mad monk whose brain had been infected by the French pox. The crazy defrocked friar killed me—get this—for my *cloak,* of all things.

Our third convergent existence happened a little closer to home. I was a subsistence farmer on the shores of Lake Huron in Ontario. This was around 1860.

Let me give you a taste of shared-past-life-number-three. Remember, I was rolling a tape on the whole thing and this is a transcript of part of that session, just the way it came out of my mouth that day at the psychic fair. If you listened to the tape you'd hear the heavy, sluggish, drugged-out (but without the drugs) voice of yours truly answering the question, "Where are you now, Harold?"

"I'm in bed. I hurt my leg. I hurt it on the farm. We were taking a tree from the field. It jerked out of the ground suddenly and fell on me and crushed my leg. The surgeon comes and he . . . my God! he . . . he cuts off my leg! My stump never properly heals and I . . . I . . ."

I stop talking for a while but the tape isn't quiet. You can hear me hyperventilating. I'm literally gasping for air. When I do start talking again I still sound drugged, but now there's panic in my voice. It's obvious that I don't want to face what's coming.

"M-m-my stump gets infected. It starts to . . . smell! I . . . I gag from the stink it smells so bad. I gag and choke. It is painful and unpleasant and then . . . thank God I . . . die."

Helen Massingham had heard enough. She knew this was difficult for me because she could sense my pain. She called a halt to the proceedings and brought me out of my trance. She was deft, incisive and direct in explaining my visions.

"The scenes and the lives that you and Arthur have gone through are quite interesting. The flamboyant man who captured and abandoned you when you were a servant girl? That would have been Arthur. He was a smelly and rough Mongolian and this was a man who obviously liked authority and power and abusing it. When you were talking, Harold, I could see this man standing there in this strong stance with his legs apart and his arms folded across his massive chest. He wasn't going to take nonsense from anybody and if you didn't do what he wanted, that was it. Your life was over. In the next one, Arthur was obviously the friar. There was a lot of rage in that man because of his being cast out of the monastery and because of his getting infected by the French pox. This time Arthur rather enjoyed killing people. He had a sort of thirst for it.

"And in the last life, where he was the surgeon, Arthur had to shut down his emotions, as a doctor must. He did things in a sort of efficient way as best he could with the primitive tools available to him. He was very frustrated with not being able to do more, but I have no doubt he was a very caring man. He did try to save you. He didn't just leave you to rot like the Mongolian or the monk would have done. This shows me that there is growth," Helen continued. "Arthur has changed and I would surmise that now, in his current life, if you ask him, he would admit that he probably doesn't care for hospitals and places like that. He doesn't like the smell of people dying."

Now, you have to remember Helen's taped reading was all going out live across the country. This is where Arthur jumped in.

> *Arthur:* Let me get this straight, Harold. I've killed you three times, is that right? Once as a smelly, power-mad Mongolian—
>
> *Fiske:* Well, the first death was more by *neglect* than actual commission.
>
> *Arthur:* Yeah, I just sort of let you die after treating you like dirt. Okay. But there's no two ways about that second guy, the defrocked friar. I outright murdered you there and in life number three I was a blundering surgeon. I killed you with incompetence.
>
> *Fiske:* Yeah, that's all true. One way or another you were directly implicated in my demise on at least three occasions.
>
> *Arthur:* What do you mean, "at least?"
>
> *Fiske:* Well, you heard the tape. Helen cut me off. She made me snap out of it early because of the high level of stress I was under. If she'd allowed me to carry on there's no telling how many more murders I could've pinned on you. Actually, you ought to consider yourself

lucky that the statute of limitations has run out on all of the ones we *do* know about.

Arthur: I'm counting my blessings even as we speak.

"That's the idea," I told him. "Be positive. Look on the bright side." I mean, let's face it: if the reason we're reborn is so we can graduate into more perfect human beings, if each new body we inhabit means another shot at being better, then Arthur Black stands as living proof that reincarnation really and truly does work.

He started out as a smelly, power-mad Mongolian, came back as a somewhat flawed man of God, and then a healer—yes, an incompetent healer but a healer nonetheless. And look at him now. He's an award-winning broadcaster, he's loved by millions, and, best of all, he doesn't stink any more.

CHAPTER THREE

ANIMAL ANTICS

Cuban crocodile farm near the Bay of Pigs:
"Silent sentinels waiting to bite off legs of
U.S. invasion force." (See Chapter Nine)

I: THE BEAST BEAT

"Fiske, you're full of horse manure!"

I F I'VE HEARD that insult once I've heard it a million times. And guess what? I love it! It's a badge I wear proudly. Nosing around in animal dung comes with the territory when the tabs assign you to what I affectionately like to call the beast beat.

Let's not get confused here—when most people think of animals and the tabs, they're usually thinking Bigfoot or the Loch Ness monster, but those guys are really more part of the science beat.

No, the beast beat is mostly concerned with your more domesticated creatures, everything from horses to house pets. See, the people who read the tabloids love cute fluffy animals: dogs and cats and furry little mice and bunnies—things that you can cuddle up to.

One of the reasons these stories work is because they're very visual, and rule number one is, you *always* run an adorable picture with these items, because let's face it, there's no such thing as an ugly puppy.

I remember a story I wrote for the *National Examiner* about a man who lay helplessly crippled in an iron lung. To cheer him up, the hospital took a little puppy dog and put it in the iron lung with the guy and the dog licked his face and slept with him and really improved the man's quality of life. You had human interest, great pictures, a health angle and a happy ending. How could you go wrong?

We also did plenty of stories about those strange birds who harbour scores of animals in their homes. My favourite was a Canadian story out of Hull, Quebec.

This woman was just crazy for dogs. She had raised a bunch of them and had taken in strays, so all told, she kept thirty-plus mongrels with her in her house. One day she had the misfortune to die.

Well, the lady left a will and in it was a clause saying that when she died every last one of those darling doggies was to be escorted to the pound and put to sleep. She, of course, saw this as an act of love—sort of like a suicide pact. For her part, she could never imagine life without her puppies and she assumed they'd feel the same way.

What she hadn't counted on was dropping dead *inside* the house with the dogs locked in there with her. Now, because she was friendless and a bit of a recluse, nobody (except the dogs) noticed. Naturally after two or three days the hounds started getting hungry and—"man's best friend" be damned—their survival instinct kicked in and they started to eat her up.

A couple of weeks later, when the cops burst in on this cozy little scene, they found no trace of her—and only discovered the truth a couple of days later when the dogs' poop was analyzed and tested positive for human remains.

The *Examiner* headline went something like **"Dogs' Revenge: Hounds Cheat Executioner by Dining on Cruel Mistress's Dead Body!"** But that grisly tale was something of an aberration. Normally, the *Examiner* didn't much go in for the ugly. There were, however, other tabloids owned by our parent company, the Globe Newspaper Group, that *did* cater to the slightly more bent consumer.

I will admit that on occasion I did dip my pen into the muse's inkpot and, under an assumed name, did write a story or two for our downmarket sister paper, *Close-Up on Crime.*

I recall one headline, **"Junkyard Dog Digs Up Mom's Head!"** It seems this woman living in a trailer in Amarillo, Texas decided she wasn't going to take her medication any more, and this really annoyed her hubby (who had long since stopped taking his). So he went to the drawer in the kitchenette and . . . oh, never mind! That story is a complete bummer. If you want the rest call the cops in Amarillo—I'm sure they still remember the details. Or, go look it up yourself in *Close-Up on Crime.*

II: DERBY DEMONS

**Dr. Mitchell Bedford is a racehorse exorcist
with a booming business in demonic deportation.**

DON'T SCOFF. Dr. Bedford is a *very* learned man. He has doctorates in educational psychology and theology and they both come in handy in his line of work. He lives in Lexington, Kentucky, which, of course, is where the vast majority of the world's primo horseflesh hangs out—horseflesh that Dr. Bedford says is easy pickings for little devils with mischief on their minds.

Some people think the Doc is missing a few marbles, but others aren't so sure. They're the ones who'd just as soon hedge their bets. Let's face it, when you spend multimillions breeding or buying a racehorse the stakes are astronomical. You have to look for every possible competitive edge you can find to get you in the winner's circle. The last thing you want is to have some pesky demon possessing your favourite mount, gumming up the works and causing it to lose those big-money races. Dr. Bedford makes sure that doesn't happen.

When I talked to him he explained how he cottoned on to this curious phenomenon in the first place.

"Several years ago, a horse named Demons Be Gone was running in the Kentucky Derby and was the overwhelming favourite to win the race," he told me. "Well, I predicted—live on a television program—that Demons Be Gone would definitely *not* win the race. Why? I simply figured out that the demons were simply not going to tolerate that type of insult and that they would ultimately interfere with his running ability. And, of course, Demons Be Gone did *not* run well in the Derby."

Bolstered by that successful prediction, Doc Bedford decided to take a closer look at the whole thoroughbred scene and came up with a particularly devilish theory.

"I argued that *all* winning horses are cursed! And a cursed horse will not be able to run efficiently in the next race. Which is why very few horses are able to carry on to win the Triple Crown."

I told Dr. Bedford that he was moving a little too fast for me. I got the bit about these so-called demons being ticked off at a horse so blatantly running with an in-your-face name like Demons Be Gone. I mean, what self-respecting devil would take that lying down?

What I wasn't too clear on was how we got from there, from one arguably justifiable demonic possession, to the bigger idea that once a horse wins a race he gets saddled with a demon.

"Invariably a winning racehorse gets cursed," he said. "It gets cursed by the grooms of the other stables who may not even know what harm they're doing—but some do know. Just as bad, the winning horse is always cursed by the losing betters who get mad at it."

Dr. Bedford's theory is founded on what I have chosen to dub the "Psychic Sour Grapes" principle. For every winner out there, you've got dozens or hundreds or even thousands of sore losers saying stuff like, "Damn you, Secretariat!" and "Go to hell, Northern Dancer." (*Note:* I use these names for illustration only—I am not representing here, nor is it true, that these animals are, in fact, possessed by demons.)

Every one of these curses is a crack in the thoroughbred's psychic armour, a foot in the door of demonic possession. Naturally, the bigger the race and the higher the stakes, the more sour grapes you get. The curses add up. The more curses, the more damage done to the winning steed. It makes sense that the better the horse, the heavier the karmic handicap.

But if virtually every triumphant horse walks away from the winner's circle possessed by a devil, how come nobody glommed onto this before? Dr. Bedford told me that these demons can be very sneaky.

It's not like in *The Exorcist*. Just because a horse is possessed doesn't mean it projectile-vomits pea soup while its head spins around like a top. That's all just movie guff—real life demonic possession is much subtler than that.

Once a tricky little devil gets its horns into a sure-bet, can't-lose, odds-on favourite, the horse might go off its feed or come up lame or get skittish or throw its jockey. He might bump another horse mid-race and get disqualified, or he might just run out of steam and fade in the stretch. "Unless," Dr. Bedford told me, "he gets 'cleansed' between races.

"Well," he went on, "at least I call it getting cleansed. Others call it exorcism, but it's the same concept. After a horse wins any major race, that horse should be cleansed."

That cleansing process is actually very simple, although it does require a trained exorcist, like Dr. Bedford, be in attendance. What the exorcist does is evoke the name of an appropriate biblical figure and order the demon to "get out and be gone!" from the afflicted animal. He claims that once it's been expelled, "The air feels cleaner, fresher, something like after a storm when you have negative ions dominating the air." (I know it's counter-intuitive, but negative ions are the "good" ions that make you feel better.)

That's pretty much all there is to it, except for one little problem. What happens to the demon—where does it go once he's cast it out?

Dr. Bedford explained. "I just tell it to get out of this area, out from the farm or the neighbourhood. Where it goes after that I don't particularly care. Jesus did this, if you remember."

Indeed, I did remember. It's the tale of the Gadarene swine—one of my favourite Bible stories from boyhood—and I proceeded to recite the appropriate passages from scripture. (It's in Matt. 8: 28-32.) The story tells how Jesus came to the "country of the Gergesenes, and there met him two possessed with devils, coming out of the tombs, exceeding fierce, so that no man might pass by that way." Those devils "besought" Jesus, who noticed there was "a herd of many swine feeding" a short way off, so he cast the demons into the pigs.

"That's right," Dr. Bedford said. "Jesus ordered the spirits out of somebody possessed by the devil. But instead of sending them back to where they came from he put them into a herd of swine and then the pigs did something stupid like jumping off a cliff. But that's another problem. In other words, the demon isn't *my* problem once it's out of the horse."

I wondered, did he ever worry about unscrupulous organized crime types keeping tabs on him, charting the horses he's cleansed and maybe using that knowledge to place bets that might be more favourable to them? "Naw," said Dr. Bedford. "That's none of my business. My business is to clean situations up. To make animals healthier, to make the atmosphere healthier."

But Dr. Bedford did admit that any time you dabble in demons there's always a chance you might abuse your power. "For example, if I happen to get mad at a politician then I could lay a curse on them. Actually, let's put it this way: I could request—that's a much kinder word than curse—I could request that spirit powers destroy that person politically. In other words," he continued, "the whole psychic world can be used negatively if one wants to do that and if you take the time to train yourself to master the discipline. Then, like money, you can either use it for good or bad."

Well, since Dr. Bedford brought it up, I asked him about money. Did he charge for cleansing these cursed thoroughbreds? You bet!

"Yeah. Generally I expect my expenses to be paid and on top of that I ask about US$40 an hour and the average cleansing takes about that long."

Let's see. Your average track runs about ten races a day. Every race has a winner. Every winner has a curse. Every curse comes with a demon. And every demon has to be exorcised—at forty bucks a pop. It's a living.

Plus, racehorses are only the tip of the demonic iceberg, as it were. Dr. Bedford casts out demons from all kinds of farm animals and pets and people, and he even has a sideline casting out demons from houses. Dr. Bedford told me that the demons in cursed houses go by a special name.

Elementals, he calls them. "Elementals breed in houses filled with friction. I can think of one house I cleansed in Hazard, Kentucky. Seven out of the eight families that lived there since it was built ended up divorced. The divorce causes emotional friction and the emotional friction creates an energy force we call an elemental.

"An elemental is not *quite* a lawless spirit, not a full-fledged demon, but kind of a half-being. That elemental dwells within the house that bore the friction and it feeds off that friction. So when somebody new comes and buys the house the elemental tries to upset the family that moves in.

"You often hear people say a house is haunted by ghosts or poltergeists, but they're not ghosts. On gradation, a ghost is different—it's a little bit stronger than an elemental. But the point here is that the elemental seeks to energize itself by getting the family fighting with each other or making them ill or upset or disturbed. It could be very dangerous."

Dr. Bedford says that cleansing a house of elementals is a whole different ball game. For one thing, unlike expelling demons from living creatures, he doesn't actually have to go to your house.

"In the case of that woman in Hazard," he said, "I told her about a German technique which involves using fresh eggs—real fresh eggs that have just been laid right off the farm, not the ones you get at the supermarket. What you do is put a couple of eggs in each room, in the corner, out of the way, where they won't be stepped on."

Dr. Bedford went on to tell me that fresh eggs are to elementals what baking soda is to bad odours in your Frigidaire. Eggs have the ability to absorb contrary energy. They suck up the excess acrimony that's floating around the house and, in effect, starve out the elementals.

He explained that the eggs work best in tandem with a more

mundane cleanser. "You pour a couple of cups of Clorox [that's bleach] down each drain to clean those out. The elementals don't like that because they can't hide in a clean drain. Ultimately you open the windows, and depending on how ornery they are, they probably will leave."

And of course right away they start looking around for somebody else's dysfunctional house to call home. But like the good doctor says, that's not his business—at least not until *they* need an exorcist.

III: CLONING AROUND

Edinburgh, Scotland, February 24, 1997
—"Hello, Dolly!"

AN WILMUT and his colleagues at the Roslin Institute in Edinburgh had just announced to a stunned press corps that they'd successfully cloned the world's first adult mammal, a sheep named Dolly.

When I heard the news I had a hunch that half a globe away, in a town called Port Townsend, Washington, a guy named Paul Asmuss must've felt like his ship had finally come in. Long before Dolly was a gleam in her geneticist's eye, I interviewed Paul about a company he owned called Genetipet.

As the name suggests, Genetipet is dedicated to the notion of cloning man's best friend (and all his other pets, too). Let's say you have a dog. We'll call him Rin-Tin-Tin. Rinty's getting on and you can't bear the thought of life without your favourite mutt. Well, one of these days, in the post-Dolly universe, you won't have to—thanks in no small part to Paul Asmuss's visionary work at Genetipet.

I talked to Paul about his "pet" project in 1994, three years B.D. (Before Dolly) and right off he was totally up front about the fact that he had no intention of doing any actual cloning himself. He was leaving that to the heavy hitters in the genetics business. No, Paul sees himself more in the role of keeper of the keys, guardian of the family jewels.

"It's actually pretty straightforward," he told me. "What we do is take blood samples from people's pets and we freeze the samples down to a point where the DNA is, you might say, in suspended animation. Then when the day comes that cloning technology is perfected—and," he added prophetically, "that could be any day now—then geneticists will be able to extract this DNA out of the blood sample and use it to create an identical twin pet.

"The clone will be an *exact* genetic match to the donor pet. That means that the dog or cat clone's temperament should be the same as the original's as long as the environment is the same. In other words, if the pet's owner or the master cares for the clone in a very similar way to the original pet, then it should turn out about the same. Unfortunately, that means it's going to have the same problems too. If your cat died of cancer the first time, it'll probably die of cancer again."

Hey, no big deal. We're talking clones here. So you just run off another copycat any time you feel like it. Same thing if you make a mistake in rearing your pet—say you botch the toilet training or whatever. No problem. You just dump the loser, order up another clone and start from scratch with an unspoiled, neurosis-free pet.

Now in case you're wondering, Genetipet doesn't just cater to cat and dog fanciers. They'll take blood samples from your goldfish, your turtle, even your snake. In fact, Paul says that *those* pets actually have a leg up on cats and dogs, because in theory the cloning process works much better when you start with a less complicated organism like a fish or a snake.

Anyway, Paul's operation sounded like sheer genius to me. After all, who among us hasn't fantasized, "Gee, if only I could have my favourite pet cocker spaniel (or whatever) back from when I was a kid." Well, if Genetipet was on the level, it looked like someday soon that fantasy could come true. And that's just the beginning. The mind boggles at the possibilities.

The whole notion of breeding racehorses, for example. It's all a crapshoot. You put a Northern Dancer out to stud and what do you get? Son-of-Northern-Dancer *might* turn out to be a winner. But the nag could just as easily be a prime candidate for the glue factory. You pays your money and you takes your chances, because there's no telling what's swimming around in the gene pool.

But with cloning technology we'll be able to reproduce an actual mirror image of the great horse down to the last little hunk of DNA. And suppose you didn't tell anybody about it ahead of time. You could make a killing at the track.

Anyway, getting back to Paul Asmuss and Genetipet, there was one little snag in all this. As far as I could tell, all Paul really did at his company was store blood samples. Was there any reason why I couldn't do that myself and cut out the middleman? You know, draw some blood from my dog or cat, dump it in a zip-lock bag and toss it my own freezer and presto—instant DNA popsicles.

"No, that wouldn't work," he said, "because a household freezer just is not cold enough. In your neck of the woods, up there in Canada with the metric system, cryogenic freezing requires a temperature of minus 196 degrees centigrade."

Translation: really, really cold. I mean even hell could finally freeze over at those temperatures. In Paul's words, "the cryogenic samples are so cold they almost turn into glass."

That was a whole other issue. Wasn't there such a thing as too cold? So cold that when you thaw out the sample to revive the DNA it would be dead?

"Not at all," Paul said. "Cryogenics, the technology of it, has been around since the 1940s and the thing about it is that it slows the cell molecular activity down to where it virtually comes to a standstill so that you can freeze something and keep it indefinitely."

So yeah, okay, I guess cryogenics is a tad beyond the range of your average household icebox. But other than a really *deep* deep-freeze, I wasn't clear on Paul's qualifications for running a cutting-edge cryogenics company like Genetipet. So I asked him if he had a background as a scientist.

"No," he said, "I just read up on it. The basic principles are readily available in the literature. It's quite simple really." And Paul went on to describe the process. "We put the blood samples in big jugs, or actually they're more like Thermos bottles. There's liquid nitrogen inside them that keeps the DNA cold. You just pour that in. The liquid nitrogen *does* evaporate over time, so you have to keep replacing it.

"But anybody could do this. Let's face it, whether you're into cryogenics or fixing an airplane or doing surgery, anything is pretty easy to do once you've got the equipment. The thing is, ask yourself how many people want to go through the hassle of investing in all the costly high-tech equipment. It's an awful lot easier and cheaper to have somebody like me do it for you."

That made sense and when I asked him how much it would cost to get my pet's DNA stored with Genetipet, Paul was more than happy to talk price and, all things considered, it *was* pretty cheap. "We charge US$175, which includes the first year's storage and $75 of that is for the shipping, handling and preparation work. Then it's a hundred dollars a year thereafter."

Unfortunately Paul was a lot less forthcoming when I asked about his clientele.

"That's a trade secret," he said. "Everybody asks me that and I decline to answer. It's best to be that way, what with the competition and all. We do have customers here in the U.S. and overseas but it's something we don't promote too much because that's never been what this is about. I will say this much: we started Genetipet with our own animals. That's really why we did it—for *our* dogs."

So Paul Asmuss was his own first, best customer. He actually entrusts his own doggy DNA to a cryogenic chill chamber. If that doesn't inspire confidence in a company, I don't know what does. Still, there was one nagging question. What about long-term maintenance? What happens if—God forbid—Paul Asmuss were to drop dead tomorrow? I know he made the whole cryogenic process sound like a no-brainer, but *somebody's* still got to keep topping up the jugs with liquid nitrogen until cloning catches on, right?

"Well, I don't guarantee anything," he said. "Hopefully there are people around who'll take it over, but there's only so much you can do. I mean, what happens if a comet hits us tomorrow?"

Well, that was a while ago and so far (knock on wood) that kind of Armageddon hasn't happened. But cloning? That's another matter. I tried to contact Paul again in the spring of 1999, just to see how his business was doing in the wake of the Dolly experiments. His company number is no longer listed in the Port Townsend directory where I got it in 1994. And an Internet search revealed no trace of Genetipet anywhere in the United States, and no clue about what happened to all those DNA-pet-popsicles preserved forever in liquid nitrogen.

IV: FREEZE-DRIED FIDO

Ever since that day I dug up the family dog
I've had a morbid interest in pet memorials.

A ND I'M interested in the way we *Homo sapiens* like to cling to our dearly departed furry friends. If you think pet cloning is out there, you better think again. I've been to pet seances and pet funerals, and done items on a pet casket company. I've held in my hand a myriad of beastly body parts—everything from a bronzed puppy-dog tail to a turtle-shell candy dish to a cat's-paw key-chain. But this story tops them all.

There's a company in Clearwater, Florida called Preservation Specialties. It's run by a fellow named Jeff Webber, and if anybody has a finger on the pulse of the pet memorial business, it's this guy. Jeff Webber is in the business of freeze-drying your dead dog or cat for permanent, decay-proof display.

"Some people think I'm a little strange when they first hear about the notion of freeze-dried pets," he told me. "And I admit it takes some getting used to. But freeze-drying has been around since the early sixties. For years it's been used only for the food industry, but we are now finding just a lot of new applications for it.

"Anyway, I have had some very negative reactions from people, but you'd be surprised what happens three months later when their favourite dog dies. They'll turn up at my front door saying, 'Hey, it's not such a bad idea. What do I have to do?'"

Jeff tells them that once they've "committed" to freeze-drying Fido, they need to get the pet frozen as soon as possible after it dies. The idea there is, of course, to arrest decomposition and to keep your pet in as close to mint condition as you can. So as soon as the pet passes on, you have to toss it in the freezer until you can make the proper arrangements. If you're not comfortable keeping Rover on ice in the family freezer next to the frozen peas, Jeff Webber advised me that your veterinarian "can take care of that for you."

"Once they're frozen," he continued, "the next step is you just wrap the pet in plastic, put it in a Styrofoam-type container with dry ice and ship it air freight right into Tampa—and we'll take care of business from there."

And business, according to Jeff, is great. He started signing up clients in February 1989. By the time I talked to him, just three months later, he'd already taken in over a hundred pets. As he put it, "Things are kicking!"

How do you freeze-dry a dead animal? Jeff told me the technique he uses is, for all intents and purposes, not much different than processing freeze-dried coffee.

"It's exactly the same," he explained. "Once we get the frozen pet we thaw it out, then put it through a three-step chemical process which basically cleans the hide. Next, we dry the pet, groom it and position it any way the owner wants it, sitting, standing or lying. That's their choice, but once the pet is freeze-dried it's too late to change your mind. The position it's dried in is going to be the position it'll have forever.

"Anyway, after we position it, the pet is then refrozen for about forty-eight hours. At that point, it is placed in a large vacuum freeze-dry machine where all of the moisture is gradually removed from the animal. Of course, the larger the pet, the longer the process takes. For the average ten-pound cat or dog you can look to anywhere from sixteen to twenty weeks. I know that seems like a long time, but keep in mind this is a very gentle process."

There was only one thing bothering me about the process as Jeff described it to me. It was clear that the pet remains frozen for the whole drying time. If that was true, won't the whole thing sort of melt and go limp when it thaws out?

"Oh no," Jeff said. "Not once all the moisture is gone. Freeze-drying is the removal of all of the moisture in an organism. Once that moisture is gone there is nothing left to melt."

The way Jeff explained it to me, what you're left with is a body filled with an elaborate honeycomb of dry porous fibres with air where all the water used to be. It's a bit like one of those bubbly candy bars that looks like a regular chocolate bar and costs the same, but actually gives you a lot less candy because it's full of air bubbles.

Jeff says that, on average, once you extract all the water, the animals weigh approximately 70 percent less than they do when they go into the dehydration chamber. All of which makes for a pretty portable pet, light enough to tuck under your arm and carry around with you wherever you go.

So far so good, but if you suck out 70 percent of the body weight of an animal, don't you run the risk of Fido or Fifi or whoever coming out looking like a prune? According to Jeff, there's "no shrinkage, no wrinkles, no distortion, no hair loss. That is the beauty of this process over taxidermy.

"Don't get me wrong," Jeff hastened to add. "Taxidermists do great work, but we're dealing with a pet you've had for fifteen or even twenty years—a member of your family. If you took it to a taxidermist it would sort of resemble the animal when you got it back but it wouldn't look exactly like your pet. Ours do. Perfection. That's the big advantage freeze-dry has over traditional taxidermy."

Perfection? Well, almost. Unfortunately, there's nothing Jeff can do about the eyes because they're almost nothing but water, so they pretty much evaporate in the process. That means the eyeballs have to get replaced with artificial peepers, custom-matched for colour and size to the originals.

Once that's done, the dead pet that comes out of Jeff Webber's freeze-dry chamber looks a lot more alive than it did when it went in. And by the way, size is no object. Jeff can freeze-dry your pet hamster or your Great Dane. But don't ask him to tackle Jumbo the elephant.

"The Smithsonian Institute," he told me, "did an elephant about fifteen years ago. First they froze it and then they quartered it. They had to cut it into four large pieces because it wouldn't fit into the chamber. After that they freeze-dried the animal piece by piece and reassembled it. So technically it can be done, but I don't want to do an elephant because it takes a tremendous amount of time and room. What we will do is anything up to a small pony."

Now I assumed that, as with all of such experimental, cutting-edge advances in the funeral sciences, Jeff's new process was bound to be a bit pricey.

"Well," he told me, "that depends on the size of the pet. The prices start at US$400 for anything up to and including eight pounds. Then, if you get into, say, a sixty-pound dog, you're looking at about $1,600, because a dog that size is going to take from six to eight months. Obviously a pony would run a lot higher than that because basically what you're paying for in the freeze-dry process is time in the chamber.

"Now, number-wise, the most popular pet we do is your regular ordinary run-of-the-mill house cat. We do about 60 percent of our business in cats. Probably another 30 percent is dogs, and the rest is just an assortment of other pets—birds, hamsters, gerbils, snakes and lizards."

Jeff told me that some people like to keep their favourite freeze-dried pet on display under glass—much as the Commies did with Lenin—but "that's not necessary. In fact," he went on, "they're the exception, not the rule. Actually, most people like to move their freeze-dried pets around from room to room."

So you don't have to treat these things like delicate *objets d'art*. It's perfectly okay to let Bowser collect dust while you've got him posed sleeping next to the couch, or begging for leftovers at the dining-room table, or at the front door fetching your evening paper. And the upkeep is no big deal. You just dust him once in a while or run the vacuum over him, and he's as good as new.

Jeff told me about "a commercial pilot who we did a cat for. The pilot says that his cat, Fred, loved to fly, and when the pilot is out on the job, Fred the freeze-dried cat usually sits up front, right alongside him in the cockpit."

How comforting to glance over and see the familiar friendly face of your beloved companion ever at your side. More comforting still is the certain knowledge there are no strings attached. A freeze-dried pet is a user-friendly pet. No more flea-bites, no more litter boxes, no more going into hock so Fred can scarf down gourmet grub while you nickel-and-dime your way through yet another Kraft Dinner.

I think Jeff Webber's really on to something with Preservation Specialties. And it's only a matter of time before he ups the ante. I asked him if he planned to start running human corpses through his dehydration chamber.

"Absolutely. It could be today, tomorrow or next year. We are already prepared to go into that sector. We've had a tremendous interest from the funeral industry in the U.S. as well as from individuals around the country. Some of these people are heads of corporations, and some are housewives and bus drivers. They all look at it as a healthy alternative to cremation or burial."

It dawned on me that price might not matter to a CEO or some other corporate honcho, but a bus driver? Could your average working stiff (and I mean that literally) afford to have himself freeze-dried?

"Well," he said, "initially, it's going to be quite high—somewhere in the neighbourhood of $20,000. Of course, as more and more people get into it, the price will drop. Eventually it should come into line—costwise—with traditional burial. I'm sure that the day will come when *everybody* will be able to afford a freeze-dry funeral.

"My main interest, however, lies in seeing people like, say, Elvis Presley get freeze-dried. Can you imagine the *real* body of Elvis lying in state at the Graceland mansion? And Ronald Reagan! When he dies he'll be another perfect candidate. The public wants to see these people," Jeff said warmly. "Why pay to see a tacky replica in a wax museum when you can have the real McCoy. It *is* possible."

And that's freeze-dried food for thought.

CHAPTER FOUR

KING CLONTZ

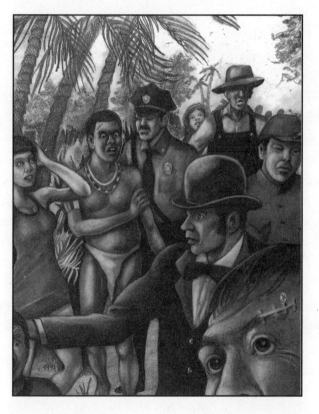

The illustrator lives on at the *Weekly World News*!
See how hard it is to distinguish this lifelike pencil
drawing from a photo. It illustrates an August 1988
story on alien implants around the world. The picture
was a gift to Harold Fiske by WWN artist Dick Kulpa.

I: PILGRIMAGE

It's only 10 A.M., but it's already
90 degrees in the shade.

BOCA RATON, FLORIDA. FEBRUARY 27, 1992

THE AIR-CONDITIONING'S busted in my cheap rental so I'm
sweating like a pig driving north out of Boca, heading for the editorial offices of the *Weekly World News.*

Weekly World News is one of the few great Florida tabs still defi-
antly publishing in glorious black-and-white. Boca Raton, and the surrounding area, is North America's tabloid coast. And I've made the
2,500-mile pilgrimage—all the way from Canada to this supermarket
tabloid Mecca—just so I can grovel at the feet of Eddie "King" Clontz,
the editorial genius behind WWN. I worship the ground this man walks
on. Eddie may not be a household name, but in the tabloid business he
is royalty, and the name Clontz is the stuff of legends.

Now, I want to confess right up front that in spite of all my years in
the tabloid trenches, I've always been a little bit in awe of Eddie Clontz.
According to the old cliché, imitation is the highest form of flattery—
that goes double for the cutthroat world of hack journalism, where you
don't just imitate, you outright steal the other guy's story, do a quick
rewrite and slap on your own byline.

Well, over the years I've ripped off more than my share of Eddie's
ideas and I have to tell you that I'm a little nervous about meeting the
guy. I'm worried he may try to kill me.

See, rumour has it the King packs a loaded pistol in his desk
drawer. I don't know if that's true, but everybody else down here in
Florida seems to be packing heat—one town even has a by-law that

obliges local residents to carry guns. As a matter of fact, this whole corner of south Florida has been built on the "armed camp" concept of municipal planning. The place is one endless string of controlled-access compounds, sort of like the one in *The Godfather*. Only more subtle.

All the houses face in on each other, and they're ringed by stately palm trees and magnificent sculpted shrubs that artfully conceal the *real* Boca Raton. (Brick walls, barbed wire barricades, attack dogs and a security force armed to the teeth, manning a gatehouse to keep out the riff-raff.)

If you do somehow happen to talk your way past the guards and the Dobermans—watch out! The good citizens of southern Florida have got more than skeletons stashed in the hall closet. These folks are all knee-deep in domestic arsenals. Hell, half the cars have got guns. And make no mistake about it—this is car, as well as gun, country.

You drive or you don't belong. There are no pedestrians, no sidewalks, no jogging paths, no bicycle lanes. You go anywhere, you take the car because, in Boca Raton, it's your God-given right to drive—*and* to park.

That's why you won't find a single parking meter in this burg. There's so much free parking it's sort of like living in one of those Hollywood movies where the hero, in a huge Mack truck, pulls up in front of Grand Central Station at rush hour and just happens to find a parking spot.

Anyway, parking's not an issue for me at the moment. I'm stuck in traffic, backed up half a mile, waiting to cross the famous intracoastal waterway. I sit here cooling my jets while some rowboat goes through the canal and they raise the entire bridge. This goes on all day long in "beautiful Boca Raton."

Before I flew down here I phoned the local chamber of commerce. I thought I'd get a businessman's package pointing out the local sights and free passes to stuff—common courtesy for a visiting journalist, right? No way! All they sent me was this miserable little package with a couple of pamphlets promoting some stupid butterfly zoo. That was about it.

Plus, they were really short with me, and dismissive and shirty over the phone. I came away with the distinct impression that the city fathers really don't encourage people like me to come into their community and delve into—what? Their sordid and empty lives? Talk about paranoid. No wonder everybody's packing heat in Florida.

Speaking of paranoia, I can almost smell it when I finally pull up in front of my destination—the *Weekly World News* in Lantana, Florida.

The wwn operates out of the same building as that granddaddy of the tabs, the *National Enquirer*. (In fact, they're owned by the same company.) Anyway, once I clear security, I head inside, hang a left when I should hang a right, and end up in the bustling newsroom of the *Enquirer* by mistake. Only it isn't bustling for long. Those guys take one look at me—a stranger with a tape recorder—and you can hear a pin drop.

Maybe they figure I'm a corporate spy sent in by the competition. Maybe they take me for some sleazy private dick digging dirt for one of those celebrity lawyers that're always suing the paper. Either way I'm *persona non grata* at the *Enquirer*. Which is fine by me, because I hate that whole self-important, sycophantic celebrity beat they specialize in.

A couple of the *Enquirer* "suits" corner me, ask me a lot of questions, triple-check my credentials and make sure I haven't taped any of their top-secret shenanigans on the sly. Then they escort me through the corridor that constitutes the no man's land separating the *Enquirer* from it's low-rent cousin, the *Weekly World News*. One of the suits warns me, "Don't come back! We don't want to catch you wandering over here again."

I'm thinking, "You got that right, fella," when I turn a corner and finally come face to face with . . . Eddie "King" Clontz.

II: AN AUDIENCE WITH THE KING

Eddie Clontz does not shoot me!

NSTEAD, I GET a firm handshake, a pat on the back and a refreshing promise of free rein. Eddie's a smallish, balding, middle-aged guy wearing one of those pastel-coloured cruise-line polyester leisure suits with an open-necked collar. As far as King Clontz is concerned, the *Weekly World News* is an open book for Harold Fiske.

Eddie turns out to be as good as his word. He tells me the idea for the *Weekly World News* was the brainchild of Generoso Pope. Pope is revered in the trade as the father of what, in the early seventies, became know as the *supermarket* tabloid industry. The tabs were around long before that, however. Pope founded the *National Enquirer* way back in 1952. He only conceived the *Weekly World News* in 1979 as a kind of bastard offspring of the *Enquirer*.

Back then the *Enquirer* had just switched over to colour printing in order to compete with the then New York–based *Star*, which was its major competitor. (These days, it operates out of the same building as the *Enquirer*—both tabs are owned by the same company.)

At the time the *Enquirer* was selling about five million copies a week and the *Star* was inching up to three million. The colour in the *Star* seemed to be the reason for that, says Eddie, so the *Enquirer* decided to go to the mattresses in an all-out circulation war. They'd switch to colour, go bigger and better, spare no expense—whatever it took to combat the *Star*.

But that left them with their black-and-white presses sitting idle down here in Florida. So Generoso Pope started the new paper just to use up the press time—a pretty sharp business move.

Maybe so, but, Eddie says, at the time it was seen as nothing more than "a sort of a make-work project, and editorially it appeared to be just that. The celebrities, the beautiful actresses, simply don't look the same in black-and-white as they do in colour, and the paper sat there not selling for three years."

With nothing to lose, they went back to the old archives of the *Enquirer*, back to the turn of the century, to see how the original old-time tabloids did it in the good old days of yellow journalism.

"Very *sensational* yellow journalism," Eddie tells me, "and that's what we tried to emulate. We brought back the great mysteries of our world—the Devil's Triangle, Bigfoot, ghosts, space aliens, and things of that nature. Stories which, by the 1980s, were all considered 1950s material. People warned us, 'Aw, nobody wants to read about that any more!' But they did. And the *Weekly World News* went from 250,000 in March of 1982 to 1.3 million by May of 1988."

The *Weekly World News* never looked back. I ask Eddie if he remembers the headline for that issue, the one that sold 1.3 million copies. "Sure. 'Elvis Is Alive'—that's the one headline that I guess I'm famous for and, to be honest, I didn't think it would sell.

"It was a slow week at the paper so I went in to see Mr. Pope—he was still alive at the time. I said to him, 'We really don't have much for page one except a woman in Kalamazoo, Michigan, who claims that she was in a Burger King and that Elvis was in line behind her and ordered a Big Mac.'

"He kind of chuckled and said, 'Is that *all* you've got?' I said, 'Yes, sir' and we went with it anyway. We sold out in three days, nationally—and in Canada. As you know, that 'Elvis Is Alive' headline went around the world and has become a part of our phraseology. It was a phenomenon."

A phenomenon that Eddie is quick to explain. "We found it to be a fascinating subject for people. I mean, how nice to think that your hero, whether they be politician, entertainer, close relative, whatever, might still be alive after publicly dying, so to speak."

The Elvis-is-alive phenomenon was so big that Eddie couldn't resist the temptation to try the gimmick out on another larger-than-life dead American hero. Only this time, "I was very, very nervous and concerned about it. Particularly when we got a photograph that showed a white-haired man in a wheelchair with a dark-haired very pretty woman. The picture was very grainy, very out-of-focus. The photographer claimed it was John F. Kennedy at the age of seventy-four.

"Jackie was rendezvousing with him in Poland at the secret hide-out, the JFK compound where he had lived all of these years after he was supposedly shot in Dallas. The reason for the cover-up being that Kennedy's advisors feared that he would be the constant target of assassination if anybody knew he was alive. The story I was told is that JFK does in fact still advise the government in times of crisis.

"I was very nervous about the story. I didn't scrutinize the photograph too closely, but that's the way we sometimes do business when something may be of great value, and may in fact be true, even though the odds may be against it.

"Maybe it's a true story, maybe it isn't—but we sold another record number of papers. And the letters were great! It was a refrain: 'Isn't it nice to think that our greatest president of the twentieth century is at least there to take a phone call when help is needed. Wouldn't it be nice if that were true?' And that is what the *Weekly World News* does so well."

Although I didn't tell Eddie this during our talk, I know those JFK shots all too well—they'd been published back in the mid-seventies long before King Clontz got his hands on them. The story they originally ran with was slugged "JFK—Alive and Well In Skorpios." (Skorpios was Ari Onassis's island in the Aegean, in case you've forgotten.) The story originally ran in the tab *Midnight*, precursor to today's *Globe*. *Midnight* was a sister paper to my old tabloid the *National Examiner;* it was published in Montreal.

The pictures for "JFK—Alive and Well In Skorpios" were actually taken in Montreal's Mount Royal Cemetery for no better reason than the graveyard was handy and boasted a pretty convincing Greek-looking column.

It was rumoured around the office that the guy playing JFK was none other than John Vader, later the editor of the *National Examiner,* and my boss. The "Jackie" pushing him in the wheelchair was a woman called Roz, who worked in the office at the time. The photographer was a Polish guy called Michel, and I suspect he's still got the negatives and is still trying to flog them to other tabs (and more power to him!).

Michel shot those pics with a wide-angle lens on grainy film. He was across Camilien Houde Boulevard in Mount Royal Park shooting into the cemetery—and the pictures looked like they'd been shot from a boat in the Aegean off the coast of Skorpios.

Obviously, this Michel guy could work miracles with a camera. I once went with him to a Montreal press conference where the Dalai Lama was speaking. We needed to get an "exclusive interview" with His Holiness, but the trouble was, I couldn't get within fifty feet of him because he was surrounded by security people—I think the Chinese government was trying to kill him or something.

Against all odds, Michel managed to get a picture of Harold kneeling in supplication at the Dalai Lama's feet, with the Great Enlightened One gesturing vaguely in benediction. Actually I was *way* across the room at the time, but Michel used one of those ultrahuge lenses, which eliminated depth of field and pulled me right up next to the Dalai Lama.

The photo ran with the Great Enlightened One's remarks on reincarnation. Now, the Dalai Lama sometimes uses his formidable telepathic powers to conduct his interviews with journalists, which is what happened on that day with me. His Holiness was good enough to answer my questions about his multiple past lives while all the other reporters in the room were snarling away about Tibetan politics. But I'm digressing here—let's get back to my historic meeting with Eddie Clontz!

"How do you get your stories?" I say, asking him the dumbest question in all journalism. "I mean the germ of an idea. Does that usually come from a freelance photographer like the Kennedy thing, or what?"

"Well," he tells me, "number one, we get stories from newspapers around the world. We try to read through a thousand publications a week. For example, we were reading a really dry little article in the *Scientific American*. One of my reporters clipped it out and showed me. It was about this scientist from the University of Iowa, a Professor Abian."

Once again I recognize the story Eddie's talking about, because *I* interviewed Professor Abian for *Basic Black*. Eddie stole that story from *Scientific American* and I stole it from Eddie. (It's in Chapter Eleven.) Abian was terrific fun. He had a wild theory and a great, thick, absent-minded professor's foreign accent. But I'll let Eddie tell it:

"Professor Abian claimed that if you take out some chunks of the moon with some explosives you could change the weather on earth, to the point that the deserts would bloom, hunger would disappear and everybody would live happily ever after. Now this was the driest little piece of writing I've ever seen in my life. It even had some mathematical equations at the end of it.

"That was not *Weekly World News* territory, but when we did our front page, "Scientist Plots to Blow Up Moon," that *was* our kind of story. Now, I do find that some of the more esteemed and academic of our story subjects aren't always too pleased to end up in *Weekly World News*, but Dr. Abian was quite a good sport about it. He didn't mind at all and I just thought that was one of the most intriguing stories we ever had.

"We go after these stories—the weird science, the medical mysteries, the people exploding on operating tables—we go at it with the same zeal and enthusiasm that a Washington reporter would go after a Watergate story.

"By the way, we get terrific story ideas from our readers. In fact, when the Elvis phenomenon really got going we had some people complain, 'Oh, you guys made up those stories.' Not true.

"Back then we were getting five hundred letters a week on Elvis alone. I had on my desk, with telephone numbers, addresses and signatures, three hundred Elvis sightings within two months after we ran the "Elvis Is Alive" story. 'Elvis washed my car.' 'I sat beside Elvis at the movies.' 'Elvis came by and mowed my lawn.' It went on and on. We had our pick.

"We got a letter from a waitress who said she lived with him from 1981 to 1983. If that was true then Elvis certainly wasn't dead. Her name is Elizabeth Prince and she truly believes that she lived with Elvis. She had photographs. We gave her a lie detector test and she is just totally believable, so we published her wonderful story."

And it all started with a letter to the editor? Sensing a quick-and-dirty source for bootleg story ideas, I hint around how I wouldn't mind a little peek inside his mailbag. Did I say mail*bag*? Eddie points to a small mountain of canvas sacks in the corner. "You're welcome to browse through those," he tells me. "See what you can find. If you *do* see any promising stories in there, please get back to me and we'll get to work on them."

III: HIS MAJESTY'S MISSIVES

I might as well be panning for gold in Fort Knox.

HITTING PAYDIRT in Eddie Clontz's heap of virgin, untouched, unexpurgated, unopened letters to the editor is almost *too* easy. It's a no-brainer.

I pull out everything from an obsessively detailed twenty-five-page document about a monumental CIA conspiracy to take over the *Weekly World News,* to a fan letter from a five-year-old, scratched out in purple crayon and covered in hundreds of happy-face stickers.

Let me show you just a few of the gems that I dig out of the pile. The first one, I'm happy to say, comes from Canada:

> Dear Editor,
>
> On the morning of June 30, 1993 my friend Marlon and I witnessed a sight we couldn't explain. Four rather GIANT BEETLES were eating a parked limousine on the street in front of my house.
>
> They stopped the damage when they got to the engine. One of the beetles though was stupid enough to chew on the engine wires and HE GOT FRIED!!
>
> The other big bugs turned and glared at us. Their abdomens were hairy and brown. They had fourteen eyes and three pairs of hands, each ending in large talon-like claws.
>
> I saw them fly to a cloud and then an explosion like that of a hydrogen bomb explosion occurred. I haven't seen the creatures since but I sent you a picture I drew of the dead one . . .
>
> WE STILL HAVE THE CORPSE IN OUR FREEZER.
>
> > (name and address withheld)
> > Welland, Ontario, Canada
>
> P.S. You can use the picture if you want to.

Okay, it *is* a cool drawing (check it yourself—it's the picture that's at the start of Chapter Ten), but c'mon guys. You've got the *real* thing in the icebox. You too cheap to send a photo?

Moving right along: Eddie Clontz says that this next letter is a response to another one of his dead-celebrity-is-still-alive campaigns.

Dear *Weekly World News,*

You're right. He's not dead! We met HIM!! On the day our encounter happened we were hiking in the woods. We had just sat down with our lunches of peanut butter sandwiches and candy bars when we heard a low deep growl behind us.

It was a BIG BLACK BEAR! The bear stumbled out of the woods and pinned down Casey. It was nosing for her candy. It consumed the chocolate in an instant then turned to Molly and me. Of course we were screaming and paralyzed with fear so we didn't move.

Then we saw him. MICHAEL LANDON appeared out of nowhere. He knelt down next to the bear and started speaking in a language we did not understand. I guess the bear understood though because when Michael finished talking the bear kind of nodded and then lumbered off.

After that Mr. Landon turned to us and said, "You girls be more careful," and then he walked away.

We told our friends and EVERYONE THOUGHT WE WERE CRAZY!! I mean, we knew Michael Landon died last year so we thought maybe we were having some weird hallucination or something. But then we saw true accounts of other people's experiences in the *Weekly World News* and we knew it HAD happened for real.

MICHAEL LANDON SAVED OUR LIVES!

(name and address withheld)
Spokane, Washington

Here's one more. This time the letter is printed, in pencil, and it looks like it was a rush job because it was done in a very *shaky* hand. Not hard to figure why once you read this thing.

Dear Sir,

Two weeks ago a farmer I know was going out in the morning to milk the cows when he spotted ... SATAN! He appeared to be eating the farmer's corn crop. This Satan figure did not see the farmer or anyone else so he went into the farmhouse.

The farmer followed the Devil and when he got inside he saw that Satan had sat on the couch and turned the TV on and was watching *Sesame Street*. When the show was over Satan burned the letter "A" and the letter "W" and the number "10" on the farmer's forehead. Then he TORE OUT THE FARMER'S EYES so that the last thing that he saw was Big Bird, Oscar and the Devil.

Yours sincerely
(name and address withheld)
Sterling, Colorado

Let's face it, you don't see stories like that in the *New York Times*. Actually, you won't see them in the *Weekly World News* either, since I pocketed those suckers and took 'em with me.

IV: THE KING'S COURT

Every king needs his loyal subjects.

EDDIE "KING" CLONTZ tells me he has "a staff of over 120 reporters and photographers working on the paper day and night." I only make out about twenty people while I'm here, but who's counting?

Eddie says that if I want the full scoop on why his paper sets the industry standard for black-and-white yellow journalism them I'm just going to have to get down in the trenches with the people who do the grunt work day in and day out on the *Weekly World News*. "You might as well start with Dick Kulpa. He's that gentleman working up the headlines for our next edition."

Good idea. The paper's justly famous for snappy, funny and sometimes disturbing headlines like

HOW TO TELL IF YOUR HEAD'S ABOUT TO BLOW UP!

or the equally unsettling

SPONTANEOUS HUMAN COMBUSTION!
Girl bursts into flames . . . In the shower!

If Dick Kulpa's the guy who turns out copy like that, then I want to meet him. I introduce myself and pump him for his take on hatching headlines.

"Each story," he says, "is case-by-case. Everything's played differently. We're not going to laugh at the misfortunes of people but we do print a lot of outrage stories, such as the one about the father who burned his son.

"That was sick. It makes anyone who reads it angry. We're *not* going to have fun with that with a goofy headline. But we *do* want the people to know what kind of really bad people are out there and how bad it can get.

"Of course, another reason we run these stories is for the out-pouring of sympathy we're able to generate for the victims. Sometimes the victims will get a little donation from our readers and we're more than glad to do that for them. So in our paper you get a whole variety of things, whether it's crime or religion or goofball. You name it, we've got it.

"If it's a serious story you're not going to see a clever headline. But you get stories about some of the really stupid things people do—how can you resist?

"There was one great story we ran several years ago where a whole bunch of body parts—limbs and organs—were found in a man's home. The headline practically wrote itself—'Home Is Where The Heart Is.' If the story asks for it, we'll give it to them.

"Another example: we have a situation right now where what we're reporting on is a brand-new yuppie fad for all these thirty- to thirty-five-year-old people with money and time on their hands and nothing better to do with it. These people used to smoke pot to get high, but now they're sniffing lizard poop! So our headline's going to be, 'What Will They Stink Of Next?'"

The headline's a real attention-grabber and any good hack will tell you getting the reader's attention is half the battle. Dick Kulpa says that you can hook them with a clever headline (and a really bad pun), but if you want to reel them in you better have a good *picture* to go with it.

Susan Chappell picks the photographs that end up in the *Weekly World News*. Dick introduces us and gets Sue to show me some of her prize pictures.

The first photo is part of *WWN's* "Baffling Gallery of Human Wonders." It shows this lady from Detroit, Mary Beth Lacker, eating an ice-cream cone and doing it the hard way. She's holding it down about chest level and her *nine-inch tongue* is snaking out like a cobra and taking a real good lick.

"That's one of my favourites," Sue admits. "It's a world record tongue. And I was so shocked when I finally *saw* it because at first when they called me on the telephone I was like, 'Yeah right!' I didn't believe it *until* I got the picture."

I skim through Sue's portfolio. There's another amazing shot in a feature called "Superhumans." The headline for this one says "Guru drives 3-foot sword through his head!" and they're not kidding.

The guy's got one of those Ali Baba-type curved sabres going in one temple and coming out the other side. And it's not pretty. There's blood everywhere. I've heard of body piercing, but a three-foot sword?

"Well, you know," Susan said, nonchalantly defending her picture, "over in India and places like that (if I'm not mistaken this article came out of Ceylon), over there they have religions where people do this kind of body piercing all the time. As you can see, he lived."

Gee, you must have to be really sharp, really on top of things, to spot which are the fakes and which are the real thing.

"Oh, we can always spot those," she replied confidently. It's a confidence forged from years in the tabloid trenches. "We have readers who are constantly sending us photos like, 'I took a picture of a ghost,' and what they send you is a lame picture that looks like the flashbulb just flashed on the wall and they'll say, 'I'll sell you this picture for $500.' I mean, *give* me a break."

Obviously, the really *authentic* bizarre photographs that the *Weekly World News* specializes in don't come cheap—and sometimes they don't come at all. I ask Susan Chappell what happens when the paper gets a hold of a great tab *story* but then comes up empty in the picture department? For the answer to that one Sue sics me back on to Dick Kulpa.

According to his official *Weekly World News* bio, "Dick is a world-famous artist, a brilliant graphic designer and nationally syndicated cartoonist," so he does double duty as both the paper's headline guy *and* its in-house artist.

"At the *Weekly World News*," Dick points out, "we're living proof that the artist will never become obsolete. You know, when cameras came around back at the turn of the century a lot of newspaper artists became unemployed. I'm proud to be able to say that we are one of the last great newspapers of this century to still employ a full-time artist on staff for action illustration.

"For instance, recently we had reports about a space alien abduction of a woman in New York City. She gave us a very descriptive account as to her encounter with the aliens after being taken aboard a spacecraft. Some rather nasty stuff happened there—some medical examinations, etc.—and of course she wasn't allowed to bring a camera on board.

"See, it's like an auto accident. You *never* get a photo of the *impact* of the auto accident. So I fill that need here. With one drawing (which of course is worth a thousand words) I *can* show the reader what happened."

He's got a point. Dick hands me an astonishingly lifelike artist's rendition of the alien abduction he just described.

It shows a woman strapped down on a table being "examined" by a nasty-looking extraterrestrial critter. Through a porthole I can make out that we're obviously up in the sky, floating over a large modern city full of skyscrapers. I take it that's New York, the woman's home town.

"Right," Dick concurs. "We try to accurately depict what the abductee reports. I'm especially careful about the mechanisms aboard the flying saucer. What will amaze us is that a lot of the eyewitness accounts tell us that the engineering inside the spacecraft isn't that much different from the engineering on earth. They see pulleys and pipes and wires and toggle switches. All the basic simple machines *we* use down here."

Quite a coincidence, and perhaps a positive sign that we're on the right track, that we already possess the basic tools for intergalactic space travel.

I ask Dick about another coincidence I detect in his drawing. That alien space jockey looks awful familiar.

"Oh sure, a lot of people say, 'Gee all your aliens kind of look alike.' Well yeah, that's because the eyewitness descriptions are all the same. Like in this picture. Big buggy eyes. Round bulbous head. Large mouth. Little slits for the nose. Veins sticking out of the head. From the reports we get, there *is* such a thing as a 'standard' alien, because they're obviously all from the same planet. Therefore I don't have a choice. I'd love to give that guy three heads, six arms and twenty fingers but that's not what we got from the eyewitness, and here at the *Weekly World News*, we're bugs for accuracy—I guarantee it."

I check out another picture. There's one truly fetching photo— sorry, *drawing!* They're so good you want to call them photographs— that's how realistic they are. Anyway, this picture looks like some kind of barbarian-type Amazon woman. She's all decked out in armour with a spear and a Mongol-style hat.

"That," Dick explains, "is Genghis Khan. Now you already noticed that he's dolled up in female gear because it turns out that the great conqueror Genghis Khan was, in fact, *a woman!* See, back in those days it was very common for people of different sexes to masquerade as the opposite sex. And of course no self-respecting warrior would have followed Genghis Khan if they knew she was really a woman. So she had to go in drag. And back then you didn't have autopsies, you didn't have medical records kept about these people, so who was to know?"

It's a good point but it raises another question. How did Dick Kulpa find out that Genghis Khan was a *femme fatale?*

"From historians," he told me. "It's historians sifting back through old records and archaeological digs. Remember, a lot of today's history is based on translations of old-time texts. It's like with the Bible. They keep going back and retranslating that and finding different things. That's what the historians have done here."

I'm willing to buy that until I notice Genghis's footwear. Her

Mongol boots are, in fact, high heels—nice kinky *stiletto* heels, in fact. Isn't that kind of a modern touch?

"Well, yeah," Dick admits. "That was one touch I couldn't resist. I just had to add that. And you'll notice the spikes on her bra, there? I confess I did take a *few* liberties."

So much for Dick's guarantee that the staff at the *Weekly World News* "are bugs for accuracy." I find that a tad troubling, so I make a point of checking back with Eddie to find out exactly where King Clontz stands on the issue of editorial honesty.

"Well, like other magazine editors, I will admit that I do put out story ideas from time to time and I really don't care *how* they get back to me. Such as I will tell our reporters, 'You know there've been all these dinosaur sightings. If anybody ever hears about one I'd really love to publish one of those. So let's get out there and really beat the bushes and get us a real good dinosaur attack.' And wouldn't you just know it, lo and behold, a week later I'll look down and there's this wonderful dinosaur story, with photographs, sitting on my desk."

I'm shocked by this admission. "And you don't care how it gets there?" I ask.

Eddie didn't bat an eye. "I follow a credo: *Don't ever question yourself out of a good story.*" It's a credo Eddie's happy to pass along to any wet-behind-the-ears journalism student who walks through the door looking for work at the *Weekly World News*.

"The first thing I tell them is it's not what you ask someone about their story that makes it a *Weekly World News* item, it's what you *don't* ask. You only ask questions until the story starts to fall apart. Then you stop. It's not what you put in a story. It's what you *don't* put in.

"A gentleman climbs up a telephone pole—we did a story about this guy—he climbs up the pole and walks two-and-a-half miles on the wire. An absolutely off-the-wall, inexplicable, human action that is funny and intriguing. If you put in there that the person had one too many drinks or had been smoking something—basically you've killed the story for the *Weekly World News*. Because what you want is for this gentleman to be an average person just like you or me. We want the reader wondering, 'Why in the world would anybody do that?' We don't want to tell them why. We want it just *out of the blue!*

"If we get a call—and we get many—about a UFO, for instance, the first thing you listen for is intercoms. If you hear intercoms or loud-speakers in the background do *not* ask what mental institution they're in. You just go on as if they're sitting in their living-room. If you hear, 'Paging Dr. Smith,' you just ignore that. If they've got some space alien sitting in their living-room, you *don't* ask for the number of their psychiatrist. You say, 'That's great. We'll send a reporter right over.' Then if they say, 'Well the alien may be gone when you get here,' you tell them, 'That's okay. We'll take a picture of you pointing to where they were just before we arrived.' *That's* what I call not questioning yourself out of a good story."

CHAPTER FIVE

ENCORE ELVIS

Philip Stonic, a.k.a. "Elvis Aaron Presley Jr.," in his days as a circus lion, well, leopard, tamer.

I: THE ELVIS-IS-*STILL*-DEAD BEAT

Eddie Clontz brought Elvis back to life, but Harold Fiske put him right back in the ground where he belonged.

EDDIE CLONTZ and his *Weekly World News* cornered the market on those "Elvis-is-alive" stories, but over at the *National Examiner,* we couldn't have cared less. Not because we didn't think Elvis was good for business.

There was no doubt that Elvis had that mythic intangible *je ne sais quoi* that can sell a mess o' papers. I mean, the man has all the properties of a god. If you read the tabs faithfully you'll find that since his death there have even been miracle cures performed at Elvis's Graceland digs in Memphis, Tennessee.

So yes, we worshipped the King over at the *Examiner* too—it's just that we preferred him dead and buried, because the dead don't reach up and bite you back. That's why we nurtured our *own* Elvis angle. We called it the "Elvis-is-*still*-dead" beat. The name evolved from its predecessors. After Presley died in 1977, the old Elvis beat became the "Elvis-is-dead" beat, and by the early 1980s, this had changed into the—well, you get the idea.

The beat had a dead-stupid formula. You'd basically say, "Now that Elvis is dead, the truth can finally be revealed about [*insert your favourite drivel here*]!" All you have to do is let your imagination run wild and fill in the blank.

We tended to zero in on the seamy underbelly of the Elvis industry, those shameless parasites with gimmicky marketing devices who try to make a profit on the King's corpse. We latched onto the impersonators who steal his songs, the psychics who steal his soul and the self-professed bastard Elvis offspring who try their best to steal a piece of his estate.

They were all grist for our tabloid mill and there were so many of these cons and kooks coming out of the woodwork that we always had our pick of the litter. The Elvis-is-*still*-dead beat never lacked for fresh material. The funny thing about "dead" beats is they don't work with all deceased celebs. When Elvis turned out to sell more tabloids after he died than before, the directing minds behind the *Examiner* tried to get a "still dead" beat going with other celebs, including John Wayne and, later, Steve McQueen. But it just didn't work, and I don't know why. I've also seen tabs trying to do the same thing with Frank Sinatra lately, but my impression is they're not having much luck. For some reason, tab readers really loved Elvis—he seemed to touch some basic primal chord in their lives that others couldn't reach (except maybe Hitler or JFK or personalities of that calibre). Go figure.

Having said all that, and in spite of the wealth of *authentic* newsworthy Elvis items to choose from, I'm a little embarrassed to admit that during the four years I worked at the *Examiner*, the only story I ever saw completely faked (but not by me!) was an Elvis story entitled: "Elvis's Ghost Seen at Graceland." Good headline, right? The problem was, the headline was all they had. (A lot of the time we worked backwards like that. The editor would come up with a snappy title or a funny picture and then assign somebody to write around it.)

The people on the Elvis beat spent a couple of months on that one, looking for somebody who would both corroborate the story and let us record their testimony on tape. We taped everything at the *National Examiner*. This was crucial because the paper's publisher wanted to be able to *prove* we didn't make this stuff up, and we didn't—not usually.

Anyway, the staff worked like maniacs buttonholing every Elvis fanatic on file, but no dice. We didn't get anywhere until one of the women who worked in the office called up the features editor, and while he rolled his tape she started cooing in her best Southern belle accent (which wasn't very good at all), "It was so weird when I seen Elvis's ghost hovering over the pool at Graceland." That was the quote that got used when we ran the story with a file shot of the pool and that was that.

So yes, it *was* faked, but it was a *forgivable* fake because three weeks after we ran that story we found out it was true! We got all kinds of readers calling and writing in saying that they, too, had seen Elvis's ghost at Graceland. Plus, we actually had a few letters from people who thought the whole thing was a contest. They sent back the shot of the pool with little pen circles indicating where they thought they saw the ghost in the picture—they figured it was one of those "spot-the-ball" contests the British tabs run all the time. Some actually drew the ghost in, along with poolside furniture or accessories.

Of all the Elvis-is-*still*-dead stories I worked on at the *Examiner*, I'm especially proud of a rework job I did to spiff up a tired old story that had been kicking around our office for years. Now, at the tabs you recycle everything . . . to death. That means that every couple of years somebody would haul this one particular war-horse out of mothballs and rerun it under a shocking new headline, something like "Experts Predict: America Will Split in Half!"

Now this story is essentially true. If you read journals (and who doesn't?) like *Geological Quarterly*, you know that every reputable member of the scientific community knows that there's a huge geological fault that runs right down the Mississippi valley, smack dab in the middle of the United States. It was responsible for the largest earthquake ever in U.S. recorded history, in the early nineteenth century, and sooner or later the thing is going to snap open again. That's a certifiable fact. It may take a couple of centuries, but you can bet the farm it's going to happen.

My problem was, how could I work Elvis into this story? In a word

—Graceland. Graceland's in Memphis and Memphis is on the Mississippi, so you do the math: "Scientists Warn: Massive Earthquake Will Flatten Graceland." That was the headline. The lead ran something like, "Concerned geologists warn that a time bomb is ticking under the beloved home of the King of Rock 'n' Roll. Any day now, Graceland will collapse in a pile of rubble." The rest of the story wrote itself. It worked like a charm.

It's funny how memory works. Of all the fools and hucksters pushing Elvis-related junk, the one I best remember (and I'm not sure why) was a guy from Arkansas who was trying to market an Elvis wine. He'd imported a whole tanker full of cheap red plonk, which he'd put into bottles with a label reading, "Always Elvis."

There was just one problem with his brilliant scheme—Elvis *hated* wine. He was more of a bourbon-and-branchwater kind of guy, and many of his fans knew it, including Donna Flint, who held down the Elvis-is-*still*-dead beat at the *Examiner* when I was there. She confronted this guy, quite aggressively, with the fact that the King couldn't abide wine, and without missing a beat the guy shot back; "Yeah, that's true—but this is the kinda wine that Elvis wouldda liked if Elvis hadda liked wine."

II: APING ELVIS

If imitation is the highest form of flattery, then Elvis Presley is the single most sucked-up-to guy in history.

MEAN EVERYBODY—the good, the bald and the ugly—"does" Elvis these days, and the good ones sure know how to draw a crowd.

I remember one Elvis impersonator we covered at the *Examiner* who advertised that during his act he intended to hold a seance. He was going to try to raise the spirit of Elvis to sing a duet with him. All hell broke loose when a bunch of fundamentalist Christians burst in screaming sacrilege and started a riot. The whole thing was a debacle.

There are so many Presley wannabes out there trying to make a few bucks off his memory that they actually hold conventions exclusively dedicated to the art of aping Elvis. The craze hit its zenith in the 1992 movie *Honeymoon in Vegas* when Nicolas Cage and the flying Elvises did a synchronized parachute drop onto the Las Vegas strip.

Big deal. Elvis impersonators were old news to Harold Fiske by then. Heck, I'd already done the definitive radio documentary on the subject a year earlier on CBC's *Basic Black*. The show's producers were hot on the idea because I'd promised them that I would at least try to incorporate an affirmative action angle on the subject—minority mimics. If they were out there doing Elvis, and if they were any good, I'd put them in my doc. CBC producers love that kind of stuff, so they gave me a deadline (one week) and *carte blanche* with a Bell Canada calling card and told me to get on with it.

When I was done I told them it had been a tougher assignment than I'd expected. I'd slaved away for the whole week tracking down leads, working the phones, talking to dozens of *ersatz* Elvises from all across the continent. I'd put in countless hours weeding out the chaff from the wheat, the chumps from the champs. There were plenty of both but I was looking for the best of the best, the *crème de la crème* of the Elvis clones. And did I find them.

Well, actually, that's not quite true. Oh, I *did* come up with three absolute gems. It's just that I kind of exaggerated the effort it took. Truth is, I didn't break a sweat. See, all along I had this really cool book called *I Am Elvis: A Guide to Elvis Impersonators*. It was full of bios and pictures and, best of all, phone numbers for sixty-five of the greatest Elvis mimics in the world. So I read the bumf on these characters, called the most likely candidates, knocked off the interviews in a couple of hours and had the whole documentary in the can in less than an afternoon. I just didn't bother to tell my producers. That way, I got to dog it the rest of the week and go nuts with the calling card. Nobody was the wiser.

And the documentary? If you ask me, it was awardworthy work, an equal-opportunity radio triptych featuring three remarkable human beings whose stories are all the more noteworthy when you consider the high calibre of the Elvis impersonators who *didn't* make the cut— including *Baby* Elvis!

Baby Elvis was a real cute three-year-old who I was all ready to use until I found out he only *lip-syncs* Presley's songs. That kind of thing just doesn't cut it on radio, so when it turned out the kid was a phony, I cancelled. He was crushed but, hey, that's showbiz, kid.

Anyway, without further ado I give you Fiske's triumphant trio of Elvis apers.

THE LADY ELVIS

Janice Keye is a wee little slip of a thing. At five feet, five inches and 105 pounds, she doesn't try to walk in the King's shoes and let's face it nobody would ever mistake this diminutive damsel for the bloated disgusting porker that Elvis had become by the time he kicked the bucket. But what the Lady Elvis lacks in girth she more than makes up for where it counts—inside.

Janice takes impersonating Elvis way beyond the rhinestones and the ducktails. This woman sees her role as spiritual. For her, the whole Elvis thing is an otherworldly exercise, a journey into the very heart and soul of the King.

The spiritual kinship she feels with Elvis stems from a momentous occasion in her life. It happened on December 17, 1983, more than six years after Elvis died. Now Janice doesn't usually talk about what happened on that fateful and fantastic day, but I was able to charm some of the pertinent details out of her.

"I was in the kitchen here in Exeter, Nebraska and the image appeared in the screen on the outside of our kitchen window. There was this image of Elvis's face. It was just his face. It was about one-and-a-half times bigger than normal and it wasn't in colour, it was in black-and-white. It was just so spooky. I watched it all night. I'd glance up and he'd still be there, looking right in at me. And he always looked sort of a little hostile—well actually, no, he wasn't really hostile, but he wasn't ever smiling, not the whole time, not even once.

"Then about two or three days later I finally noticed. Behind that same window screen we had this evergreen tree that had kind of taken over and blocked the window. Well that evergreen tree was scorched all the way through, like it had been burned behind that face on the screen. And you know, I thought, 'My gosh do you suppose some kind of force come through there and it was Elvis?'"

Well, on that note a light bulb lit up over my head and my internal entrepreneur kicked into high gear. I told Janice that if I were her, I'd turn that kitchen into a shrine. The neighbours would be lined up around the block and paying big-time to get a look at the holy site where that epic visitation had taken place.

Sadly, Janice told me that stuff "just isn't me." In fact, she doesn't like to go around broadcasting the incident because, "You tell people about that and on average they'll just think, 'Aw, she's nuts,' you know."

Yes I do. I know all too well the cynical depths to which our culture has sunk! There are disbelievers everywhere. Well, I could sense Janice's discomfort with the issue, so I didn't press. Instead I changed the subject back to her Elvis act. Since Janice was the only lady Elvis I'd ever interviewed, I wanted to know if she made much of an effort to look like the King when she was on-stage?

She said, "No, I really don't. It would be preposterous to think that I would try to look like Elvis. In fact, I have noticed I've been starting to have a little trouble with people saying, 'Do your sneer!' Well, see, I don't have an Elvis sneer because I'm a very bubbly type of person."

Bubbly doesn't tell the half of it. Janice is the very definition of perky. She giggles a lot and says things like "golly" and "okey dokey" in a light, girlish Nebraska twang. In fact, I couldn't imagine that sweet little voice even attempting to do Elvis. So I asked her if it changes when she sings.

"It seems to, yes. It just rolls out of me in a different, much lower pitch than my talking voice and it feels sorta Elvis-y. Something comes over me and Elvis spills out. It's a miracle and I think it's just a blessing from God, I pray."

I say amen to that and I'll attest to the miracle that comes out of Janice's mouth. She sang "Heartbreak Hotel" for me over the phone and "sorta Elvis-y" doesn't come close to doing her voice justice. Even the lousy phone line couldn't blunt the passion, the pain, the raw sexiness and, yes, dare I say it—even the sneer. This was Elvis on estrogen. Long live the Queen!

AFRO-ELVIS

Clearance (as in clearance sale) Giddons hails from a tiny Southern town called Melfa, Virginia. He's a professional house painter by day, but at night he trades in his brushes and rollers for a brush with rock 'n' roll stardom. I asked him how he got started in the Elvis impersonation business and how he likes to bill himself.

"Well, I couldn't go under no other name than just the Black Elvis because I guess folks wouldn't know who they were talking about if I didn't use that title now. See, the title was given to me by my friends and my home-town folks. They're the ones who thought it up. As for how I first started out, at first it was kind of like a joke. You know, in your own hometown the folks are used to seeing you around all the time just being yourself. Then one day all of a sudden you're on stage doing Elvis at the county fair and they start coming on to you like you're from L.A. or something. That threw me for a loop. I couldn't believe it was really happening."

But he pinched himself because it *was* happening—and he liked it. So he worked up an entire Elvis act: hair, costumes, the whole shootin' match, including a back-up band. "We bill ourselves as 'Black Elvis and the White Trash,'" he told me.

I told him that must be quite a sight—the Black Elvis up there on-stage in the King's white sequinned jumpsuit, surrounded by white trash.

"Yes sir," he agreed. "The only thing is my jumpsuit doesn't have all the rhinestones that Elvis had. I kind of put my own personal touch to it. Mine sort of gives you a dressy tuxedo look with tails. When I goes into my concert I kind of rip the tails off and it reverts back into an outfit that gives you that jumpsuit look."

In homage to the King, Clearance doesn't just rip the tails off. He flings them to the screaming women in the audience. A nice, authentic touch. Another Elvis-y touch is that Clearance has the Elvis sneer down pat. And, maybe more importantly, he's nailed the hair. His secret? "I guess a lot of chemistry goes into that, man!"

You gotta love this guy. And a lot of people do. I'm told that real aficionados of the genre regard Clearance Giddons as the Elvis mimic who most exactly sounds like the real thing. And they're not talking about the flabby drugged-out Elvis near the end, but the swivel-hipped bad boy we all know and love from the fifties and sixties.

Well, the experts won't get any argument from Harold Fiske. Oh, I admit I was a tad skeptical when Clearance offered to give an exclusive command performance of the King's signature tune, "Love Me Tender," for my radio doc. But when he started wailing away, I just closed my eyes and floated off to hound-dog heaven. I was entranced. The guy is that good. So good, in fact, that the Black Elvis even has his own fan club. Naturally enough, they call themselves the Blackheads.

THE MEXICAN ELVIS

My third and final Elvis clone is unique in the firmament of Elvis apers. He's so good, not just at doing the King, but as an entertainer in his own right, that he routinely opens for top acts like Linda Ronstadt and Santana, and has a recording deal with Big Pop Records. I'm talking, of course, about El Vez, the Mexican Elvis.

El Vez is, of course, a stage name. The guy was born in East L.A. with a much more mundane moniker—Robert Lopez. Lopez was in high school when he joined his first punk band, the Zeroes. After that he was spinning his wheels in the punk scene as a member of Catholic Discipline and then Bonehead before he saw the light.

It was 1988. Lopez was working as a PR flack in an L.A. art gallery. They were running an exhibit of Elvis-related folk art and Lopez was blown away. He took it as a sign—Elvis, he decided, had been "the first punk and the first glitter rocker." And now a Bonehead punker would be the new Elvis. It was his calling, and El Vez was born.

El Vez hasn't exactly gone for the authentic Elvis look. In fact, he told me that he actually goes out of his way *not* to look like Elvis when he does his thing, costumewise.

"I do the jumpsuits too sometimes, but I want people to know that Elvis Presley is more than just a jumpsuit. I do my own interpretations of Elvis Presley outfits. You know the 1968 comeback special that he did with the black leather outfit? Mine is like that, only it's *patent* leather so it looks kind of shiny. And then I wear traditional mariachi pants, but mine are breakaway mariachi pants so I can have the Elvettes tug at my pants, which they do lots of times, and with a slight tug the pants rip away."

I stopped him right there. "The Elvettes?" I asked. "Who are they, and why are they ripping your pants off?"

"The Elvettes are my women, *las mujeres dos El Vez*. They are like the Mexican version of the women in Elvis's life. They're my back-up singers too, and boy, can they dance, and sometimes on purpose they pull off my breakaway pants and underneath I'll be wearing gold lamé pants. It's sort of like a Chippendale's Elvis."

He's not far off with that description. El Vez stages some pretty wild production numbers. The Elvettes—Priscillita and Lisa Maria—have been know to blast away at the audience with plastic Uzis while they strut around in spike heels and brassières made out of little sombreros.

El Vez prides himself on never putting on a dull show. Like Elvis, he's showbiz savvy. But, also like Elvis, he knows when to be serious.

"Like with my jumpsuits. I have a white jumpsuit, only my rhinestones and studs are red, white and green like the Mexican flag. And on my back? You know how Elvis always had the power symbols, like the eagle? Well, I put the Virgin of Guadalupe because she is the symbol of Mexico. She's my patron saint."

Interestingly, El Vez doesn't really see himself as an Elvis impersonator. He says, "I'm an Elvis *translator*. What I do on-stage is, I take Elvis's songs, which are all my favourites, and I give them the Mexican feeling. Songs like "In the Ghetto" to me is "En el Barrio." I talk about the gang problems in East L.A.—you know, the homeboys and drug wars and bad situations like that. I take "Suspicious Minds" and for me it becomes "Immigration Times," talking about not just my people, but people from all over the world trying to get to the promised land, the melting pot that is the United States."

El Vez does all kinds of Latino rewrites on the Presley classics: "Esta Bien, Mamacita" and "Blue Suede Huaraches" and "G.I. Ay Ay! Blues." "One I like to do," he told me, "is 'Hound Dog', but I sing 'You ain't nothin' but a chihuahua yappin' all the time!' That's really fun. You have to see it on stage with the visuals and me dancing in something shiny and the Elvettes all around me. It's a good show.

"One of my favourite places to play is in Memphis at Bad Bob's. Once I was performing there and this very large woman—she was about 275 pounds—she comes up and she was going crazy, as the women do. She's dancing with me, kind of like doing the Lambada in front of me, real sexy, and I said to myself 'Whoa! She's kind of embarrassing. I'll go lower and see if I can embarrass *her*.' Then *she* went lower, so I went all the way to my knees and my pants split all the way from the back all the way to the front. So I had, like, crotchless pants. After the show was over they had a count—twenty-two pairs of panties thrown on stage! Elvis has been *berry, berry* good to me."

And El Vez isn't modest about the fact that, in his fashion, he's been very, very good to the memory of the King. When El Vez belts out that old Elvis rouser, "The Battle Hymn of the Republic," he takes a few liberties with the final line. He sings, "Glory, glory, hallelujah / To the legend I'm adding on!"

III: ELVIS'S OFFSPRING

Love-child's shocking claim:
Nun Gave Birth to Son Elvis Never Knew He Had.

THAT'S THE GIST of just one of the literally dozens of paternity claims made about Elvis Presley. And it's not as far-fetched as you think. Let's face it, Elvis had more romantic encounters than he had hit songs. He himself personally boasted of five thousand conquests during his all-too-brief lifetime. Think about it. Five thousand sexual partners, but only one kid—little Lisa Marie. Who's he kidding?

More and more claimants to the Presley throne pop up every year and from all over the world too. We had one of them come through Toronto back in 1988 and I was intrigued enough to check his story out. It was a corker.

Philip Stonic had every kid's dream job. He was a lion tamer, working the centre ring under the big top with the internationally acclaimed

Vargas Circus. Born in Yugoslavia, he'd been raised in the circus by his loving parents, Anita and Jacob Stonic. Philip revelled in his circus family. He had his mum, his dad, his cats and his comrades. What more could a boy ask for? Life was grand and Philip Stonic's universe was unfolding as it should. That all changed on his twenty-first birthday.

On December 25, 1982, Anita and Jacob Stonic gave their son a gift. It was the gift of a new life. They told him a shocking secret. For twenty-one years they had lived an elaborate lie. Philip was *not* their child. He wasn't even Yugoslavian. The boy was, in fact, a careless "mistake." Philip was the unwanted fruit of the loins of a fleeting night of passion between Elvis Aron Presley and a mostly forgotten actress named Dolores Hart.

Dolores Hart did two movies with Elvis. She was his co-star in his second picture, *Loving You* (1957), and the following year she was back for an encore, in *King Creole*. The two, it's alleged, were really hot for each other, and she got pregnant. Elvis's manager, the legendary Colonel Tom Parker, got wind of it, covered the whole thing up and kept Elvis blissfully in the dark.

The Colonel had Dolores spirited away to Chicago (her hometown) for a "rest." On Christmas Day, 1961, she slipped across the state line and gave birth to little Philip in Gary, Indiana.

The child—Philip—was handed over to the Stonics. They agreed to hide the truth from the boy until he was twenty-one. They had kept their promise—and now he knew.

Philip was naturally stunned. He told his fraudulent folks: "This is amazing news. Now I'm going to have to change my name to Elvis Presley, Jr., dress up in a sequinned suit and go out and sing in bars." Which, of course, is where I finally ran into him.

Is he any good? Well, he's no El Vez and I don't think he's ever going to get rich doing his "Daddy"—unless he can prove paternity. That might take a bit of doing.

First of all, when I asked Elvis himself about the Stonic claim, he was *really* vague on the issue (check out my interview below with Elvis's ghost: "The Haunting of Heartbreak Hotel") and Dolores Hart disappeared from the public eye decades ago.

In 1963, without warning or fanfare, this vivacious young starlet shrugged off the glitz, glory and glamour that are part and parcel of motion picture stardom and became . . . *a nun!* That's right. Mother Dolores Hart resides in the Abbey of Regina Laudis in Bethlehem, Connecticut, and to this day, she's not talking. And I mean that literally. She's taken a vow of silence and remains cloistered from the prying eyes of the outside world.

As Sister Rita, another member of her order, said to writer Mark Lambeck in the November 1983 issue of *Connecticut* magazine, Mother Dolores "is kept under protective custody. She's not to be exploited for her past worldly life."

Amen to that, sister.

IV: ELVIS'S GHOST

The Haunting of Heartbreak Hotel:
You Can Talk to Elvis from Beyond the Grave

T HAT WAS THE cover story in the December 1, 1987 issue of the *National Examiner*. It sounded promising, so I decided, for old times' sake, to rip off my former employer and recycle that article for radio. This was going to be my first close encounter with the ghost of Elvis Presley—at least on radio.

The gist of the story was that a Chicago psychic named Irene Hughes was supposed to be in daily contact with Elvis's ghost. It seemed that, being a psychic, she was surfing the ethereal airwaves one day and just sort of bumped into Elvis on the other side. Their auras intersected on the astral plain and they really hit it off. Elvis, it turned out, liked to talk, Irene was a good listener and before you could say "blue suede shoes," they'd gone into business together.

See, because Elvis was dead he was free to float around the cosmos unfettered by the limitations of space and time that we mere mortals have to face every day. Translation: Elvis's ghost was clairvoyant—he could see into the future!

Now, predicting the future is the backbone of every good psychic reading, and Irene's Elvis angle was a cute gimmick, so I booked them to do a (free) live radio reading for me. They way this worked was that I never actually got to hear Elvis talk. I would toss questions to the King and Irene acted as his interpreter, relaying his words of wisdom back to me.

First things first, I told Irene: I wanted to clear something up. I told her about the recent reports in the press (that's right, the very same reports we had faked at the *National Examiner*) about Elvis's ghost or spirit being seen at his stately Memphis mansion. I wanted to know if Elvis would confirm or deny these rumours. Was he really hanging out at Graceland or were those reports just the product of the overactive imaginations of his loving fans?

"Well," she told me, "Elvis is appearing to me at this moment as I'm talking with you, so his spirit certainly can make itself seen."

(Just as a little aside here, the revelations in my interview with Elvis's ghost took place a full five months prior to the time Eddie Clontz kicked off his "Elvis-is-alive" campaign in the *Weekly World News,* as reported in Chapter Four. I don't like to brag, but since I'd scooped Eddie, I could have burst his bubble when I talked to him in Florida. Instead, I did the decent thing and kept my mouth shut.)

"By the way," Irene continued, "Elvis is wearing one of his favourite outfits. This one is white and it has a lot of gems or flash things on it." Irene explained that as a spirit Elvis of course doesn't need to wear anything, but he has the power to put on what Irene calls "thought clothes." That sounded like a nifty trick and I was comforted by the fact that the corpulent calorie King had the common decency to cover up whenever he appeared to Irene.

By the way, when we got around to the reading, Elvis turned out to be a pretty lame fortune-teller. He told me all the usual stuff. I was "going on a long journey" and could look forward to a "happy" career change. You know the routine. That didn't matter, though, because I wasn't interested in that stuff anyway. The *Examiner* article said I could "talk to Elvis from beyond the grave" and that's what I kept trying to do. I was looking for dirt.

I asked Elvis about his drug overdose, the orgies of fast food and faster women, the paternity suits, and then Irene relayed back that "Elvis is telling me that he didn't die of an overdose. He died from disappointment. He's indicating that he always was and still is very, very deeply in love with Pris—that's what he called his wife Priscilla privately. He's very disturbed and hurt over the tales in the tabloids about all the wild nights with other women. That only happened now and then. When Pris divorced him, it broke his heart. He was never the same from then on and he felt that since he had already reached the peak of his work it was just his time to go.

"As far as drugs are concerned, he's admitting to me that he did use drugs and it disturbs him that he *had* to do that because he was terribly depressed. He wants to pass along this message to all the young people: drugs are not the thing to do. Use your talents to bring you highs."

A message to America's youth! Ho hum! I felt like hollering, "Gyp!" Here I was digging dirt, and Elvis was working on a whitewash job.

V: ELVIS SINGS AGAIN

I was waiting for a blind date
with death warmed over.

BOCA RATON, FLORIDA, MARCH 1, 1992

I WAS FIDDLING with that stupid little pink paper umbrella they always stick in your Mai Tai. The Mai Tai was my third and even it was long gone. I was killing time out by the pool of the Radisson Suites Hotel with my pal Arthur Black, my producer John Stinchcombe and our ace sound technician, Barb Dickie. We were scheduled to do an interview with a guy named David Darlock, but to tell you the truth, the sun shone, the beach beckoned and we all kind of hoped David wouldn't show.

We'd just spent the last three days busting our butts on the investigative behind-the-scenes look at the inner sanctum of the tabloid industry that you read about in Chapter Four. And I for one was "tabbed out." I mean, we already had tons of great stuff in the can, but Stinchcombe complained that it was all "too theoretical." We needed, he said, at least one actual real-life tab *story* "for balance" (whazzat?), and David Darlock was going to give it to us. Rumour had it that David was a man possessed—literally—by the ghost of Elvis Presley.

I know what you're thinking. Been there, done that, and it was all a big snore the first time 'round. I thought so too, but I wasn't holding the purse-strings, so like it or not, I was going to that well to drink one more time.

David eventually showed up with his wife, Diane, and they joined us poolside for drinks. I was disappointed, but I figured if we got through this quick there still might be time to hit the beach and catch a few rays. So I got right down to business. I started by asking the obvious question. When did David first discover his spiritual connection to the King?

"I had a dream," he said. "It was right after Elvis Presley passed away in 1977. In this dream he spoke to me, and after that dream I was able to channel him. By channelling (Chapter Ten, "Channel Surfing," goes into great detail on this whole channelling thing) I mean that, in the process of going into a meditative state, I'm somehow able to produce or manifest what I believe and countless other people now believe to be Elvis Presley.

"As strange as it sounds, I discovered that Elvis Presley did not die. He was not really dead. He *is* alive." Right. Okay. Fine. Next question: why him? Why would Elvis want to get inside David Darlock's skull?

"I asked that question too, because I hadn't really paid much attention to Elvis before that. I knew about him, of course, but I was never real familiar with what he did. I guess I like to think the reason he came to me is that he felt there was an openness and a sensitivity in me."

Yeah, but there was something else. The longer I stared at David the more I noticed that, without make-up or hair gel, and with no attempt whatsoever to dress the part, David Darlock had a striking resemblance to the young Elvis Presley. David is a little taller but he's got the same general features. They wouldn't pass for twins, but brothers? Maybe. Cousins for sure.

I figured the ghost of Elvis took one look at Dave and got nostalgic. So I put the question to him. "David, do you think maybe Elvis saw in you a glimpse of an earlier version of himself, unspoiled, with all the years and all the fat burned away and said, 'Hey, there's the guy I'm going to possess?'"

Dave said "No. I'm sorry and I appreciate the compliment but I don't think so. I mean, I've never been told that I look like Elvis before."

I found that hard to believe, but didn't press the point. Instead, I asked him how he actually gets in touch with Elvis. What has to happen before the King makes contact?

"What you want to do is quiet yourself down. It has to be very quiet. It's just like when I had that dream only I want to get myself not quite into the dream state. I want to be awake, but not totally awake."

Unfortunately, we happened to be outside at the time, sitting around the hotel pool. There was too much noise and too many distractions. The vibes were all wrong, so it just didn't work. We moved our group up to my air-conditioned hotel room and in semi-darkness, with the blinds virtually shutting out the sensory overload of southern Florida, we tried again.

"First of all," David explained, "the thing that gives me an idea about whether I'll be able to do this on any given occasion is I need a sign. I need to see *something* happen. And it usually does. People's watches stop. Other things malfunction. Inanimate objects seem to develop a life and a mind of their own."

With that in mind, David asked for a cup. I offered him my plastic glass full of Diet Coke and ice but he turned that one down, saying, "No, I don't want to spill anything on the carpet." So I found an empty glass in the bathroom and gave him that.

David set the glass in the middle of a coffee table a good foot and a half from the edge. Then he told us, "I know this sounds really strange but the only thing I'm going to ask everybody to do with me now is, in your mind, I want you to just believe. Not necessarily that Elvis Presley is in this room, but that what I like to call spirit energy is in this room. There is a form of spirit energy in this room right now."

There was silence. David closed his eyes and concentrated very hard. You could see the tension in his neck and face. Then he stretched his hands out over glass the way you see the faith healers do it on TV, only David didn't touch anything. He kept his distance. His hands never once got within six inches of that glass. But they moved, in slow motion, as if they were caressing the air or manipulating some invisible forcefield.

Then it happened. Almost imperceptibly at first, then in jerky, tentative steps, the glass *moved*. We all saw it and we all sat there bug-eyed as that glass inched its way to the edge where—and there's no other way to describe this—it literally jumped off the table and crashed to the floor.

We all sat there stunned, marvelling at this feat, when David collapsed from the effort. His eyes were welded shut but they twitched the way they do in REM (Rapid Eye Movement) sleep.

David groaned and I was worried about him but his wife warned us not to touch him. "He's in transition. He's falling into a meditative state and it might take a few seconds. If you touch him, it'll break the spell."

A minute passed, maybe two, and then the eyes were still shut but the unmistakable voice of Elvis Presley came out of David Darlock's mouth. Elvis wasn't in a hurry. He meandered as he spoke, with long pauses between ideas, and sometimes even between words. I couldn't tell if the halting nature of the conversation was because of the trance or if Elvis was measuring each word, aware that he was being recorded for posterity. Probably a little bit of both.

> *Darlock/Elvis:* When I was a child, I had nothing. Many times, I believe, this can make you a little nicer human being.
>
> *Fiske:* Elvis, are you in heaven?
>
> *Darlock/Elvis:* It's not what you think, man. It's not what you think.
>
> *Arthur Black:* Elvis, what's happened since you've died is there have been Elvis sightings all over the world. Elvis is serving burgers in Wyoming, he's washing cars in Idaho. What do you make of all that? Is it true?
>
> *Darlock/Elvis:* I'm here with you. I'm here with you now. That's all that matters.

Fiske: Where you come from, what is it like there?

Darlock/Elvis: It's different. I learned that you cain't . . . you cain't please everybody all the time and it's . . . it's hard to live up to an image.

Arthur: Are you with friends? Do you see people you know?

Darlock/Elvis: Mama's here.

Fiske: The Colonel, is he there?

Darlock/Elvis: Mama's here. That's all I need.

Arthur: Can you see things that are happening back on earth? Can you see Priscilla's movie career?

Darlock/Elvis: It's not up to me to decide any type of anything. I'm jus' . . . I'm jus' here with you now.

Fiske: Do you have a message for Priscilla or for Lisa Marie?

Darlock/Elvis: They already know. They know that I love. They know. They know everything, that time has no meaning. That it's only the closeness of friends that means anything.

Almost as if he were trying to punctuate that last point, David/Elvis picked up the guitar that I'd brought with me, just in case. He expertly noodled around a bit on it, decided it was in tune and started singing very slowly, and with a touching sadness that was beyond anything I'd ever heard from Elvis while he was alive.

"'Love me tender, love me true' . . . I thought I had something and now . . . now I'm telling you it's not what you think." At this point, Elvis got real quiet. Then we heard a whimper that sounded more like David than the King. It was the kind of sound you make when you're coming out of that twilight zone between sleep and consciousness and you're not quite sure which one's going to win out.

Then David shook his head, cleaned out the cobwebs and opened his eyes. He looked at us expectantly and said, "What happened?" He didn't know. David couldn't remember a thing. So I filled him in on the whole conversation and told him about Elvis's impromptu concert.

He laughed (a little uneasily) and had a look of disbelief on his face. "I can't sing," he told us, "and I sure can't play the guitar. The only way I can explain it is that I'm like some sort of telephone to Elvis. I'm the open line and his call just flows through me."

"Dave used to be able to control the entity." This was his wife, Diane, piping up. "Now it seems like the entity controls him. That gets a little scary," she continued, "but living with it is part of my love for David. I mean, I love him and I bought the whole package."

Diane got down to specifics. "One time we were shopping like any ordinary couple. I walked in the food store with David and walked out with Elvis. I remember I was reaching for the peanut butter and turned to Dave to ask him if he wanted plain or chunky and—I was looking at Elvis's face. Just like that he'd gone under and hadn't even realized it. Another time we were in our living room and Dave levitated. He went right off the ground, at least two-and-a-half feet off the carpet. I think that was the most frightened I ever was. I ran out of the house screaming."

The day he levitated turned out to be David Darlock's watershed encounter with Elvis. "I had a vision. I saw Elvis Presley walking through what seemed to be mansions. And I saw hundreds if not thousands of angels, and he was speaking to them, reciting what I at first perceived to be a poem. Then I began getting some kind of melody in my mind, too."

After David came back down to earth he wrote down the words that Elvis had recited to the angels. Then he hummed the tune that had been planted in his head to a couple of musician pals. They transcribed it into sheet music. "We put that together with the words and what I thought was a poem actually turned out to be a very beautiful song that Elvis wrote for his daughter, Lisa Marie."

That was a *real* shocker, because as far as I knew, Elvis never wrote any of his own material. If the King had gone to all the trouble of penning a posthumous pop song, then I wanted in on the scoop. David didn't disappoint. He was kind enough to let me have a copy of Elvis's "Song for Lisa Marie." Here it is, in print for the first time anywhere.

SONG FOR LISA MARIE

You try to face another day,
Dreaming I'd be here to stay,
But when you wake I'm far away.
Tears were borne, you beg me to stay

Honey, I know, I know you tried
To end the hurt you felt inside.
Don't you cry, not one more day.
I'm here with you, I'm here to stay.

Our hope, our dreams may still be realized.
I see it in your face, I hear it in your cry.
Please don't be sad, not one more day.
I'm here with you, I'm here to stay.

They may take you away from me,
But they can't take our memories
Of the special times when we cared,
Special times that we shared.

For you are everything to me,
My Lisa,
My Lisa,
My Lisa Marie.

As a father myself, I was moved by those powerful words of loss, longing and hope. I told David we should make history and record "Song for Lisa Marie" for posterity right then and there. Would he be willing to reopen the telephone line to heaven and ask Elvis to do the honours?

"No, I'm afraid I've never tried to channel twice in one night because it's very, very draining on me. But I would like to get the word out that I am looking to find someone in the recording business to do a professional job on this song, because I think it's something that Elvis would want. I believe that he chose me to create this in the physical world so that it would be heard. I think it's something that he's looking forward to."

So now the truth can finally be told. Elvis is alive and well, living in heaven and looking for a record deal.

CHAPTER SIX

THE DEAD BEAT

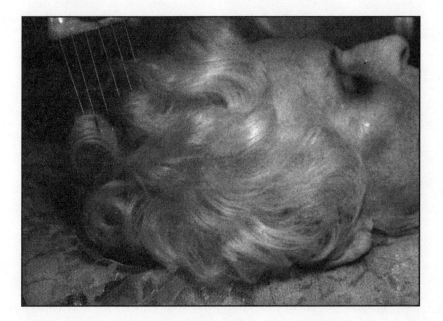

A "hands-on" photo from Noella Papagno's book
Desairology: Hairdressing for Decedents (See Chapter One).

ET'S FACE IT, when you're a tabloid hack like me, you get used to grinding out six, seven, eight stories a day, so you can't afford to be choosy. You have to be versatile enough to cover the whole range, everything from titanic tumours to talking trees. It's a bit like when some political toady finally lands his plum patronage job, and the reporters say, "Hey, you don't know *anything* about pollution control in the steel industry! Why did you, a know-nothing parasite, get appointed to that government agency?"

Like the wise tab hack, the appointee always gives some idiotic answer along the lines of, "It's best not to approach these things with any preconceived notions." Still, just for survival's sake it's always wise to specialize. Once you glom on to a vital area that no one else can cover as well as you, your job security is virtually guaranteed—that's why it's a good idea to develop a beat.

It's nice (but not always necessary) when your personal preferences and your beat come together—when the beat becomes something that does more than just pay the bills, when beat stories haunt you and obsess you and almost seek you out, when you're drawn to your beat like a moth to the flame. *That's* what the dead beat has always been for me.

I've been fascinated by death, in all its manifestations, ever since I was a small child, and I hope I've passed on to my own children that same fascination for the enthralling elaborate rituals that we, as a race, have devised to dispose of our dead loved ones. And in all honesty, after more than twenty years as a funeral sciences reporter (first for the *National Examiner* and more recently for *Basic Black*), I've gotten pretty good at covering this stuff.

1: DADDY'S DEAD!

You're dog-tired, done in and
downright dead on your feet.

YOU'VE HAD A tough week, slogging through three gruelling days just to earn a few thousand bucks to put bread and cheese on the table. You come home and all you want to do when you walk in the front door is kick off your shoes, put up your feet, suck back a couple of martinis, then pass out in front of *The Price is Right* until supper. But can you do that?

No! There's "quality time" to be spent with the kids as they come down from their after-school sugar highs. You want to lie down and rest but the only thing in the whole wide world the adoring little beggars want to do is play with daddy. And what do we play? A quiet game of checkers or Go Fish?

No. It's roughhousing the kids love—wrestling or piggyback rides or hide-and-seek, and, natch, daddy's always got to be "it."

Well, not in my house. The minute I walk in the front door I immediately suffer a fatal heart attack. I clutch at my heart, fling my briefcase across the room, gag, then fall dead in a heap on the living-room floor. The kids just love it when this happens.

We call this game "Daddy's Dead"—it's a laugh-a-minute, fun-filled time for the whole family. After I drop dead, I get to lie down and my three kids get to play ambulance attendant, pathologist, mortician and embalmer while they prepare my body for burial.

First they straighten me out in front of the TV (where I conveniently happen to have keeled over). Then they put a plastic flower in my hand and cross my arms over my chest. After that they place a couple of coins on my eyelids to keep them shut. Loonies work great for this, and like all good undertakers, the kids steal the coins from the dead person's pockets.

For embalming fluid we keep a couple of vodka martinis (shaken not stirred, tinted with red food colouring) in this plastic juice bottle in the fridge. It's got a long straw in it so we pretend it's an IV bag that I get to suck on while the kids work me over. Eventually (always after a few drinks) *rigor mortis* sets in and one stiff arm starts to slowly rise up in the air and the kids have to force it back down again, with much giggling. When they do, just like with a real stiff, the other arm (or maybe this time it's a leg) starts to come up.

Sooner or later the kids get to say a few touching words over their dearly departed dad, then bury me by heaping a whole bunch of sofa cushions on top of me. It's very cozy in there, and I often drift off to sleep.

The whole thing is a hoot and a holler. The kids get to burn off some energy *and* they get quality time with Dad. And me? I get my beauty rest, plus, when the kids aren't looking, I take back the eyelid loonies. Good thing, too, because I need every cent I can get my mitts on. When that fateful days arrives and I really *do* kick the bucket, you can bet I'm planning to go out in high style.

11: COMMONER COPS KING'S COFFIN

Got a hankering for a royal resting-place?

I T COULD HAPPEN. There's a company in Nevada where any average Joe or Jane can get buried inside King Tut's sarcophagus—and it doesn't cost a king's ransom.

Just in case you're not up to speed on your funeral sciences history, a sarcophagus is a very elaborate ornamental coffin. They were a big deal in ancient Egypt, where they were used to bury pharaohs like King Tut. Their big selling feature was a life-sized carving of the deceased king stretched out in all his glory on the lid.

Anyway, Margaret and Donald Northway of Genoa, Nevada have taken to manufacturing genuine knock-offs of King Tut's coffin. They got the idea from that big King Tut craze that was all the rage back around 1978. You probably remember the old boy-king's dreary arti-facts touring the world's best museums to long line-ups while the *haute couture* of the moment saw women decked out as Cleopatra clones. Steve Martin even had a hit song about Tutmania climbing the charts.

Well, like everybody else, the Northways got caught up in Tut fever, only they were never cured. They had it so bad they decided that when their time came they both wanted to be buried in King Tut coffins.

Easier said than done. Where do you start? Well, Margaret and Don started by heading to a Rosicrucian theme park in Santa Barbara, California. Now the Rosicrucians are that weird cult that has those little ads in the back pages of major magazines, the one about releasing your mind power through ancient Egyptian knowledge and stuff like that. Apparently, they had an exact replica of King Tut's sarcophagus on dis-play and they graciously allowed the Northways to take precise meas-urements. From those, the couple were able to make perfect dead-ringer copies of the original for themselves, the only difference being that Tut's sarcophagus was crafted out of beaten gold and lined with sandalwood. The Northways settled for fibreglass.

Anyway, even crafted on the cheap, those coffins were still a knock-out. When their friends and neighbours got a look at them, everybody wanted one. So the Northways went into business cranking these things out.

"Our King Tut sarcophagus is pretty much the same size that your regular caskets would be," Margaret Northway told me in an interview. "It's six foot two inches long and twenty-three inches across."

Well, I'm six foot *three* and "big-boned" so I'm no pipsqueak, and to be honest, I never much thought of myself as a "regular casket" kind of guy. I wondered if I was going to have any trouble getting into one of these things. It sure sounded like a tight fit.

"Don't worry," Margaret assured me. "We had one gentleman who thought the same way. He was a touch over six foot two and we were able to put him in it and he was really kind of amazed. We had to flatten his hair down a bit but other than that it was fine."

Margaret added a little-known fact. When King Tut's coffin was first opened, they discovered that the sarcophagus-maker hadn't done his homework and His Royal Highness had to be folded up a little to make him fit. So there's good historical precedent for flattening hair or even bending knees (you should do this **before** *rigor mortis* sets in, if possible) to fit larger guys like me into off-the-shelf coffins.

Now since Margaret's coffins are made of fibreglass, I wanted to know how they hold up to the ravages of Mother Nature—to worms and stuff—once they're planted in the ground.

"We understand from our research," she assured me, "that next to stainless steel, fibreglass is the only substance that will go in the ground and will stay indefinitely without disintegrating, so we're really excited about the material we have him made in."

"Him" meaning King Tut, of course. I liked the sound of that. The way Margaret humanizes her coffins, that "him," speaks volumes about the personal bond she and her husband, and I suppose, her customers, feel with Tut. It goes a long way towards explaining what makes people want to get buried in a replica of his casket. "One of the things people feel so good about," she said, "is that our casket depicts the living King Tut. It shows life rather than death. This is very important to some people, because it takes the usual idea of a coffin right out of the picture. Other people want it because you can put it into your home as an art object. We've had ours in our living-room now for eleven years and it's a wonderful conversation piece."

I'll bet it is. All of a sudden I had visions of the Northways' neighbours coming over and climbing inside and posing for great novelty pix. And Hallowe'en must be wild at their house.

"Oh no!" Margaret protested. "We look on it as something that is very much in the concept of art, rather than saying, 'Let's play with it or lay around in it.'"

But if it's such a unique art object, why would anybody ever bury it? It turns out that not everybody does.

"Oh, my husband and I, when we took on this challenge, right from the beginning we knew we wanted to be buried this way *in the ground.* But other people have decided that, since our sarcophagus has been certified as safe to go into mausoleums, what they would like is to have theirs placed in some kind of a drawer that can be pulled out."

That way their loved ones can see and appreciate the craftsmanship down through countless generations. What a beautiful idea. And how much do I have to pay for the privilege of being entombed in one of Margaret Northway's exquisite King Tut sarcophagi?

"It's going to run you right around US$3,500, which is pretty competitive. Regular coffins can go anywhere from $200 up to $9,000. So when you see that you have a coffin that will not only last indefinitely but can also become an art object and a conversation piece in your home at the same time, it's like getting two for the price of one."

Plus, what I love about it is that, in a pinch, your King Tut coffin can also do double duty as a linen closet or a laundry hamper. It's a bargain at $3,500. And, believe it or not, that's just the *low* end of the burgeoning Egyptian funeral market. Read on.

III: I WANT MY MUMMY

Don't you laugh when the hearse goes by
For you may be the next to die.
They wrap you up in a big white sheet
And throw you down about six feet deep.
The worms crawl in, the worms crawl out,
The ants play pinochle on your snout.
Your body turns to a glassy green
And slime pours out like whipping cream.
Damn! And me without my spoon!

—*Song from my boyhood*

LIKE A LOT of you, I learned that charming little schoolyard ditty all the way back in kindergarten. I was five, and it was my first childhood encounter with the grisly God-awful truth that lay beneath the thin veneer of pretty speeches and gaudy floral arrangements that pass for a funeral nowadays.

My folks used to tell me; "Life is short, young Harold. Take care of yourself and lay off the junk food. Your body is a temple." Yeah? Well, six feet under, everybody's potentially just junk food for worms. It doesn't have to be that way, though. Not if you've got deep pockets and you know a couple of guys named John Chu (a full tenured professor at the prestigious Lynn University in Boca Raton, Florida) and his colleague, Summum Bonum Amman Ra, known to his intimates as "Corky." (Corky Ra told me his full name is half Latin, half Egyptian, and translates as "the source of all good and the creator of all life." In fact, the name on his birth certificate is Claude Mellow.)

John and Corky happen to be two of the leading practitioners of actual, full-scale, contemporary mummification. This is the real McCoy, folks. For the right price, these guys will bundle you up nice and snug, and guarantee you a worm-free eternity, resting in peace, not in pieces.

When I called them up they agreed to spill the beans on the nuts and bolts of modern-day mummification for the discriminating dead. But before I could get into all that stuff, Professor Chu figured I needed a crash course on how the Egyptians did the deed back in the glory days.

"Their method," Professor Chu explained, "was dehydration, using salt. They just packed the body in salt. Many countries around the world have salted things like beef jerky and pork and salt cod. But with the Egyptians, it's just the way it was applied and the beliefs that went with it that made it really something very special.

"The ancient Egyptians had a value system that said life would return to the body. The concept came from when the Nile River would flood. The dung-beetle would form a little shell around himself. He'd float around all over the place during the flood and when the water went back down he would actually break out of this capsule. The people saw this as a resurrection. That's why they preserved their dead.

"Everybody knows the pharaohs were preserved. What *isn't* so well-known is that there were actually over 600 million people mummified in Egypt. A man and a woman would save all their lives to be mummified. You would wrap them and at night sneak into the Valley of the Kings and bury your loved ones so they could be with their pharaoh, who was a god to them."

But if 600 million Egyptians were mummified, how come we've only got a handful kicking around today? According to Professor Chu, it's grave robbers. "Many mummies were used by the English for fuel when they put the railroads into Egypt. They literally cut the mummies up and burned them like firewood. Remember, these bodies are totally dehydrated by the salt. They're so dry they burned with intense heat."

That was a daunting image. I mean, I *was* actually thinking about signing up for one of Professor Chu's modern mummy treatments, so you can imagine how thrilled I was at the prospect of somebody somewhere down the line hacking me up for kindling so they can roast wienies. But I digress.

"Other times," said Chu, getting me back on track, "the grave robbers would take the bodies, grind them up and make mummy powders for medication to spread on wounds." But by the twentieth century, the grave robbers started running out of mummies, so they improvised.

"It was discovered," Professor Chu explained, "that modern man was cheating. He was taking living people who were dying of disease, drying them out in the sun, grinding them up" and palming off their fake miracle mummy medicine as the genuine article.

Anyway, since Professor Chu's history lesson got us back to the twentieth century where we belonged, it was time to find out more about the current practice of mummy memorials. Corky, Professor Chu and I had a lively chat about how modern man goes about getting the full King Tut treatment.

> *Corky Ra:* First of all, your body will be placed in a vat and soaked in solutions designed to preserve your cell tissue.

> *Fiske:* Is that anything like what my mother used to do when she was pickling cucumbers in the kitchen?

> *Corky Ra:* No, you won't see this in your kitchen. That's a completely different kind of chemical process. What *this* does is set up the proteins within the body so it remains the way it looked when the person passed away.

John Chu: And because we use oil-based chemicals instead of just salt, *our* bodies never get as dried out as the Egyptian mummies. The Egyptian mummies always look burned, whereas ours, after being soaked in the vat for seven to twelve days, look more like the actual person.

Corky Ra: Then, after the body is removed from the vat, it's wrapped.

Fiske: Like in the horror movies, where they're all wound up in bandages and stuff?

Corky Ra: No, it's *much* more permanent than that. They're wrapped in gauze-type sealings that are soaked in resins like the kind used in the fibreglass cast they wrap you in when you break an arm or a leg. But before we wrap the body we coat the whole thing, inside and out, with polyurethane. To do that, we remove all the intestines, the lungs, the liver and all the organs—with the exception of the heart.

John Chu: We leave the heart intact to go along with one of the traditions of the ancient Egyptians. To the Egyptians, the heart was the seat of intelligence. So we just respect that and leave the heart where it is. All the other organs are coated with polyurethane and then we wrap them up in canopic packages and put them back in the body.

Fiske: So it's sort of like a turkey with the giblets, in a way?

John Chu: Right! Same thing.

Fiske: Okay, so you've got the organs coated and bundled

up back inside the wrapped corpse. What's the next step?

Corky Ra: After the body is all wrapped it's placed inside what we call a mummy-form. The mummy-form is a statue that is usually cast in bronze. It looks exactly identical to the deceased individual. Once the body is inside the mummy-form it's welded closed. Then it's purged with argon.

John Chu: The argon gas displaces the oxygen. That way, there's no chance of any type of life form continuing inside, because most life needs some form of oxygen or some way of generating it.

Corky Ra: Then the bronze cast is finally sealed for a permanent and unique memorialization that allows a person to make a statement about their life that will carry on for thousands of years, because the mummy-form is a full body statue of the client. It can be designed to wear a business suit or a favourite dress or a clown costume—whatever they prefer.

Fiske: So if I want the world to recognize and remember Harold Fiske as a tireless crusader, I could have my bronze mummy-form decked out like Don Quixote or Gandhi or Batman?

Corky Ra: As long as you're paying for it, we can do you any way you like.

John Chu: The *really* unique thing is, when we make the arrangements with somebody to do this, we make a life mask of them.

Fiske: This is while they're still alive?

John Chu: Yes. Then when the person dies that life mask

will be placed on the customized mummy-form. We have one here on display that follows the King Tut style but the client's face would replace Tut's. Some people want something a little different. They may want an Oscar with their face on it. We're even designing one right now for a couple that's a companion type where when they die, they'll be joined.

Fiske: Wow! His-and-hers Siamese twin mummies?

John Chu: Yes, and that's a couple who will be truly in love for all eternity.

Fiske: Sounds like business is pretty brisk. Do you guys get many takers?

Corky Ra: We've got some world leaders and we have people that are in the entertainment industry who are going to be permanently preserved by us. Unfortunately, our contracts restrict us from naming any of our clients. The reason being that not all media are responsible journalists like you.

Fiske: Yeah, I know you've got a lot of those *National Examiner* types out there—dreadful yellow journalists.

Corky Ra: Yes, and they harass these people once they find out they're doing something that's a little bit different.

Well, this certainly qualifies as different, and I admit I was interested enough to bite the bullet and talk turkey. How much would it set me back to be mummified and then immortalized in this magnificent fashion? Corky Ra told me, "It's approximately US$32,000."

John Chu broke that down for me. "The mummification itself runs between $7,000 and $7,700, depending on how big the body is.

But the mummy-form is another matter." The sky's the limit there. "If you want it made in gold," Chu cautioned me, "it's going to be maybe $200,000."

And the last word on the subject? That goes to one of Chu's satisfied (although sadly anonymous) customers. "During my life I haven't been able to live like a king—but I sure will die like a king."

IV: DO-IT-YOURSELF FUNERALS

Bold Brit's claim: There's a "funeral trade Mafia" in Merrie Olde England.

ACCORDING TO Nicholas Albury, the United Kingdom's undertakers are involved in a "conspiracy of silence" to keep Britain's aging population ignorant of its legal right to a cheap no-frills funeral. And although Albury lives in London, England, his observations apply over here in the colonies too.

Now, I've got no problem with honest up-front entrepreneurs turning a good buck in the mortuary market. Take those guys selling King Tut coffins and modern-day mummification, for example—sure, they charge an arm and a leg, but there is *no* pressure because their eccentric clients sign up years in advance.

But we've all seen undertakers in action. Most of the time you or (if you're the one who's dropped dead) your grieving family doesn't even meet the mortician until you're at your most vulnerable—confused, shattered, lost and loaded with the insurance money.

By the time you turn up at the undertaker's gaudy showroom, he's got you in the well-greased palm of his hand. That's precisely when he gets the hook in and guilts you into hocking the farm to give the dearly departed an outrageously overpriced fond farewell. The problem is, these guys almost *never* bother to tell you about all the great cost-saving options that are available out there for the frugal funeral-goer.

Well, Nicholas Albury says it's time somebody stood up for mourners' rights and he figures he's the man for the job. So he's started over in London. Nick says there are two distinct trends of the 1990s driving the Natural Death Movement.

First, there's ecology. As environmental activists get older and begin to face the limits of their mortality, they come face to face with the need to think about how they want to be disposed of when the time comes. Pretty soon they discover that funerals pollute, and are a terrible waste of the earth's valuable resources, on top of being a rip-off.

Trend number two: the do-it-yourself movement. Everybody's fixing their own house, canning their own fish, brewing their own beer. Why not dig your own grave, too?

What we are, in fact, finally talking about is a melding of the two trends into what is best described as the "green" funeral. Not only is it green for the non-polluting ecological correctness of it ("May you rest in greenpeace"), but also for the *green*backs you'll save by going the do-it-yourself route.

Instead of paying an undertaker zillions of dollars for funeral services and a fancy-schmancy coffin, for example, you *could* be buried in a biodegradable cardboard box. And you can also avoid the whole drippy graveyard scene. It's a commonly held belief that you *have* to be buried in a cemetery. Not so.

Nick says that in England you can be buried in the vegetable patch in your own backyard if that's what you want. Instead of daisies you could be pushing up tomatoes. When I talked to Nick, he told me that over there funeral options are limitless and they're all laid out in his Natural Death Movement's *Natural Death Handbook,* which is full of handy dandy tips for anyone thinking about a DIY (do-it-yourself) funeral.

"Seventy percent of the funerals people choose in the U.K. are cremations," Nick told me, "so if you're having a DIY cremation then it's just a matter of putting the deceased on the roof rack and . . ."

I stopped him right there. Did Nick expect me to believe that some Brits actually stick Uncle George on top of their car and then cruise on down to the crematorium?

"That's right," he said. "Maybe with a suitable drape."

It turns out that in England, at least, there aren't any laws against that sort of thing. Over there *anyone* can conduct their own funeral. You don't have to use an undertaker. But there are obstacles and that's what the *Natural Death Handbook* is for. It helps you wend your way through the treacherous minefield of morticians that stands between you and your eternal resting place.

Nick offers an example. "By law you *can* buy a coffin from an undertaker without having him conduct the funeral, but it's difficult because there's a sort of funeral-trade Mafia over here. We surveyed 2,800 undertakers and only twenty-nine were actually prepared to sell a coffin direct." (And they're all listed in the *Natural Death Handbook*.)

But the *Natural Death Handbook* even goes one better by offering detailed plans on how to make your own coffin. You can get a local carpenter to knock one up for you, but it's so simple you could probably bang it together yourself out of plywood and scrap lumber or, as Nick explains, "out of pine or birch if you want to have something a bit more magnificent." Better still why bother with a coffin at all? It seems like such a terrible waste of wood.

"Yes," Nick was quick to agree, "it is a waste. And there *are* one or two crematoria in this country who will accept a body even in a body bag as long as there's something to keep it stiff, like a little plank of wood, underneath. The plank," he informed me, "is for dignity in carrying the corpse," because the crematorium doesn't want to see the body slumped with the butt dragging on the floor while it's being carried in. That kind of thing tends to put off some of the mourners.

But enough about cremation. Suppose you're the demure conservative type who'd rather not go out in a blaze of glory. Let's say you're looking for a good old-fashioned farewell—six feet under, going toe-to-toe with the red wigglers. Nick says your low-cost natural death options for plain old getting buried are as unlimited as your imagination.

"In my own will," he said, "I've instructed that I'm to be buried in a plain white sheet on a piece of land I was given as a wedding present. Then an apple tree is to be planted right on top of me. And that won't cost anything. That'll be absolutely free."

I love it. It's simple, elegant, dignified, dirt cheap and probably greener than moss on a maple tree. I mean, a dead guy decomposing right under a sapling's got to be a whole lot better than Miracle-Gro, right?

"Well, yes," Nick concurred. "It *would* be a form of fertilizer. When you boil down to it the body *is* made up of 90 percent water and 10 percent fertilizer, really."

Yeah, well actually with some of us the fertilizer count would be a lot higher, but never mind that. One of the things Nicholas Albury is really pushing right now is an offshoot of his own burial plans. He wants Brit farmers to start up nature reserve burial grounds (NRBGS) where a new tree will be planted on top of every corpse.

According to Nick, farmers in the U.K. already get a £1,575 grant from the forestry commission for each hectare of new broadleaf trees they plant, so what have they got to lose? "The commissioners," he adds, "assure us they don't mind if those forests are also used as natural reserve burial grounds," because as far as they're concerned, "the more forests, the better."

The best news of all is that NRBGs don't look *anything* like graveyards. From a distance they're all just virgin forest. That's because the NRBG does not allow any gaudy monuments, tombstones or statues to spoil the view. All it has are discreet little markers next to the trees. That way your loved ones can still find your sapling, pay their respects and, while they're at it, maybe hug a tree for good measure.

One thing I really like about the Natural Death Movement is the way it uses death as an instrument of ecological social activism. Want to strike a blow against the ever-spreading menace of urban development? Think about this: once you plant a human body in the ground—it doesn't matter if it's in your backyard or the back forty of your alfalfa farm—that ground is then and forevermore considered sacred. It is, in fact, a graveyard. You can't put a highway through it. You can't build a tacky shopping centre on top of it.

But although going green is obviously a big deal for Nicholas Albury's Natural Death Movement, the main argument in favour of do-it-yourself funerals, he says, "is that they're more personal. DIYF's help with the grieving process because the more contact you have with the body the healthier it is for the survivors. It's always a lot more intimate to dig the hole and lower the body into the grave yourself."

V: SHOTGUN FUNERALS

It's not exactly taps and a twenty-one gun salute.

BUT JAY "Canuck" Knudsen of Des Moines, Iowa offers a unique personalized memorial that's plenty loud enough for any diehard gun nut who's gone to that great hunting ground in the sky. It's safe to say that Canuck will take your mortal remains where no man has gone before.

I talked to him back in 1992 and we really hit it off once I told him I was calling from Canada.

> *Canuck:* Y'know what? Canada is my love. Every moment I get free I go to Canada huntin' and fishin' and I just love that country.

Fiske: Well, hey, the people up here are hunting nuts.

Canuck: Oh yeah!

Fiske: Well, after all, what sane man doesn't like going out into the woods and firing off a gun?

Canuck: That's right.

Fiske: Which is why I like your story. Tell me about what you guys do, because I'm all ears.

Canuck: Well, we work with the loved ones of the deceased sportsperson or we work with the sportsperson while they're still alive to plan their prearranged memorial. What we do is actually incorporate the cremated ashes of the deceased into a regular shotgun shell with a charge of shot.

Fiske: You actually put the shot, the pellets, in there with the ashes?

Canuck: Oh yeah. And then we go out and hunt with them, whether it be birdshot or a deer, bear or wild boar load.

Fiske: Oh, so you don't just go after birds and squirrels? You go after bigger game too with your personalized ammo with the ashes of the deceased in there?

Canuck: Yes, of course.

Fiske: Oh wow! Now, how do you work this? Do you just load up one or two cartridges or do you use *all* of the ashes of the deceased on a whole mess of shotgun shells?

Canuck: No, not unless they really want to load that many shells. That's an awful lot of ammo.

Fiske: Well, how many shotgun shells would you get from your average dead hunter?

Canuck: Well, I never sat down and figured it out but it would have to be a couple of cases.

Fiske: And you don't need that many for your typical shotgun funeral?

Canuck: Not really. Generally what the widow decides to do is have us load a half a dozen rounds for the actual hunt. Then we might be directed to take the rest of the ashes and put them into a hollowed-out duck decoy or a stuffed pheasant or a covey of quail or something of that nature.

Fiske: So that way one of the husband's favourite hunting trophies becomes the repository for his ashes instead of some dumb urn. That's a lot more personal. In fact, it's quite touching.

Canuck: Right. And another one of the things that's been getting more and more popular lately is our gun-dog memorial. That's where a hunter has become extremely close to a very loyal huntin' dog. Well, when the hound deceases we take the cremations of the dog and load them in shells just like we would do for a deceased hunter. Then we go quail hunting or goose hunting or chucker hunting or whatever.

Fiske: That way, even in death, the loyal pet gets to go along on one final special hunt. I love it. Tell me, Canuck, do you have any kind of ceremony you go through or any special eulogy you perform when you're on one of these shotgun funerals?

Canuck: Well, once again, it depends on what the

deceased asked for or the widow wants. We are going on a bear hunt in the spring. In that situation we have been asked that before we get into our sleeping bags that night we are to drop a handful of ashes in the fire and recite the twenty-third psalm.

Fiske: I know it well:
> "The Lord is my shepherd, I shall not want,
> In verdant pastures he gives me repose,
> And I shall dwell in the house of the
> Lord for years to come."

Very tasteful and, again, I have to say, very appropriate as well. So then I assume it wouldn't be a problem if, say, I wanted to write my own funeral ceremony? You guys would go out and do whatever eulogy I wanted?

Canuck: That's right. We would go out of our way to carry out the detailed specifications that you provide us with.

Fiske: Canuck, do you mind if I ask you how much it's going to cost me to get one of your customized funerals?

Canuck: Well, we can go on a bear hunt in northern Saskatchewan and do your memorial service up there for around US$7,000, give or take a few.

By the way, just in case that's in your price range and you're tempted to sign up for one of Canuck Knudsen's shotgun wakes, he cautioned me that, for $7,000, the grieving widow does *not* get to go along on the memorial hunting expedition.

And forget it right now if you're thinking Canuck will just hand over his special handcrafted crematorium-ash ammo to your hunting buddies. It *would* be great for old time's sake (not to mention male bonding) if you and your pals could bag one last moose together, only that "ain't gonna happen," he told me. That's because Canuck is out-right spooked by the litigious American legal system.

As a long-time hunting nut himself, Canuck has seen more than his share of dumb hunting accidents. He says an awful lot of them are caused by people who don't know what they're doing. They abuse their weapons, don't clean their guns and then—pow!—one day the damn thing literally blows up in their face.

There's no way of getting around the fact that by packing cremato-rium ashes into shotgun shells Canuck is hunting with highly uncon-ventional ammo. He figures that all it'll take is one gun misfiring in one widow's face and he'll get sued around the block and back again.

But he *is* more than happy to take that risk himself. It's a danger-ous job, but somebody's got to do it. So Canuck leaves the grieving widow back at home where she's safe while he goes off with his team of crack mourners on her $7,000 memorial safari.

> *Canuck:* Of course, the price includes guides, nonresi-dent licence, a trapper friend and his dogsled. You see what I'm saying?
>
> *Fiske:* Yeah, I see all right. One thing I'm wondering about is, do you get into any conflicts with the client when you do this? I mean, you shoot some game using a special shell packed with the ashes of the bereaved's husband. Is there ever any trouble with the widow or the estate of the deceased person having a claim over the game that you kill?
>
> *Canuck:* No, sir. We always give them that option. We feel that is their choice.
>
> *Fiske:* So you'll give the widow . . . the dead carcass?
>
> *Canuck:* Well sure, if that's what she wants. Like on this bear hunt I mentioned that we're doing in the spring . . .

it's been left up to *our* discretion to do what we want with the meat. We happen to like bear meat, so we'll keep the meat for ourselves.

Fiske: Well, the widow probably wouldn't be too keen on eating bear meat riddled with her hubby's ashes. But what exactly does she get?

Canuck: She would like, and in fact has requested, the hide and so she has agreed to pay the difference to have a bear rug made out of it.

Fiske: That seems fair. Have you thought about expanding up to bigger game and more exotic funerals or moving up to larger-bore weapons?

Canuck: Sure. We're talking to a fellow presently in Phoenix on a possible memorial lion hunt in Africa. We will go anywhere in the world and carry out any hunt there is or do anything with your ashes, so long as it's legal and ethical. As far as I'm concerned, anything beats the morbidity of an urn on the mantelpiece."

And "anything" is the operative word here, folks. Canuck told me about some of the stranger requests he's worked on over the years. A lot of them don't even involve hunting at all.

"We signed up one fellow who, when he's cremated, he wants his ashes put in an hourglass and regulated to run for thirty minutes. We had a lady whose father was a big golfer. She wanted her dad's ashes put into the hollow metal shafts of his golf clubs."

And my favourite? The guy who had his ashes shipped to Canuck with instructions to insert them in his favourite bowling ball.

CHAPTER SEVEN

CAR CRAZIES

The Trabant 501 "De luxe."

I: MY CAR, MYSELF

True confession: Harold Fiske sells out!

A ND ABOUT time too! I mean let's face it, the high-minded hot-shots who run CBC Radio as a commercial-free enterprise have had me under their corporate thumb for years.

"Send it back, Fiske!" is the oft-heard refrain around these hallowed halls whenever some freebie happens to cross my desk—a case of fine wine, a summerweight suit, some cosmetics for my lady. Even worse, I've lost track of how many lucrative endorsement deals I could have had if these guys hadn't squelched them, "just to keep you honest, Harold."

Well, after years of scrupulously avoiding even the slightest whiff, the merest taint of a conflict of interest, I finally decided, to hell with integrity. I was going to start cashing in on my celebrity status and take my first ever corporate junket.

I was whisked away (okay, actually I had to drive the two hundred kilometres myself) to lovely snowbound Huntsville, Ontario where, as part of a select group of "media VIPs," I was privileged to test drive a bunch of very new and, I might add, very expensive sports utility vehicles.

For two days, we "automotive journalists" got to tool around in four-wheel drives from every major car company. We put those suckers through their paces on a disused airstrip that was laid out like an obstacle course.

We got to burn rubber and skid out of control on the ice-encrusted tarmac. The whole thing was a glorious throwback to my old hotrodding days in the sixties. But don't get the wrong idea. It was hard work, too, and treacherous. Luckily, in between those gruelling test drive sessions we got to recuperate in spa-like splendour at the well-appointed Canadian Pacific resort hotel, the Deerhurst Inn.

The whole weekend was sponsored by Nissan and they footed the bill. Nissan was looking to showcase their new Infiniti suv in head-to-head competition against all the other top-of-the-line four-wheel drives on the market. Now, I want to make it clear that Nissan wasn't putting *any* pressure on us. We were free to come to our own independent conclusions about these cars. However, I'm sure Nissan hoped we'd all go home well wined and dined and plenty grateful, with nothing but kudos for the Infiniti, and plug the hell out of it.

Hey, no sweat. I was all ready to shill for Nissan on the public airwaves, but when I showed up at the CBC, ready with an in-depth radio documentary on the event, my producers flat out warned me: "Harold, you might, in a stretch, be able to justify that junket as an investigative undertaking, so we will allow you to discuss and deconstruct your experience on air, as an abstract philosophical concept." (These guys really *do* talk in this way.) "However," they droned on, "you will refrain from any and all brand-name identification, especially involving the sponsor, Nissan. We won't permit the slightest hint of impropriety."

So I had to be pretty careful on air and although I did manage to sneak in a couple of innocent lines like "I'll probably have to wait from now until *infinity* before I'll ever have that much fun again," I pretty much resigned myself to concentrating on other less controversial aspects of the junket. For example, I explained that while I was there I got to rub elbows with a lot of automobile writer-types, one of whom turned me on to a fascinating new piece of car research.

The research findings indicate that a curious, almost spooky symbiosis exists between car and car owner. It turns out that the physical condition of your car might just be a window to your soul and a mirror to your psyche. This startling revelation is contained in a huge, six hundred-page book called *My Car, Myself.*

My Car, Myself is the painstaking work of Narayan Singh Khalsa. This gentleman is a self-proclaimed "sacred teacher" out of Boulder, Colorado. One of his principal teachings is really more like a mantra. It goes: "It's no accident, even when it's an accident."

Narayan Singh Khalsa's revolutionary idea is that every time something goes wrong with your vehicle (your clutch is slipping, you get a flat, you blow a gasket), the car's mechanical breakdown is directly linked to, or more accurately, mirrors something going wrong inside you. In other words, your car's not the lemon, *you* are!

This curious teaching is supported by the ancient Hindu theory of chakras. Chakras are sort of lumps of energy that run down the front midline of your body and emit auras of energy from your belly button and other places higher up and lower down. What these chakras do is hook you up to a universal power source. It's sort of like having a gigantic cosmic halo hugging the world. The power is invisible to the human eye but it permeates everything—animal, vegetable and mineral—and it allows us to channel our psychic spiritual energies and links us together with all things, including our cars.

Narayan Singh Khalsa admits that a lot of people think he's missing a few spark-plugs of his own. He knows his theory is controversial and he's not surprised. "Heck, I've been controversial all my life," he boasted.

A shrink for more than thirty years, he describes himself as "a super-scientist type" and "one of the founders of behaviour modification. B.F. Skinner was an acquaintance of mine."

Khalsa figures all those years as "a superscientific behaviour-mod headshrinker," bent on probing the mechanisms behind tortured minds, led him to his offbeat theory of a psychic link between man and machine. "When we take possession of a car," he said, "we get into the thing, we drive it, we have our experiences in it and you know how intense we are in our cars."

I certainly do. I'm well versed in the fine art of road rage. It's rampant in this country and, quite frankly, people are car crazy. Nowadays, nobody can afford a house, so a man's *car* is his castle. I mean I know guys—real slobs—who *never* do the dishes or clean the apartment. But every weekend they're out there in the driveway washing and waxing and detailing. And it doesn't matter if it's a Bug or a BMW—they fondle it and pamper it and put it on a pedestal. These guys are closer to their cars than to their wives.

My Car, Myself goes a long way toward explaining this intimate relationship that people have with their wheels. The way the author puts it is, "Since we, as people, are the living and ensouled being in the relationship, our intense feelings and our aura effectively modifies or fuses with and changes the structure of the car's aura."

English translation: We become one with the car.

"And that means what happens to us affects the car's aura. You see, a car's aura, like our own aura, has different components, like our liver and spleen and all that stuff. But when there's a perturbation in our aura it affects the car's aura in a particular vibrational frequency and whatnot. It causes it to go out of sync with itself—and it breaks."

Translation: if you're having a real bummer of a day or have the flu, your car, in a fit of sympatico, might blow a gasket. And, according to Khalsa, it's reciprocal. "Oh, absolutely, because your car is a *being*. All physical objects are. Believe it or not," he said "there is consciousness in everything. So if the car is really battered and dinged up it can get you going real intense too, especially if you're vulnerable at the time. There is that kind of interactive thing. You know how sometimes you get into the car and the damn thing doesn't want to start and it drives you up the wall? In its relatively primitive way, it's pissed at you!"

I could relate to that. Unfortunately, I usually get ticked right back and slam the hood down or something. Khalsa says that's a bad idea because the ill will snowballs, and before you know it, both of us are in for repairs.

Getting down to specifics, this connection between car and driver is precise and literal and easy to chart because different body parts and body functions link up with similar workings in the car.

"Your two hands," Khalsa explained, "are your left and right front wheels. Your feet are the rear wheels. Your butt is the trunk. Your teeth are the grill. The hood is your forehead. The headlights are your eyes. And your abdominal cavity is the passenger compartment. The gasoline tank is the stomach. The manifold and the muffler and the exhaust pipe are the intestines. So you literally *are* your car, and it *is* you."

If that were true I could test out Khalsa's premise (and get a free reading) with a couple of examples from my own life. I had, in fact, just spent $350 having my car fixed. It turned out I had a blown spark-plug and the mechanic hit me with a lot of grease-monkey jargon about how the ignition wire's resistance was way too high. I asked Khalsa what *My Car, Myself* had to say about a burnt-out plug, a cockeyed ignition wire, and me?

He flipped to the chapter on spark-plugs and read, "Action suppression. You won't let things go into action. You feel you have to be in complete control of everything. But you're freaked out and distrusting of the universe, so you're bollocksing things up. It comes from growing up the sane one in a dysfunctional family."

Translation: I come from a screwed-up family and I'm so freaked out that I'm afraid to do anything. My sluglike existence caused the spark-plug to blow, and now, just like me, my car can't do anything either.

Next I told him about a small crack in my windshield. Actually, it started as a small crack but it was getting bigger and bigger.

Khalsa looked up "cracked windshield." "Slightly off base," he read. "You have a tendency to distort the meaning, import or significance in events and situations. You're fearful or agitatedly nervous, which leads to a magical mystery tour experience of life. It arises from having grown up in a denial-dominated family in which seeing, knowing, telling and acting on the truth were tantamount to suicide."

Translation: My windshield's cracked because I lie a lot? Not only that, it's congenital. I come from a long line of liars?

There was an embarrassed silence on the other end of the line. Finally Narayan Singh Khalsa came back on and in a timid voice said, "Well . . . yes."

It was clearly time to change the subject. I had an idea for a radical medical breakthrough (and smelled another endorsement deal). "If what you say is true," I told Khalsa, "it should be possible for somebody to take their jalopy down to Canadian Tire for a tune-up, get it scoped on one of those electronic diagnosis gizmos, and then use the readout to draw significant conclusions about their own mental health. Wouldn't that mean . . ."

Khalsa cut me off. He was way ahead of me. "That your mechanic is your shrink? Yes, of course!"

II: PEE-PEE POWER

Every day, with every flush of the toilet, we're pissing away the fuel of the future.

THAT STUNNING news comes to us from south of the border courtesy of a fellow named Lee Crutchfield. Lee's a telephone technician at the Cherry Point Marine Air Station in Newburn, North Carolina. But he's also a part-time inventor who claims to have discovered a limitless and previously untapped energy source—the human kidney and bladder.

Lee Crutchfield calls his discovery Urinol and it just might revolutionize the way we live. Urinol will fuel our vehicles and just about anything else you can think of, long into the new millennium. According to Lee, Urinol can "cook your food and heat your home and make your lawnmower go." But most of all, it will keep North Americans rolling down the highway at a fraction of the cost we're paying for gasoline or propane or even diesel fuel.

Lee refines his miracle fuel by using a "urine reactor" (patent pending) that "lets me extract a highly flammable vapour gas from ordinary everyday liquid urine. Mixed with air, Urinol can do anything gasoline or any other fuel can do."

Lee is understandably a tad guarded about his reactor. He's worried about industrial spies swiping his idea, so he was keeping his cards pretty close to his vest when I asked him about the nuts and bolts of precisely how his Urinol reactor works.

That said, he was willing to talk in general about the basic starting principle behind Urinol. It's really just a new twist on an old tried-and-true process known as electrolysis. Lee's running electricity through common run-of-the-mill urine. I'd never heard of anybody trying that before, so I asked Lee how he got the idea. He quite candidly admitted that, as with so many of the really great scientific discoveries, he stumbled on Urinol by accident.

"I had a mishap," he confessed. "One day I was working on an experiment in the bathroom. I was running a current through some water in the tub, trying to break the water down into hydrogen. I took a pee break and I was wee-weeing there in the bathroom and I missed the commode. Some of the urine spilled into my experiment and when the current ran through it I ended up with a white gas that hadn't been there before. The next day I was changing a wet baby diaper so I decided to run a current through that and the diaper gave off the same white gas."

That white gas was an early impure stage in what would eventually turn out to be Urinol. That's where Lee's mystery reactor comes in. He calls it a "high-speed, low-power reactor" that refines the pee-gas and shuttles it through a series of ten interlocking and sequentially larger chambers to accommodate the ever-expanding volume of Urinol.

There are two bonus by-products of the reaction process. First, Lee says, "the reactor gets very, very hot while it's breaking down the pee." The extra heat can be siphoned off and used in any number of ways. Second, Lee found out that "once the urine is turned into gas it leaves a residue. It's sort of like a fertilizer that you can put in your garden, and that will end up being the greenest part of the garden. I noticed that when I did it last year."

But those are only sideshows to Lee Crutchfield's amazing discovery. The main act, of course, is the gas and what he affectionately calls "pee-pee power." Lee says his family relies on pee-pee power every day. "I've already got one Urinol reactor set up in the house and another one hooked up in the car."

So, he told me, he's actually running his car on urine right now. He says "a quart of pee would probably take a car about fifty miles." That works out to two hundred miles a gallon. I tell him that's unheard of!

"Uh-huh, yeah," Lee casually agrees with my math. "And you know I'm in the process of doing a lot of things with the car. I'm thinking of putting little rocket engines on the back to push it along, because I would like to show everybody that I have something different in my car. It will be similar to what happens on *Star Trek* when they go into outer space. It'll just be a big boom and then I'll take off.

"Another thing I've done is I've sent a proposal to your Department of Energy up there in Canada. I've offered to build special heaters for you guys because I know how cold it gets there in the winter. And with this heater you don't have to go to the bathroom. All you have to do is wee-wee right into the heaters."

I love it! I mean, suppose it was thirty-two degrees Fahrenheit (zero degrees Celsius) outside and all you had was a single quart of urine. Lee says he could heat your average two-bedroom house to a comfortable seventy degrees Fahrenheit (twenty-one degrees Celsius) for about three hours. With a simple conversion unit on your gas stove he could just as easily cook your Christmas turkey and all the trimmings on that same quart of pee. Not too shabby.

And that's only the beginning. The best part about Urinol, of course, is that once you've installed the reactor, the raw fuel is free. Urine is an endlessly renewable resource that can be collected from every member of the family—pets included.

Plus, it's got a long shelf life. Lee's tests also indicate that urine, just like a fine wine, gets better with age. "That's right," he told me. "For some reason, the gas refined from *older* urine burns better than the new stuff."

Actually, Lee has an even better source for what could turn out to be sure-fire premium Urinol. The idea is to use the washrooms in bars as urine collection stations. "We should hook up every urinal in every toilet in the clubs and bars, because some of the best urine samples I've collected are the ones containing alcohol and also sperm," he points out. Lee says that the added alcohol content from all that booze would make for high-octane Urinol. Factor in the way the hosers up here suck back the suds and we might never run out of fuel. By the way, Lee's not too sure what sperm adds to the mix—but he's keeping an open mind on the subject.

So am I. I mean, if only half of what Lee says turns out to be true then this guy's going to be famous and plenty rich. There'll be a Urinol conversion reactor in every household and pee-pee power in every car across North America, if not the world. And you'll never have to worry about running out of gas again. Just pull over on the side of the road, pee into the tank and off you go.

The possibilities are endless. The ramifications, staggering. This could turn Lee Crutchfield into the next Thomas Edison. I asked him if he ever thought about that, or about maybe some day picking up the Nobel Prize?

"I hope so, yes. I wrote to the President [of the United States] about this invention quite a few times and hopefully I will get the recognition I deserve sooner or later."

Lee's still waiting for the Oval Office to get back to him.

III: TRABANT TRIBULATIONS

London, England, October 2, 1993— Harold Fiske humbled!

IT WAS A sight to see. Me down on my knees in the middle of Fleet Street (not easy to do in heavy London traffic!), prostrate before the shrine, ready to kiss the pavement in homage to the great god of tabloidism.

I go through this ritual every couple of years, whenever I get overwhelmed by the utter inanity of what I do for a living. I take the cure: I head back to my spiritual birthplace and get my batteries recharged (and while I'm at it, steal as many good stories as I can) by basking in the reflected glow of Fleet Street's tabloid empires.

But this time something was missing. The *Sun*, the *Mirror*, even the *News of the World*—they were all gone. The British tabloids had picked up and moved east, lock, stock and barrel, to cheaper digs on the Isle of Dogs, down Wapping way. Still, I was able to track down a couple of my old chums—the ones who weren't dead of alcohol poisoning, or (a fate worse than death) down in Florida working for the *National Enquirer*. We got together over warm Guinness and bangers and mash and then I started pumping my old pals for any leads I could recycle back home. That's how I picked up news about Oliver Walston.

What's special about Oliver Walston is that he collects Trabants. There's a good chance you've never heard of the Trabant. If so, you're not alone, because for decades the Trabant was hidden from prying decadent Western eyes by the opaque veil of the infamous Iron Curtain.

The Trabant was an East German invention, a one-size-fits-all automobile built for the proletariat. It rolled off an assembly line in Zwickau, in the German Democratic Republic, from 1957 until just after they tore down the Berlin Wall. You had to be East German and a comrade in good standing with the Communist party if you wanted to buy a Trabant. And even then, you had to wait up to fifteen years for the privilege. The Trabant's company motto proclaimed it to be "Legenden auf Rädern," which translates as "Legend on Wheels."

Now, Oliver Walston is acknowledged by his fellow car connoisseurs to be the free world's leading Trabant authority. When I spoke to him, he owned seven Trabants in all, at that time the largest known collection outside of Germany. He agreed with the legend-on-wheels tag: "It's a legend all right—a legendary lemon, the very worst car ever built!"

Trabant translates as "servant," which only goes to prove that in that day and age good help was hard to find. Oliver keeps these legendary losers on display, lined up all nice and neat in a barn on his farm just outside of Cambridge. Actually, the Trabants share the barn with a bunch of boarded horses and riding ponies, and Oliver was kind enough to give me a hands-on tour of his prize fleet of what are, by all accounts, the world's least sought-after automobiles.

"I bought all of these Trabants," he told me, "just after the Berlin Wall came down and I drove them back from East Germany. They all came through English Customs, where I paid no duty at all, because the value of the cars was so low they came in less than my duty-free allowance.

"This first one, a pale robin's-egg-blue Trabant, is called a *Limousine,* which must have been a joke, because it's pretty basic stuff. It's made of plastic. I bought it from a man who lived on the top of a high-rise building along the aptly named Lenin Alley in East Berlin.

He'd had it less than two years after waiting thirteen years to get it. He sold it to me for US$200."

Oliver went on to explain how the fellow was a literate chap who'd nicknamed his Trabant "Hannibal" after taking it on vacation to Yugoslavia. He was amazed when the little car made it over the Alps and back again in one piece, just like the warrior of Roman lore. Unfortunately, it was all downhill for little Hannibal after that. The car had less than 25,000 kilometres on it, and I was trying to be charitable when I told Oliver it looked a little bit shabby.

"Of course it's shabby!" he shot back. "It came out of the factory in Zwickau looking shabby. Shabby is invariably one of the hallmarks of the Trabant! It would be hard to argue," he explained "that they were anything other than the worst car in the world. For starters, technologically, they're crap. The worst thing about it is the engine. It's a 600 cc engine, a two-cycle engine I think you call it in Canada. Over here we say it's a two-stroke. Anyway, a 600 cc engine is a bit like a lawnmower. It runs on a mixture of oil and gasoline and makes terrible blue smoke when it goes along. So pollution-wise, it's a killer."

Oliver wasn't kidding. He took me out for a spin in Hannibal but he prefaced the adventure with an apt warning: "Prepare to be asphyxiated." He wasn't far off the mark. That Trabant chugged and jerked and backfired its way through the lovely English countryside, all the while spewing the most outrageous cloud of steel blue petrochemical slime that, I'm almost embarrassed to say, actually looked quite pretty the way it blended in with the lush green hedgerows.

There is, however, nothing pretty about the Trabant itself. Hannibal at least came in a passable robin's-egg-blue finish, but the other cars all had God-awful colours. His worst wreck was done in hangover barf yellow that somebody in the factory had apparently handpainted with a brush. You could tell because there were little bits of hair stuck in it. What's underneath the paint job? The body reminded me of the model kits I used to slap together when I was a kid.

The Trabant's exterior skin is moulded out of something called "Duroplast." Duroplast is made out of resin, reinforced with wool. In other words, it's a cheap plastic that simply will not decompose. Wait a minute! A rust-free body that'll last forever? What's wrong with that? Plenty, when it's on a car that nobody wants. To make matters worse, those ingenious East Germans somehow figured out a way to attach the permaplastic body to the car's steel frame in such a way that you can't separate the two cheaply enough to make recycling cost-efficient.

Oliver told me that these things are "virtually impossible to unload. That's one of the reasons why, in Germany today, if you want to sell or, as a last resort, just dispose of your Trabant (and everybody does), you have to pay the authorities DM100 to take it off your hands. Nobody wants to pay the ridiculous fee to get rid of them, so what happens is most Trabants are just abandoned along the roadside."

On top of the terrible two-bit engine and bad bodywork, the Trabant offers a suspension system that's a throwback to the buckboard buggy springs of the wild, wild west. I kid you not. These things bounce along on antique cart suspension. My test drive was about as comfortable as bumping down some gravel road, riding on the handlebars of my old CCM bike. It was numb-bum time. I discreetly suggested to Oliver that the car's suspension was a tad primitive.

He didn't give me any argument. "Indeed! The whole thing is primitive. The brakes are iffy. The controls are crude. There's no fuel or water pumps, no radiator, no oil filter, no timing belt, no valves, no camshaft, no points. It shows what happens when you don't have a free market and there's no competition. The Trabant was the only car an East German could buy, so they never bothered to improve it, outside of changing the dashboard every decade or so."

Actually, that dashboard is a real piece of work. It's got three buttons—choke, headlights, windshield wipers, plus a bunch of weird unused wires sticking out all over the place. Apparently, those were the result of some optimistic designer's unrealized fantasies for the Trabant. They were installed just in case the company ever got around to putting in high-tech "options" like a cigarette lighter or a radio. That never did happen. Those wires turned out to be nothing but wishful thinking in a car that has no speedometer, no mileage indicator and— get this—no gas gauge.

Which brings us to the Trabant's charming fuel system. I asked Oliver Walston how he keeps track of his petrol level without a gas gauge? He told me, "You have a little dipstick in the tank so you can tell how much gas is in there."

I said that was okay if your car was sitting in the driveway but suppose you're booting along in heavy traffic on the *autobahn*. How are you supposed to know when you're almost out of gas? Doesn't a warning light come on?

"No! The engine starts missing and you run out of petrol and the car stops." Simplicity itself.

Next I turned my attention to the car's unique upholstery and, in a stunning epiphany, I finally figured out what happened to all that Hallowe'en candy I used to hate getting as a kid. You know the ones. They were made out of some really cheap brown sugar by-product and they pulled out the fillings in your teeth when you tried chewing them. Anyway, do you remember the wrappers on those things? They were made out of orange and black wax paper that was covered in bats and black cats and witches and stuff. Well, *that's* the Trabant's upholstery—orange and black and ugly, with a real stick-to-your-butt feel to it. I had to peel myself off the seat when we got back to the barn.

By then I'd pretty much had it with Trabants, but Oliver wouldn't let me go until I got a closer look at the one true gem in his collection, his proudest piece—that beat-up model with the puke-yellow paint job I mentioned earlier.

"That's the rarest Trabant there is," he said proudly, "so it took a bit of getting. You don't see these around Germany at all any more. It's *the* original Trabant. This one was built in 1961. It only has a 500 cc engine.

"That was probably the least fun to drive back from Germany because it took forever. It has a maximum speed of seventy kilometres per hour." I thought that for the shape it was in, even seventy km/h might be dicey. It looked to me like the roofline had been pretty badly damaged and then repaired with a sloppy welding job. This was *not* the work of a professional.

"Oh no," said Oliver, cluing me in. "And it's *not* welded. Trabants are notorious for leaking. This one probably leaked at some stage during its thirty-two-year career and somebody shoved East German chewing gum in the seams."

Ingenious!

Of course, it's no mystery why East Germany's "Legend On Wheels" bit the dust. That nifty slogan didn't fool anybody. The Berlin Wall came tumbling down. Free enterprise got its hooks into the country, and just like that, the Trabant was history. Let's face it, given a choice, what kind of idiot would buy the worst car in the history of the known universe, let alone seven of them? Well actually, Oliver Walston's no idiot. It turns out there's gold in them thar lemons. Remember, all through the Cold War the Trabant was *the* car on the other side of the Iron Curtain.

Now try out this scenario: the BBC is in preproduction on another one of those Cold War spy flicks like *Smiley's People*. The movie's set in East Germany, but the Beeb can't be bothered going to all the trouble and expense of filming there. They dress up a dingy corner of London or Manchester to look like East Berlin and, if the price is right, Oliver will let them use his prize fleet of Trabants to add just the right touch of authenticity.

Oliver says the money's pretty good, but don't be fooled. He's not in this for the cash. He actually *likes* these cars. See, what the guy is, is a collector and the bottom line on collectors is, there's no accounting for taste. I once knew a fella who bragged about his international globe-spanning collection of navel lint—167 specimens from 167 belly buttons in 167 different countries—and counting.

So why not Trabants? After all, in a hobby dominated by multi-millionaires looking for that elusive solid gold Cadillac, Oliver has cleverly gone against the grain and carved out a modest little niche for the downmarket crappy car collector.

Makes sense. The field's wide open, the overhead is low and you don't need to build a climate-controlled mausoleum to house your collection. Lemons like these are right at home, fender to flank, with the ponies in Oliver's old barn, up to their hubcaps in horse manure.

CHAPTER EIGHT

ROADKILL ART

Stuffed mice play out a scene from Shakespeare's *Hamlet*.

I: ROADKILL REUNION

I've got a dead mouse hanging on
my Christmas tree.

T'S RIGHT UP there with the tinsel and the twinkly lights and the plastic glow-in-the-dark star o' Bethlehem. Every year, that dead mouse is the first decoration to go up on the tree and the last one to come down. Most of my friends hate the thing. They think it's disgusting and they think I'm nuts. But my kids love it. No surprise there. Kids love anything that'll freak out a grown-up. So do I.

I come by it honestly.

When I was six years old my family went off on a day trip, and when we came back that evening we found our family dog, Puddy (short for "Puddles" because he'd never been house-trained properly), lying dead on the front porch. What happened was he'd been hit by a car. But he had guts. He'd doggedly dragged himself home, I guess so he could die near his loved ones. Of course, because we were *out* he died all alone. Naturally I was devastated. The whole family was.

My father went to the backyard. He dug a hole and we dumped the dog in. Then we filled the hole in and said a few tearful words of farewell to our faithful friend.

A couple of weeks later my sister Joyce and I were missing the old pooch pretty bad and because we didn't fully understand the concept of death, we decided to get a shovel and dig the dog up.

We dug this big hole and looked down at the dog and what we saw was this ugly thing in an advanced state of decomposition. Joyce somehow managed to slip and fall into the grave onto what was left of the dog. Getting her out was tricky and we both ended up covered with this sticky decaying stuff.

That freaked out my mother.

She got really, really mad at us and she made us take a bath. She put us in the tub together and made us scrub ourselves clean with this great sweet-smelling national name-brand soap for kids that's still around today.

The fallout from this story? To this day, every time I get anywhere near that soap—my kids are using it, I walk past it in the drugstore, even if I just see it advertised on TV—it triggers a flashback. Not to some grisly nightmare memory, but to a sweet, clean, dreamy roadkill reunion with the family dog.

II: DEM BONES GONNA RISE AGAIN

Donna Helmsley is the Rodin of roadkill.

LIKE AUGUSTE RODIN, she too is a sculptor. And like that famous French chiseller she approaches her work with a sensuousness and a passion that almost leaves you breathless. The main difference is that where Rodin worked in marble, Donna Helmsley dabbles in dead animals that she just happens to pick up on the side of the road.

Donna lives in Austin, Texas, and the first time I talked to her back in November 1989, she was swamped trying to fill all her pre-Christmas orders for roadkill *objets d'art* (which make great stocking-stuffers, by the way). But as busy as she was, she graciously took the time to explain how she got into "the art of roadkill."

"I'm really into recycling," said Donna. In all her art pieces—her furniture, wall hangings and jewellery—she uses only things that she found or that were discarded. Dead animals on the highway are numerous in her part of Texas and not a week goes by when she doesn't find an armadillo, deer, raccoon, ringtail cat, possum or rattlesnake. But, I wondered, how did those rotting smelly dead animal carcasses get turned into art?

"It's just the bones I use," Donna told me, which meant she had to figure out how to get the flesh off, leaving a gleaming skeleton behind.

The answer? Press the dermestid beetle into service. Donna knows a cave near Austin where the floor is literally carpeted with these flesh-eating beetles. What are they doing in there, I wondered?

"This is a bat cave," Donna answered breezily, "and one of the largest bat caves in the world—with about 10 million bats in it." When they get sick and die, they fall on the floor and the bugs go to work helping to "keep the environment clean and odour-free." The bugs "will strip a bat carcass in a matter of a couple of hours," said Donna. "So when I went in there, first I got me a pair of rubber boots because the bat guano—the bat poop—is really deep there. I also had to wear a respirator in the cave because you can contract a disease called histoplasmosis if you breathe the air because it's so thick with ammonia."

The ammonia, she said, came from all the bat poop and urine, and I was about to point out that the bugs weren't very successful at keeping the cave clean and odour-free, but Donna ploughed ahead.

When she saw the "billions and zillions of little flesh-eating beetles on the floor of the cave, a light bulb came up over my head" and she realized she could use them to strip the flesh off the roadkill for her art. So she drove up and down Route 81 between Austin and Mason, Texas and harvested a rich array of roadkill, then dumped her crop of carcasses inside the bat cave.

The beetles got to work munching away to their hearts' content and all Donna had to do was drive back to the cave a couple of weeks later and bag the bones. By that time, the animal skeletons were clean as a whistle and, well, dry as a bone.

Once she's collected her raw materials Donna gets to work on her unique one-of-a-kind items. She does lots of nifty jewelry. When we talked she was wearing an exquisite pair of earrings that were actually the recycled vertebrae from a roadkill raccoon. Plus, she had on one of those skinny Texas string ties, the ones the country-and-western guys go for, only this had a clasp made out of an opossum skull.

Donna says her jewellery is really popular, but her master works, the stuff she really sinks her teeth into, are big-ticket items like her bone furniture. "It's a real southwestern kind of look, so in this part of the country I do real well. I did a whole bedroom suite for this one lady."

So how much would it cost to have my bedroom done over in early animal bone, I wondered. That depends, said Donna, but a dresser she had on display in a Dallas gallery sells for about us$1,600. "But then my earrings go for as little as $20 and necklaces for $75," she said, which is, let's face it, not too bad for handmade art.

"It's not for everyone, of course," Donna admitted, "but there are a lot of people out there who want things new and different and this is definitely new and different."

No argument from this corner on that—and speaking of different...

III: MICE-ELANGELO

Did Dale Evans have Roy Rogers stuffed?

THAT'S WHAT everybody wanted to know when the "king of the cowboys" died in July 1998. For years, urban cowboy legend had it that Rogers's last will and testament stipulated that his hide was to be stuffed and put on display atop his trusty horse, Trigger (who had been stuffed after dying in 1965), at the Roy Rogers Museum in Victoriaville, California. Sadly, it turns out Roy opted for a conventional burial.

This kind of novelty taxidermy is nothing new, however. In fact, it has a long and honourable history. Cast your mind back to those happy carefree days of the forties and fifties. Remember driving home from your Florida vacation with a trunkful of souvenirs? Remember those goofy stuffed baby alligators wearing tiny straw hats and sunglasses? Or the frogs decked out as the duelling three musketeers?

Down in Mexico, around that same time, you used to be able to pick up little stuffed lizards or horned toads wearing sombreros and playing in little mariachi bands. If you didn't like little amphibians or reptiles, there were always those bigger—but pricier—dioramas of stuffed dogs playing poker. I always thought they were the coolest things.

Those were the halcyon days, the long-gone golden age of novelty taxidermy. Then the animal activists decided that killing God's little creatures just to turn them into cheap souvenirs was cruel and unacceptable. Better to have them torn apart by vicious predators or die of hunger in the wild. The bottom fell out of the business and novelty taxidermy has been dormant for decades.

But the time is ripe for a renaissance and novelty taxidermy is making a comeback, thanks to an artist in the San Francisco area. (Her name is M—Jeanie M.) It's not an alias and it's not some paranoid attempt to hide from the PC police. Jeanie M's not ashamed of what she does because she is, in fact, an "enlightened" novelty taxidermist.

She came to her field quite by chance. She actually started out as a roadkill photographer, but soon realized that there were limitations to that particular art form.

"I saw these really cool dead animals on the side of the road and wished I could take them home," she told me. "I wanted to learn how I could do something with them so my dad signed me up for a small taxidermy class, but it turns out that it's sort of illegal to pick dead things up from the side of the road—and I don't hunt—so I had to look for another source."

In her taxidermy class she "found out how easy rodents were to stuff and that it was legal too, and they were really easy to get a hold of," and not with rat- and mousetraps, but from larger pet shops where "they have hundreds and hundreds of mice," prekilled, prepackaged "and frozen in a variety of colours and sizes. Some of them even come vacuum-packed and freeze-dried."

But do they still have their innards in them? Sure, she told me, because they're basically being used as food. "There's a huge trade in these dead mice for anybody who has to feed a pet snake or a large lizard. Plus, wildlife rescue places use them for feeding injured birds of prey. I can get them made to order, ready to go. I've got an endless supply of mice."

The best part of all this is that it's absolutely humane. No animals are hurt or suffer for Jeanie M's art because they're already dead—in fact, if Jeanie weren't stuffing mice, some snake would be stuffing his face with these things. But since snakes don't care one way or the other what the dead mice look like, I'd guess that pet stores aren't that careful about how they handle the corpses. Did that create a problem for her? Are the mice in good shape by the time Jeanie M gets her hands on them?

Jeanie said no. Even if the mice are a little beat-up and bent out of shape, it doesn't make much difference. The taxidermist only uses the skin, so the condition of the body isn't that important. "Plus, since I put tiny little clothes on them, if there is anything wrong, like there's a bald patch or freezer burn or a piece of the mouse is missing, I just cover it up with the costume. If I were a traditional taxidermist I'd need something a little more pristine."

That makes sense, I thought. A traditional taxidermist is going for realism, whereas Jeanie's going for fantasy, and the small animals she chooses—mice and rats—wouldn't be handled by a conventional taxidermist. "Regular taxidermists chuckle at that because they won't work on anything so tiny. They just think I'm crazy, which is fine. I don't mind being crazy," said Jeanie. Other than that, the process is pretty much regular taxidermy.

The stuffing process "consists of gutting out the mouse's little tiny skin then putting wires in to stiffen up the legs and the tail. Then you wrap the skin over a little cotton-body frame," said Jeanie.

She uses very few chemicals—"just a little salt and a little bit of borax, mostly nontoxic stuff"—to keep the finished product from smelling. According to Jeanie, the lack of chemicals is very important. She has a cat at home and it has chewed up more than its share of her little dead friends. If they'd been toxic, that cat would have been a goner too.

The big question is, how do Jeanie M's stuffed mice stack up against the classics? Can her work hold its own next to those duelling frogs of yesteryear?

A piece of cake.

Her *oeuvre* knows no bounds. She's done everything from a punk-rock-rat to a prima ballerodent who spins around in a tiny pink tutu on top of a music box. She has a real soft spot for Shakespeare because, "For this to work, people have to be able to figure out what the mouse is supposed to be. Shakespeare's got really identifiable Elizabethan costumes, so it's easy to do those." Jeanie crafted a terrific Hamlet figure doing "to be or not to be" and holding a little mouse skull in his paw. And she's working on the balcony scene from *Romeo and Juliet*.

There's almost nothing she won't tackle. She got a request to decorate a wedding cake from a friend who "begged me to do it." So she got a couple of dead mice and made "a little bride in a dress and a tiny groom in a top hat and a cape that they put on top of the cake. They loved it, but their parents were mortified by it."

Her most ambitious project was Santa Rat and his eight tiny mice reindeer. "That was really intricate," Jeanie recalled. "Santa held the reins and the mice were harnessed to a sleigh on a rooftop with doll-house shingles, fake snow and a chimney." It was about three feet long and a foot-and-a-half wide. Her biggest artistic challenge on that one was Santa's beard. "Actually, Santa Rat doesn't have a beard," said Jeanie. "I thought about it and played around but it looked strange because rats don't really have chins. But he does have a big belly and a little red outfit with a Santa hat and jacket and everything. All the mice have little antlers made out of modelling clay." A diorama like that takes weeks to build and she ended up selling it for US$600.

But "that's a top-end item, of course," Jeanie stresses. "The less expensive ones go for about $38." That's for one little mouse in a basic outfit, dressed up like a doctor or a vampire, things she gets asked to do all the time, so she can crank them out in a couple of hours. A little white angel mouse is a little pricier and goes for $50, but that includes a tiny set of plastic buckteeth plus a pair of bird's wings sewn on its back. And the angels are just the tip of the ecclesiastical iceberg. For some reason or other, Jeanie gets an inordinate number of commissions with religious themes.

"I get a lot of requests for nuns and popes and somebody just requested a St. Sebastian," Jeanie told me. I remembered my bubble-gum cards of the saints and recalled him perfectly—he's the saint who was martyred when hundreds of arrows were fired into him, and he took forever to die. He looked like a human pincushion. Jeanie explained she was using porcupine quills for the arrows. Cool idea, I thought.

Another special request was for a *Pietà*. "Somebody wanted to give that as a birthday present," said Jeanie, "and they wanted a very elaborate scene. They wanted Mother Mary holding the dying Jesus with angels flying around, so I made a whole diorama." Michelangelo's *Pietà* (which I still remember from its unforgettable appearance on the old *Ed Sullivan Show*) is one of the great icons of our culture, I observed. Did she base her own taxidermy *Pietà* on this famous statue?

"Yeah, I did," said Jeanie. "But mice are not anatomically the same scale as humans. For example, their arms are very tiny, so the mouse Mary couldn't reach around to hold Jesus the same way, so I had to improvise things."

Such poetic licence was understandable under the circumstances, I said, then took the opportunity (as always) to ask for a free sample. Now, what I *really* wanted was a big custom-made diorama on a St.-George-and-the-dragon theme, with a mouse in armour mounted on a rat steed and lancing a big stuffed snake (I had one in my freezer at the time). But I knew it was too much to expect for free, so I gratefully accepted Jeanie's offer of a Christmas angel, since at the time we were getting on for the holidays.

"The angels go like hotcakes, not just at Christmas, but year-round," she told me. "People just love them. They don't just hang them on the tree, but put them over their beds, anywhere where an angel looks good."

And my angel now nestles among my treasured Christmas ornaments, wrapped in newspaper, waiting for my ruddy-faced children to trim the tree on Christmas Eve. We're proud to have a dead mouse hanging on our Christmas tree.

CHAPTER NINE

TABLOID TRAVEL LOGS

The Tragedy in U.S. History Museum in St. Augustine, Florida.

LIKE NOEL COWARD, I've always wondered why the *wrong* people travel, travel, travel, when the right people stay at home? It's a musical question that perfectly captures a travelling tabloid hack's mood as his mind meanders off to foreign shores in search of the next hot story. Or it would if he actually ever *did* any travelling on a story. Really, the best way to travel is by telephone—that way you steer clear of the filth and disease found in most, if not all, foreign jurisdictions.

And while it's sometimes necessary to travel, it should *never* be done unless it's in search of a story. Remember, as every professional travel writer knows, there's no vacation that can't be written off, so the secret is to convert that trip into cash—and if not cash, at least a pile of tax deductions.

There's no excuse ever to take a boring vacation. We tabloid hacks dig up all the strangest destinations because the folks who publish travel books send us only their weirdest offerings. But take care—what's promised often doesn't pay off. When people stay away in droves from a place it's usually for a good reason—the food is bad, the water's polluted and the people are hostile and sullen.

Take Cuba, for example—please. I was sent to Cuba by the *National Examiner*—well, I wasn't exactly sent. I sort of got these two package tours deeply discounted from some bucket-shop travel operator I knew. He worked out of a briefcase at Dorval Airport and had some sort of scam going with the folks at Cubana Airlines. Everyone was in on this fiddle—pilots, flight crew, ticket agents—and you could fly to Cuba really cheap. They even took blue jeans as payment. Good as cash! So I cleaned out my clothes closet and was on that plane!

Anyway, while in Cuba there was very little to see except East Germans making pyramids on the beach—plus the rum tasted like kerosene—so my then-wife and I decided to take a side trip to the infamous Bay of Pigs, where an American invasion was soundly beaten back by the Cubans way back in 1961. Remember?

We got on the wretched tour bus in Veradero—it was little more than a 1950s vintage school bus without the usual comfy padding—and as I was sucking back my fourth complimentary Cuba Libre, the tour guide on the bus ("Hello, my name is José. I'll be your guide today") came over and asked us if we wanted to visit a crocodile farm near the town of Guamà. (There's a picture of the entrance at the start of Chapter Three.)

So we stopped and got off to see these big pens full of different-sized crocs and watched the locals amuse themselves by throwing the small ones in with the bigger ones, and laughing and clapping at the ensuing cannibalistic feeding frenzy.

I got bored with this pretty soon, so while the wife was buying one of those stuffed crocodiles they make out of all the little ones they find floating belly-up in the tanks at the end of the day, I said to the guide, "Hey José, if the Americans ever invade again what are you gonna do with these crocodiles?" And he says, quite seriously, "Señor, we'll let 'em out so they can bite off their legs."

That was enough for the perfect *Examiner* story—and it appeared the following week as:

EXPOSED: CASTRO'S SECRET WEAPON TO PREVENT ANOTHER BAY OF PIGS—CROCODILES!

The kicker line ran, "Silent Sentinels Waiting To Bite Off Legs of U.S. Invasion Force." My unimpeachable source? The story alluded to "an agent of the Cuban government who would only identify himself as José," which was true enough. Hell, *everybody* worked for the government in Cuba, including our tour guide José, so the story was true— he really *was* an agent . . .

At the tabs *any* travel can be turned into a story, as the examples below show.

I: WHEN YOU GOTTA GO

**If you carry a hockey stick and
a can of pepper spray . . .**

THEN NEW YORK is a great city for "just walking around"—at least that's the accepted myth. The "Big Apple" is supposed to be full of interesting stuff to see and do, and you can get to most of it the old-fashioned way—by pounding the pavement. Personally, I hate New York—I've often worked there illegally and it's overrated and self-absorbed and overpriced. Still, it's a good place to turn a buck or two when you need some fast cash.

And the travel-writing hacks all know it. That's why they keep grinding out these lame and dreary walking guides to every out-of-the-way nook and cranny in New York City. They steal most of their material from the *New Yorker* then rehash it, so by the time you actually get to the places they mention, they're usually boarded up.

Anyway, they all wimp out on stuff you *really* need to know, like where you can take a pee in that town without getting arrested. One visit to Manhattan is all it takes and right off you'll know what I'm talking about. The routine's always the same. You've really, *really* gotta go! You spot a restaurant, then weasel your way in the door, try to look hungry and if the *maître d'* is busy, you sneak into the washroom when he's looking the other way. Except, of course, it doesn't work that way. You always get caught, because in New York, a restaurant will hang, draw and quarter you and *then* make you buy a six-course meal before they'll let you anywhere near their toilet. They're worse than the French—at least you get a decent meal in France.

The hotels are just as bad, they're just sneakier about it. What they do is *hide* their "public" toilets so tourists can't just walk in off the street and find them. That way, you have to ask for directions, and then it's "Are you a guest in the hotel?" No? Tough luck, pal. You and your bursting bladder are back on the street. And don't try to answer yes—they'll ask to see your room key.

But there is one New York walking guide that actually helps a stricken visitor with stuff you really need to know—*The Toilets of New York*. It's a book that, quite simply, cuts through all the crap.

This book tells you exactly where some of those cagey hotels have hidden their cans, and includes directions like "behind a pillar, around the corner from the service elevator on the second mezzanine." That way, you can make a bee-line right to a john where you won't get knifed, and without bumping into the snooty concierge who'll want you to grease his palm and will probably *still* throw you out on your ear.

But wait—it gets better. *The Toilets of New York* also tells you what to expect once you get your foot in the washroom door. It's got a four-star Michelin Guide–type rating system that talks about everything from the quality of the graffiti on the walls to the texture of the toilet paper in the stalls. It even tells you where you have to "pay to pee."

Now, no New Yorker would ever stop navel-gazing long enough to write something as useful as this guide. *The Toilets of New York* was put together by a guy from Milwaukee named Ken Eichenbaum. Ken remembers all too well how he got the idea for the book. What visitor to New York hasn't suffered the embarrassment, as Ken did, "of having to relieve myself in a bush in a little park outside Lincoln Center," after being shamefully turned away by countless establishments up and down Broadway.

The Toilets of New York means that, from now on, Ken and millions of desperate tourists like him won't have to put up with the kind of cruelty New Yorkers like to inflict on unsuspecting out-of-towners.

I talked to Ken Eichenbaum back in January of 1993 and right off,

I tried to get him to share with the world his personal list of New York's top ten toilets. Ken told me he didn't think there were ten but that "there might be two or three."

Wait a minute. With eight million toilets in the naked city, only two or three are fit for human use? "That's right," said Ken confidently, and he wasn't telling where they were—people would have to buy the book to find that out.

Well then, I asked, how about at least coming clean on the worst toilet in town, or was that top secret too?

Those, he said, were in Grand Central Station. They're really dirty, a lot of the plumbing doesn't work and they're populated by bad characters. Most people who'd use a guidebook in New York would want to avoid a mugging or would want to stay away from guys who are using dope. They'd want to avoid Grand Central's toilets.

"But if you are stuck at Grand Central," said Ken, "go out on one of the platforms, find a train that's just sitting around and looks like it's not planning on going anywhere for a while and use the toilet on the train. It may not be much cleaner but at least you can express your disgust in private."

Ken Eichenbaum's handy little book is full of such tips and get this: it's got a nifty little bonus section. What you do is you flip to the back of the book, to the last five pages. They're blank, they're perforated and they're designated *"Emergency use only."*

II: COME FLY WITH ME

THROW AWAY those barf bags and forget about jet lag, wind shear, flight delays, lost luggage and crummy airline food. Say goodbye to airplane crashes or getting hijacked to some horrid place for an unscheduled stopover. If Herbie Brennan's book catches on, all those things could go the way of the dodo.

The Astral Projection Workbook is the first-ever handy, practical how-to book on the ancient art of leaving your body behind while your spirit takes an out-of-body holiday. It's sort of a free, all-expenses-paid vacation, and the only downside is, no air miles.

Herbie Brennan, the guy who researched and wrote *The Astral Projection Workbook,* is an Irishman from County Kildare, and he told me that if I worked through the easy-to-follow, step-by-step directions in his handbook, eventually I could use the technique to go pretty much anywhere I wanted to.

Sounded good to me, so I wondered what I should pack for the trip. Could I take any of my stuff with me? Do I travel naked or dressed? How about the family dog? Could I bring Fido along on my astral vacation and forget about the kennel fees?

"First of all, about the clothes," said Herbie. "I have no idea why this should be, but it's one of the mysteries of astral projection—yes, it's an observable fact that when you exteriorize you do have clothes on. Now, I've never heard anybody bring the dog, although I did come across one projector who managed to take his cat along to the astral plane."

If you can take the cat along (hey, no rabies papers when crossing borders!), how about other people? Suppose two people wanted to have an affair—could they do it astrally and not have to worry about their husbands and wives catching them?

"That's a terribly interesting question," said Herbie, pointing out that there's "a marvellous body of literature—and of course it would have to be from France—that says, yes, it is possible, and it has been done. And although I blush to admit I've never managed it myself, I really should tell you that according to the French literature, the experience, when it's carried out astrally, is even better than when it's carried out physically."

This was getting better and better. And how about stuff like projecting yourself into a major boardroom and getting a stock tip, or going on an astral sightseeing tour of the shower room at the girls' dorm?

"These are marvellously immoral suggestions, Harold," said Herbie. "And the honest answer has to be . . . yes. If you're that way inclined I don't see anything that would stop you."

Book me on the first astral flight out of here, I thought, but as a dyed-in-the-wool, card-carrying coward, I needed to know—does it hurt?

"There's nothing particularly dangerous about it," he told me. "But having said that, some people have reported quite unpleasant experiences—heart palpitations, paralysis, that type of thing—all temporary, obviously, but when you're going through them you feel as though you're extremely ill. And if your corporeal body is touched while your spirit is on the astral plane, if something even just lightly brushes against it or there's a loud sound nearby, the reaction is to draw your astral body back in quickly and violently. It gives you a severe jolt, which is quite unpleasant but not particularly dangerous, unless you have some sort of pre-existing condition like a bad heart."

There's always a downside to these things. I could just see it—zooming out astrally on a two-week around-the-world cruise and you've just checked in at the Sultan of Brunei's pleasure garden for some R & R, when suddenly one of the kids comes over to the couch and pokes your physical body in the tummy. Instantly, you're jerked back twelve thousand miles to dreary old Ontario with a heart-stopping jolt! After such wonders, the psychological shock of returning to the cold cruel ho-hum-ness of home could kill you!

On second thought, maybe I'll take the train.

III: THE GHOSTBUSTING GYNECOLOGIST

D R. KENNETH WRIGHT, whom I nicknamed the "ghostbusting gynecologist," told me about a really harrowing holiday he had in the American southwest. But before we get to Dr. Wright's memorable vacation, there's one thing I want to clear up: the "doctor" tag.

Working on the tabs you learn pretty quickly to take the honorific "Dr." with a great big grain of salt. The world is crawling with self-appointed experts sporting dime-a-dozen doctorates from Whatsamatta U. and other hallowed halls of higher learning. I myself have several nicely lettered doctoral sheepskins on my wall, picked up *gratis* in exchange for a little free publicity for the "institution." Dr. Kenneth Wright, however, is the genuine article, an honest-to-God practising physician, a pillar of the Fresno, California medical community, a dedicated man of science and, even better, someone who's been pressed into service as a ghostbuster! For a hack like me, that's an irresistible combination.

A serious and respected man of science dabbling in the occult? When I spoke to Dr. Wright, I asked him right up front if he didn't see a bit of a contradiction there.

> **Dr. Wright:** Well, I had a connection with the psychic world long before I ever became a gynecologist. Actually, it doesn't make any difference what field of endeavour you're in. Most people know that there are ghosts. Most people have had some sort of encounter or ESP experience. Even you, Harold, if you'll admit it to yourself, either as a little boy or as of right now, you get an

uncomfortable feeling when you're totally in the dark.

Fiske: That's true.

Dr. Wright: And the reason you do that is that a lot of the time you're not alone in the dark.

Fiske: Okay, but leave me out of this. I'd rather talk about your ghosts. When was the first time you actually saw a ghost with your own eyes?

Dr. Wright: That would've been when I was about seven or eight in the basement of my home in Idaho Falls, Idaho. It was a new house. My dad had just built it so nothing had happened there. Nobody had died. It wasn't some old haunted house. Somebody or something had just wandered in. See, ghosts are mostly just folks, home-less people who, for some reason or other, haven't gone over to the other side. In fact, the vast majority of them are just people like you'd meet all the time because they were people.

Fiske: So homelessness affects the spirit world just like it affects our world?

Dr. Wright: Very much. That's why they attach on to a place and when the ghostbuster tries to drive them out they will fight with such vehemence because they need a place to . . . well, to be. Another interesting thing that happens is that once there is a ghost that inhabits a place, it sort of leaves a trail so that other ghosts can come in.

Fiske: Sort of like roaches? Once you've got one ghost you're going to get more?

Dr. Wright: Sure.

I got the picture. If ghosts were half as tough as roaches to get rid of, then Dr. Wright must have some pretty wild stories to tell about his exploits as a ghostbuster. He did.

The doc, his wife and their two kids, Jeremy and Megan, were on vacation. They were in their motor home driving through the dusty town of Cimarron, New Mexico, when all of a sudden some eerie feeling made them stop. They found themselves outside the St. James Hotel and they had this bizarre intense desire to spend the night.

"Bizarre?" I was skeptical. I told the doc it sounded pretty normal to me. More like just being tired after a long day driving through the desert. He said, no, the family wasn't tired, they hadn't been driving long. They couldn't explain it but they *had* to stop—right then and there—at the St. James Hotel.

They found out later that the St. James was built in the 1880s and it was the haunt of gunslingers and outlaws. By 1993, it was being run by a lady named Pat Lorrey.

Pat put the Wright clan in a suite of rooms on either side of room number 18 and the family settled in for the night. Then Dr. Wright started hearing weird noises. They were coming from number 18. He went down to the lobby, grabbed hold of Mrs. Lorrey and made her come upstairs and check it out with him.

Dr. Wright picks up the story: "She opened the door, we stepped in and I was instantly terrified," he said. "Before I walked into that room I had a pretty good idea I'd be talking to a ghost, but I was not prepared for what I saw. Over in the corner was a man cloaked in black. He had a black hat, a black beard and he had *red, red* eyes. I said, 'Oh my God!' I was face to face with the personification of evil. He exploded out of the corner and came at me with a '*gaahrrooarrr!*' And I nearly jumped out of my skin. Then Pat, the owner of the hotel, clenched her fists— not in a fighting position but down by her sides—and she said to the ghost, 'You may go now. You are free to go. You may leave.'"

According to Dr. Wright, "that made him just *crazy*! He came back at her, right up to her face, screaming and roaring. Well, I couldn't make sense out of what he was screaming but I *could* see that he was really mad at her. So I said, 'Pat, he hates your guts. *Get out of this room!*' Well, she got out of there and closed the door behind her."

But then *he* was alone in a room with an angry evil ghost who, Dr. Wright said, "wanted to tear me limb from limb. God was he mad!"

But what was he mad about? I asked. "Pat told me that a couple years earlier she'd brought in an Indian medium to drive the ghost out," explained Dr. Wright. "That's why she was chanting 'You are free to go.' She'd been told that's how you evict a spirit. And I guess . . . hey!" At that point, he broke off, and since we were on the phone, I asked him why he'd stopped telling his ghostly tale. "We just had an earthquake!" he replied. "How about that?"

I was utterly stunned by this unexpected development. "What? You mean now? There? While we were talking?" I stammered. Now remember, Dr. Wright was getting to the *really* juicy stuff about this evil red-eyed ghost and—*bingo!*—we get an earthquake. And that was just the beginning. We talked for more than an hour and quakes were going on all through our conversation.

Just a coincidence? I don't know. It's not for me to speculate about what dark forces might have been at work trying to get Dr. Wright to back off from his revelations, but God knows I wouldn't have blamed him if he'd hung up on me right then and there. To his credit, in spite of all these bad vibes, he was a real trouper and he ploughed right on with his story.

Now before we go any further, you've got to understand that Dr. Wright is different from your average exorcist. He's kind of a sensitive New Age ghostbuster. He realizes there's no point in trying to get rid of ghosts. Remember, they're actually homeless folks and they need a place to live just like the rest of us. Kick them out of your house, they'll look around for somebody else to haunt.

So Dr. Wright doesn't confront, he negotiates. In this circumstance, he went to the ghost, sat down with him and cut a deal. The terms were simple: Pat Lorrey agreed that Room 18 would be out of bounds—she couldn't rent it, she couldn't clean it, she couldn't even go into it. The ghost got exclusive possession, but that's *all* he got. The catch was, he had to stay put in Room 18—*forever!*

"You stay in Room 18 *from now on!*" Dr. Wright told the ghost. "You can't go in any of the other rooms. You can't even come out in the hallway."

The ghost agreed, said Dr. Wright, pressing on with his tale. "Anyway, the next morning I went into my kids' room and my daughter Megan said, 'Daddy who was that nice man who came in my room last night? He had a black hat in his hand and he had a black beard and he just stood and looked at me really sweetly.'"

The ghost's broken promise made Dr. Wright "really mad." He went down to Room 18, jerked open the door and told the spirit, "You leave my children alone. I'm telling you, you better understand this for sure. You break the agreement one more time and you're out of here."

The ghost just sat there and glowered.

The Wrights got out of there the next day; they finished their holiday and headed back to Fresno. A couple of months later the doc called the hotel. He wanted to check in, you know, to see how his deal with the dead was holding up.

Pat Lorrey said no problem, everything was fine. She hadn't heard a peep out of Room 18. Well, there was one little thing, though. Something Pat hadn't bothered to tell Dr. Wright when he was actually in the St. James Hotel.

The doctor asked me, "Harold, do you remember that Indian medium—the one Pat brought in a couple of years before to try to get rid of the ghost? Well, Pat said the Indian and the ghost did communicate. They had quite a little talk. The ghost told him that his name—listen to this one—was T. J. Wright. w-r-i-g-h-t!"

The penny dropped. "That's *your* name!" I cried in amazement.

"Correct," said the doc. "T. J. also told the Indian that he'd stayed at the St. James in 1880 and won the hotel in a poker game, and he had signed the ledger. So Pat did some checking. She dug up the books. They were back in a crated box that nobody had looked at for seventy years. She found the particular date, opened it up and there it was— T.J. Wright's handwriting. Well, then *we* did some checking," the doc continued. "It turns out T. J. Wright was a relative of mine and that's the reason, that night in the hotel, he broke the rules and came into my daughter's room. He just wanted to get a peek at his great-great-grand-niece, Megan."

So it turned out Dr. Kenneth Wright's faith in ghosts as "just folks like us" was justified. The "red-eyed personification of evil cloaked in black" was really only looking for a friendly family reunion on a happy haunted holiday!

IV: THE BALLAD OF BUDDY HOGUE

DEAD BIG SHOTS are big business for L. H. "Buddy" Hogue. Buddy is the owner-operator and chief curator of The Tragedy in U.S. History Museum in St. Augustine, Florida.

What Buddy does is look into those watershed tragedies of American history—those stunning moments when you say, "I remember exactly where I was when I first heard about _____." He ferrets out the memorabilia, the actual day-to-day items that played a crucial or contributing role in those tragic events. Then he buys the stuff and puts it on display.

In his collection, Buddy's got the Jayne Mansfield Decapitation Car (or what's left of it). If you remember, the way Jayne Mansfield died was that she rear-ended a flatbed truck in Biloxi, Mississippi back in the early sixties. Talk about instant convertible—the truck just sliced off the whole top of her car, and sure enough, there's the bottom half of it resting peacefully in Buddy Hogue's museum.

Then there's the Bonnie and Clyde Getaway/Death Car, a vintage 1934 Ford with—count 'em—163 bullet holes in it. For forty-five years, this icon of American folklore was lugged around America from one cheap carnival and gun show to another until Buddy Hogue got hold of it. It took a visionary like Buddy to give the B & C Getaway/Death Car the place of honour it deserved. So it's on display in his museum, along with a gallery of actual autopsy photos of Bonnie and Clyde, naked and dead, right there on morgue slabs. But as impressive as those displays are, neither one of them rates centre stage at The Tragedy in U.S. History Museum. That honour belongs to Buddy's collection of memorabilia surrounding John F. Kennedy's assassination.

When I talked to Buddy Hogue, he told me how he'd picked up these crown jewels of his emporium, the treasured collector's items that got him started in the tragedy business.

"Back when I was a young man," said Buddy, "I was a Gulf gas distributor here for the county and we were sitting at a table where the employees chewed the fat an' it come over the television that the president [JFK] had been shot, and I told the men that worked with me, 'That would make a museum,' because I live in a town that is all museums. (St. Augustine actually bills itself as the "museum capital of America." It's supposed to have more museums *per capita* than anywhere else in the U.S.) "So," he went on, "I went out to Texas and I seen the possibilities in these things, these assassination mementos."

It must have cost a fortune to get all that Kennedy stuff together, I suggested. Not really, said Buddy. "Of course, it would today. But I guess back in those days Kennedy wasn't so popular, and in Texas they were more like ashamed of it that he got shot there."

So Buddy got some great deals, including, he said, "the 1954 Chevy that the government claims without this car the crime could not have been committed." Buddy explained that Lee Harvey Oswald worked at the Texas Book Depository, and at the last minute, Kennedy's handlers changed the parade route so it would go right in front of the book depository.

"That gave Oswald the chance he could shoot the president," said Buddy, "but he didn't have his rifle in Dallas. He had to go to Irwin, Texas, seventy miles away, to get the rifle. But Oswald didn't have one penny on him in Dallas for a bus and he could not drive a car. He'd only taken one driving lesson. So what he done, Oswald had one friend in Dallas, Texas. His name was Wesley Beule Frasier. Now Wesley owned this '54 Chevrolet. Oswald talked Wesley into taking him to Irwin to get some 'curtain rods' for his apartment."

That means that Oswald's friend's auto is the very car that carried what was supposed to be curtain rods (but was, in fact, a cleverly disguised rifle) to that tragic date with destiny! "And we've got that '54 Chevy right here where the people can look at it, and we ask 'em not to touch it but a lot of people open the doors and such like that, ya know," said Buddy.

Buddy told me his other Kennedy memorabilia include "the furniture from the room in Dallas where Oswald planned this awful crime." Buddy said Oswald's landlady, Mrs. Bledsoe, "had heard Oswald talking inside the room in Russian, or it seemed to be some foreign language, anyway. Well, we have the furniture from Oswald's room in Mrs. Bledsoe's boarding house. It's here in the museum, set up just like it was in Dallas. We've even got Oswald's comb with some of his hair still on it."

And how much did Buddy have to pay for all this great stuff?

"On that particular deal," Buddy told me, "I had to rebuild the front porch on Mrs. Bledsoe's house. It was in real bad shape. It was kinda like horse trading, ya know?"

In a just and sane world, Buddy Hogue's amazing Oswald items would have put his Tragedy in U.S. History Museum on the map. Sadly, that did *not* happen—and I that mean literally, because St. Augustine's stick-in-the-mud Chamber of Commerce has flat out *refused* to mention Buddy's museum on any of the town's tourist maps.

And you know those little tourist trains, the ones that run through resort towns and show you all the local points of interest? Well, in St. Augustine, they go past all the *other* museums, *but not Buddy's*!

The city fathers are really down on the guy. Always were. Right from the start they thought his idea was tasteless and exploitative, so at first they wouldn't give him a permit, then they fought him in court, for four years.

When they lost, they used their smug little conspiracy of silence to make sure nobody ever heard of the place. And that is the *real* tragedy of Buddy Hogue's Tragedy in U.S. History Museum.

CHAPTER TEN

CHANNEL SURFING

One *Weekly World News* reader included this drawing of
the gigantic bug he keeps in his freezer! (See Chapter Four)

You CAN forget the remote control . . .

The channels I like to surf won't turn up on your TV. I'm talking Shirley MacLaine-type channelling here. We touched on this stuff back in Chapter Seven when I discussed the existence of chakras. We're all supposed to have these things inside us. They're invisible, little lumps of internal life force that link us up to a boundless cosmic power grid. Chakras are what people are talking about when they say they "feel at one with the universe." The theory goes that when you're tuned into your chakras you can talk to anyone or anything anywhere.

Now, I urge you to abandon your outdated notions of communication. I want you to suspend your disbelief and get ready for one spacy trip through the world of interspecies dialogue. The species I'm talking about (and talking to) run the whole gamut, animal to vegetable to mineral. We'll start with the vegetables.

1: PLANTS ARE PEOPLE TOO

Scientists Discover:
WE'RE ALL RELATED TO TREES!

IT WAS A snappy headline and it caught my eye while I was waiting in line at the supermarket checkout. The year was 1990, and I was killing time flipping through the latest issue of my old paper, the *National Examiner*. I've always been a sucker for a good science story and this one was a doozy.

Remember that, until late 1989, the Berlin Wall was the only thing keeping the Communist hordes from overrunning Western Europe, so you'll excuse the outdated references to what's now Russia. The article explained how a Soviet doctor named Yuri Babikov had discovered that we *Homo sapiens* are, in fact, distant kin to plants and trees!

According to Dr. Babikov, all that Darwinian stuff about apes and evolution is a load of trash, because the *real* missing link was probably a majestic oak, a shady elm or a spreading chestnut tree. So you can forget the notion that apes came down from the trees. According to Dr. Babikov, we *are* the trees.

Well, this was hardly news to me. Our human speech is riddled with references to the vegetable kingdom, something we still carry as an unconscious inheritance from our ancestors, the plants. We're "as cozy as two peas in a pod." We "veg out," get a "plum" assignment, "bark up the wrong tree" and "root, root, root" for the home team. We name our daughters "Iris" or "Heather" or "Rose." You're "a peach," "a tomato" or "the apple of my eye." I'm "a sap" or "a nut" or a real "corny" guy. Hell, if I can have a family tree, why not a tree in the family? The more the merrier, I always say.

So Dr. Babikov's research was just "peachy" as far as I was concerned, and it jogged my memory about an old science experiment that we'd actually run, nine years earlier, in the *National Examiner* newsroom. Simply put, the thesis behind our little experiment was that when we talk to plants they listen and pay attention! In fact we postulated that not only do they listen to us—they *like* to listen to us. And more than that, they actually *thrive* on it. In other words, talking to plants helps them grow. That's what we were out to prove.

Here's how we did it. We got some ordinary common variety carrots. (We used bag carrots with none of that green leafy stuff growing out of the top.) We took two equal-sized carrots and cut about a quarter of an inch off the fat ends, and then we plunked those carrot tops down, side by side on a wet paper towel. (It was crucial that throughout the experiment the paper towel had to be kept slightly moist.) We marked one carrot top with a tag that had a big plus sign and the other one with a minus sign.

Next, everybody in the *Examiner* newsroom (from the editor down to the janitor) was encouraged to talk to the carrots every chance they had. But they had to do it *telepathically*. We decided to go the ESP route because except for corn, veggies don't have ears, so there wasn't much point in everybody yammering out loud—we needed to get work done and it was already noisy enough with all the manual typewriters in that place.

The idea was to think loving, supportive, caring thoughts, and once your head was filled with positive vibes you were supposed to channel them directly to the "plus" carrot. The other carrot got your hostile, stressful, irritable, evil thoughts. That "minus" carrot was the one we were supposed to take out all our anxieties and frustrations on. We had to really give him hell.

The result was that the plus carrot grew a veritable rain forest of rich, green, healthy shoots, while the minus carrot grew scrawny and ugly and almost withered away. Proof positive that our thesis was correct—the plants are listening! Believe it or not, though, even in the face of our rigorously collected scientific data, there were plenty of doubters out there in the scientific community looking to discredit us.

They were finally silenced when a distinguished educator (and good friend of mine), Lisa Sainsbury, came to our defence. Lisa was a kindergarten teacher at the exclusive St. George's private girls' school in Montreal. Lisa read about our amazing breakthrough in the *Examiner* and decided (since all good scientific experiments have to be repeatable) to test our controversial results with the help of her kindergarten kids. When they were finished, Lisa got in touch with me and shared her findings. The following is her unsolicited testimonial.

"To tell the truth," said Lisa, "I was very sceptical when I first heard of this and I decided that I would try the experiment myself. So I went to the supermarket and bought a large bunch of carrots. I think there were twelve in all. I divided them up in class—six on one side and six on the other. I told the kids, 'Six of them are bad evil carrots and the other six were good, decent, heroic carrots.' Then I told them that over a period of ten days, 'you have to think angry nasty thoughts towards the minus carrots and good friendly thoughts towards the plus carrots.' In fact, like the tree of righteousness the plus carrots did prosper and the minus carrots wilted and were miserable. It was pretty impressive! I'm going to try it in my own garden sometime. Seeing is believing."

Ms. Sainsbury's impassioned testimonial silenced our critics. The *Examiner*'s research had been validated. We now had conclusive corroborative evidence that man can, in fact, communicate with carrots, and very likely with the entire vegetable kingdom as well. But wait, there's more—that's just the tip of the iceberg lettuce. It turns out that vegetables can communicate with each other too!

Again, back in 1990, barely a week after Dr. Babikov's stunning news about man's evolutionary link to treedom, I uncovered an interesting sidebar to all of this. I interviewed Ed Wagner, a physicist from Portland, Oregon.

Dr. Wagner was investigating something he called "W waves." In case you're wondering, the good doctor is a humble man—the "W" stands for wood, not Wagner. You see, Dr. Wagner had discovered that there are these weird wood waves that are generated inside trees and then transmitted from one tree to another.

He discovered his wood waves when he rigged up a little electronic gizmo, a sort of elaborate voltage meter, with a couple of electrodes. He plugged these things into a tree. Apparently his probes picked up a measurable voltage reading from the tree. Dr. Wagner analyzed these W waves and concluded that what they really *are* is the trees talking to each other.

"If you chop into the tree below the probes you'll see a deflection of the meter," Dr. Wagner told me. "It goes up then it goes back down."

"So the tree is sort of saying 'ouch?'" I asked.

"If you want to put it that way, yes," he replied. "The tree is going 'ouch,' or however you want to describe it. And if you chop into one tree not only does that tree itself respond but you can measure a response from adjacent trees."

What an astounding notion! One tree is talking to another tree! But this was "kind of old hat" to Dr. Wagner, "because people had discovered a while ago that trees seemed to communicate, but they've always in the past explained it by chemical communication. They observed," he went on, "that if insects attacked one tree then the surrounding trees got ready for attack too. For example, they might produce certain chemicals that tended to poison the insects."

The trees were communicating, according to Dr. Wagner, not by chemicals, but by his mysterious W waves. And there are enormous practical applications for these, he said. "If we wanted, we could prepare a forest for insect attack by producing the proper signal. But I don't know how to do that yet, except by chopping into a tree. But there is a possibility that one day, if you can produce the right W waves, you might be able to warn the forest ahead of time and prevent insect attack."

Of course, the implications for Dr. Wagner's research are amazing.

Once we've deciphered W waves, we could actually talk to the trees—and not just trees but *all* plants.

"All the plants that I've looked at have these waves in them," said Dr. Wagner. "I've measured them in house-plants and begonias and cabbage, so apparently all plants can communicate with each other."

And I immediately had a disturbing thought: remember the tree saying "ouch" when struck by an axe? Wouldn't researchers be over-whelmed by guilt if they knew they were inflicting pain on sentient communicating beings?

"I haven't given too much thought about that," confessed Dr. Wagner. "I don't think that a tree really feels any pain—it's kind of like an automatic response."

But I persisted. "If you wired me up to a voltage meter and gave me a whack with an axe, I'd probably register a change too," I suggested.

"Well, yes," said the doctor. "I have made some measurements that seem to indicate that these W waves are in animals too." But that raised the question of whether animals and trees could be interacting on some kind of level that we can't really understand yet.

"It's possible," Dr. Wagner conceded. "I think all nature communi-cates with each other."

My mind raced with a dozen questions. Suppose you started eating cabbage rolls under a maple tree. Would the distress caused to the cab-bage be communicated to the maple so the tree might decide it's 'us against them' and maybe attack somehow? Or, failing that, could the tree call in some bees or even an angry bear to do its dirty work? I put these queries directly to the doctor.

"I think," he observed, "the cabbage rolls would already be cooked, so I don't think they'd be communicating with anybody."

That made sense, but it wasn't all that comforting. If Dr. Wagner was right, if "all nature communicates with each other" and the plants and trees are already talking to the animals, well, it stands to reason that they can (and will) someday start talking to us. And I've got a hunch they're going to have a lot to say, for who among us is without guilt?

As we mow, so shall we reap. We clearcut our forests as the willow literally weeps, the carrot cries and the humble blade of grass grumbles. You and I have the sap of countless billions of innocent creatures on our hands. Let's face it, we've got a lot to answer for. I'd think twice, if I were you, the next time you head for the salad bar. Either that, or we might all be reading about "Veggie Vengeance" and "Cereal Killers" in the next *National Examiner.*

II: ROCK TALK

Rosemary Brown-Saunders has rocks in her head!

NO, I MEAN IT. That's no metaphor and she's not crazy. I mean she *literally* has rocks in her head. Rosemary is a Carmel, California psychic who actually "talks to rocks," which is no big deal since, according to her, every rock on the face of this planet is, in fact, *alive!*

Rosemary Brown-Saunders believes that every stone on earth, from the most majestic hunk of granite to the humblest piece of gravel, is a living, breathing (well, maybe not breathing), sentient being and that these "rock people," as she calls them, beam their thoughts and ideas and words of wisdom directly into her brain.

When I talked to Rosemary by phone right around Christmastime a couple of years ago, she told me how, a little over a year earlier, she was meditating on the beach in Carmel when an emissary from the hitherto unknown race of rocks contacted her. Now that signal did not come, as you might expect it to, from a local pile of pebbles that had washed up on Rosemary's beach. No! It originated a thousand miles away from the middle of the desert near Sedona, Arizona.

That's quite a hike. It sure sounded to me like Rosemary's rock pals had gone out of their way to get in touch. I asked her if she could tell me more about that fateful day when they first broke the ice.

"At that time," she recalled, "the essence of this being came through and announced himself. I say *him*self because I felt it as a male vibration as the way he came into me." But "actually they're androgynous beings—they're both male and female—but in order to present himself he came through as a tiny little boy-being."

Can all rocks can do this or just the one little fella? I wondered.

"He has introduced us to three or four different types of intelligences just from that particular area of rocks," said Rosemary. "One of them is named 'Moha,' who, he says, is a rock elder."

So these rocks have names. Did he happen to say what his own name was?

Yes indeed, said Rosemary. "His name is 'Rojo.' He indicated that name came through to him because it was an old name for that area. It's something that the indigenous culture, the Indians there, named the rocks and so he liked that name and took it and I have since found out that 'rojo' means 'red' rocks."

And now that we're on a first-name basis with our rock pals, what do they have to tell us?

"A lot of things," said Rosemary. "Rojo has explained physical ailments on an individual basis for people I have introduced to him. He talks about comets and extraterrestrial beings and just about anything you might happen to be interested in. It's fascinating, because Rojo likens us to being rocks ourselves. He says that's because we have so many minerals in our system, plus some of us have gallstones and kidney stones and all that good kind of stuff, too."

I told Rosemary I wasn't sure I'd call a kidney stone "good stuff"— I had one of those once and they hurt like hell. But she told me "if you were to ask Rojo, he would probably tell you how to get rid of them."

Did I hear that right? Rosemary had just implied that talking to rocks is not some special kind of gift that she alone is blessed with. Anybody can do it, she told me, "and Rojo has said that whatever you need to know, anywhere on the planet, all you have to do is pick up a rock and listen."

Well, I sure was ready to listen. Could I chat with Rojo or Moha (or one of their rocky friends) there and then? Rosemary was only too happy to oblige.

"It'll take some time and there will be some silence, so don't hang up," she warned. At that point things did, in fact, get very quiet for about four or five minutes. Maybe Rojo just didn't feel like talking that day, but nothing was happening and I was starting to have my doubts. I mean, this was a long distance call, back when long distance wasn't cheap—and it was on *my* nickel. I have to admit I was getting a little annoyed and actually thought about hanging up.

Then I heard something. It was faint at first but I did pick up the sound of slow, rhythmic, very deep breathing on the other end of the line. That tipped me off right away. I'd been through this kind of thing with other channellers, so I knew that Rosemary Brown-Saunders had disappeared into a deep trancelike meditative state.

The next voice I heard was not Rosemary's. Not even close. Rosemary's got a grown-up's voice, and speaks with a typical "American" accent. But the voice on the phone could only be a little girl's voice. It had to be. Plus, I'd swear the kid was Belgian or Japanese or maybe a little bit of both. Anyway, it talked slow and very deliberately, like a foreigner struggling to come up with the right words. It was Rojo!

"Hello! It is I. I am here," said Rojo. "I understand that you are a friend."

I said sure, then I told Rojo I was a journalist and wanted to ask what life was like being a rock. For starters, how about time? Did he experience the world in geological time?

"There is no such thing as time in our existence because we have been here for so many eons," he said. "We watch all of the populations come and go and, in fact, we are recorders of everything that happens in the earth. That is why your archaeologists and geologists like us so much."

"But those guys frequently break rocks and smash you to bits and cut you up. Isn't that painful for you?"

"It is, yes," Rojo confessed. "But those are sacrifices that we will make if the information that is received from us can help all of the mankind and naturekind on the planet. However, we do not enjoy being blown up by large atomic devices."

I was stunned by this admission but ploughed on to my next question. I'd recently read a prediction that huge destructive comets (like the type that struck Jupiter in 1990) were on a collision course with earth. Did Rojo have any knowledge of that?

"Do not worry," he said. "Comets do exactly what their mission is. You speak about comets that have hit Jupiter, and that is to ignite life on that planet, not to destroy."

Gee, I thought, you learn something new every day.

"The imploding of megatons of energy and the placement of new amoebas that have come in on the comet's surface have ignited life on the planet of Jupiter," Rojo went on. "This is also how your life began on your earth."

"Oh, so *that's* how it all began," I told him. "And speaking of life here on earth, do you rock people have a culture? Do you like art and poetry and music like, say, rock 'n' roll?

"We do," said Rojo. "It is that we have the ability to sense, even though we do not have ears or eyes, all sounds and all pleasantries of the planet."

Since we were talking about art and "pleasantries" I decided to tell Rojo about a rock joke I remembered reading back in the sixties. It was a "Peanuts" cartoon.

Charlie Brown and his philosophical pal Linus Van Pelt are standing on this beach looking out at the lake. Charlie stoops down, picks up a pebble and casually tosses it into the water. Linus says, "Nice going, Charlie Brown. It took that stone four thousand years to get to shore, and now you've thrown it back." Good ol' wishy-washy Charlie Brown hangs his head and says, "Everything I do makes me feel guilty."

I asked Rojo if the rock people get ticked off when people do stuff like that. I was surprised by his answer. It turns out Linus was way out of line. Charlie Brown had nothing to feel guilty about.

"It is very interesting to note that all children see us as very loving and wonderful beings," said Rojo. "It is true that they pick us up and throw us and that is the way we get to fly! It is only that you need to pick up any stone that you are attracted to, for that stone is also calling to you to pick it up. Just ask permission and it will want to be with you."

A heck of a message, eh? And one heck of a time to get it. Remember that my conversation with Rojo/Rosemary took place just a couple of days before Christmas, the season of peace, goodwill and (now that I think about it) rock-solid friendship with no strings attached.

Maybe the guy who started that pet rock craze back in the seventies was actually on to something. And maybe we all got that old wives' tale backwards. That lump of coal in your Christmas stocking might just be the best gift—and the best friend—you'll ever have.

III: THEY CALL HIM KATUBA

Trouble in paradise:
EARTH'S DOLPHINS WILL SOON BECOME EXTINCT!

THAT SHOCKING ecological news comes from the Dancing Dolphin Institute in Maui, Hawaii. Ashleea Nielsen heads up the institute and she recently told me that the dolphins are on the way out. "Yes, they are exiting the planet," she told me. "They're not happy here. They're transiting out of here by dying off then reincarnating into another energetic form somewhere else. They've told a lot of people that and they've told me that, too."

That's right, the dolphins channelled that sad message to Ashleea, and that's not all they told her. It turns out that she's in constant telepathic communication with them and has picked up and absorbed a *long* list of dolphin grievances.

Ashleea says there are all kinds of things bugging the dolphins, but what it all basically boils down to is plain old-fashioned disillusionment. They've had it up to their dorsal fins with the human race. For centuries, the dolphins have tried to be our friends and what have they gotten in return? Exploitation! The crass commercialism in what's called interspecies tourism.

The dolphins are tired of being buzzed by tour boats that take people out to swim with them. Actually, at first the sweet trusting creatures thought it was okay, but pretty soon the yahoos started showing up and ruined the whole racket. The dolphins got sick of being gawked at and poked and prodded with sharp objects and having to give bareback rides to fat tourists and being asked to pose for dumb pictures with stupid little hats on their heads.

Now Ashleea told me she learned all this one day while she was meditating. The dolphins contacted Ashleea using their ethereal codes to mind-meld with her in a kind of psychic space-docking type of ritual—I'm not exactly sure how this works, and I'm not sure I want to know.

"It must have been a hell of a jolt when that happened," I said to her. "I mean, it isn't every day that a school of dolphins comes flooding into your brain. What was it like?"

"The way it worked," she said, "was the dolphins didn't use words. They came into my consciousness with images. They put pictures in my mind with a holographic ball. It's like everything is given to you at once. You can smell it, feel it, see it, hear it, taste it. It's just like you're immersed in this energy field of knowingness."

She went on. "Then they will give you messages or pictures, and for me, the dolphins have a really strong sense of humour. They give real funny images. Like one time they were warning me of danger and in the holographic ball all the dolphins wore little shark masks and held them up across their faces and then peeked out from behind them."

I told Ashleea it was a cute story, but that it seemed like a contradiction to me. One second the dolphins are so depressed they're ready to pull the plug, the next they're joking around. She told me to look beyond the yuks for the deeper, more sinister subtext.

Even though the dolphins were joking, the joke was about "danger," and about their fears and anxieties. In fact, a great deal of my conversation with Ashleea focused on how the dolphins are concerned about pollution and ship propellers and fishing nets and our plundering of their food supply and even the canned tuna labelling laws. They're really scared and really ticked off, and that's why they're going "to exit the planet."

To us, they will appear to have just died off. But what's *really* going on is that the dolphins are going to transform themselves to higher, godlike, transdimensional beings and then move off to another plane of existence and wait for mankind to come to its senses. They *might* come back if we get our act together and clean up the social and ecological messes we've made, but otherwise it's *adios, muchachos.*

And that will be a real tragedy, because according to Ashleea, until about thirty or forty years ago, dolphins and people got along just great. She says that ancient cultures actually saw the dolphins as gods. She'd done a lot of research on that, with the help of a book by the internationally respected archaeologist Nelson Glueck, *Deities and Dolphins.* It's a history of an ancient culture called the Nabataeans, a Middle Eastern culture from the desert (you heard right, a *desert* civilization), so far away from saltwater you'd think the people wouldn't know a dolphin from a doorknob.

Says Ashleea: "He found all these broken-down temples with sculptures of busts of women wearing dolphins on top of their heads. He was exploring this culture that obviously deified dolphins and that's where he got the title of his book. Dolphins also, of course, go way back and were really respected in Greek times. Aphrodite was a dolphin who came out of the ocean and shape-shifted into a human being.

"Actually," said Ashleea, "I know some people out there who still practise [shape-shifting]. I'm not saying that I can shape-shift, but I believe it's a possibility."

So do I! In fact, I'd already interviewed a guy who dabbled in that arcane art. His name is Neville Rowe. When I spoke to him in 1989, he was a fifty-one-year-old ex-electrical engineer and, like Ashleea Nielsen, he channelled himself to a pod of dolphins swimming somewhere out in the Pacific Ocean.

Neville compares it to being like a radio receiver and it's an apt comparison when you consider that, just like the Nabataeans, he lives in the middle of a desert. Neville is headquartered in Phoenix, Arizona, five thousand miles away from his dolphin pals who frolic in the South Pacific.

When I talked to Neville about his first close encounter with dolphin kind he told me, "I went into a deep level of trance, which in other terms is going into an inner meditative space, self-hypnosis, various terms are used to describe this state of mind. And when I went into this state of trance I said, 'Hey dolphins, if you're around, come on through' and I felt the dolphin energy coming into my body and my body being physically turned into a dolphin."

That's right, Neville Rowe actually found himself transformed *into* a dolphin. And his shape-shifting was not a one-shot deal. It happens every time he talks to his finny friends.

"My whole body becomes dolphinlike," says Neville. "A very powerful muscular movement runs through the body from the feet to the head, just as you would imagine in a swimming creature in the ocean. My knees come together and I'm solid from the waist down. Basically, I have no legs any more."

I was totally blown away by that. I mean, I'd talked to literally scores of channellers over the years but Neville was the first one who actually went beyond mere psychic conversation and into the realm of empathic shape-shifting.

Okay, I know, I can hear you saying, "This whole thing sounds kind of fishy, Harold." Arthur Black said the same thing when I told him about it. So I figured the best way to silence the doubting Thomases was to put Neville Rowe's fish story under the unforgiving glare of a live radio interview on *Basic Black*. That interview was one of the most stunning and spectacular moments in Canadian radio history!

At eight minutes past ten on Saturday morning, October 28, 1989, Neville Rowe picked up the phone in Phoenix, Arizona. For the next fifteen minutes, Arthur Black and I grilled the amazing dolphin man about his outrageous claims. When Neville got to the part about the shape-shifting, Arthur asked just how complete the actual overhaul was. "Do you," he wanted to know, "actually develop a blow-hole?"

"In a sense I do," Neville replied. "They use my mouth as a blow-hole. They keep my head as human. You see, I still have to have a human head, because when the dolphins are communicating through me, they use my subconscious mind, my human vocabulary and my speech because, of course, dolphins do not speak English."

Now that we'd cleared up that issue I asked him if there was any special place that was ideally suited to channelling dolphins. Did he have to be submerged in the deep end of a pool, or did the bathtub work just as well? "No, I never do it in water," Neville said. "If I were in water I'd be in big trouble."

I told him that didn't make any sense. "You're a human dolphin," I said, "and you can't swim?"

"No, I can swim okay but I'm in such a deep state of trance, and so out of control of my physical body, I might drown. I prefer to do this in a comfortable chair."

Now Neville just happened to be sitting in his favourite easy chair when we called. After a (very) little arm-twisting, he graciously consented to try to make contact. First he had to switch over to his speaker-phone, because when Neville transforms into a dolphin his arms fuse with the rest of his body and he loses the use of his hands.

Next, he used self-hypnosis to go into a trance. He was going to try to open up a channel to the dolphins, right then and there with 3.6 million Canadians listening in via telephone and the CBC.

I want to warn you right up front that the mere printed word cannot do justice to what happened next. The sounds emanating from what we can only assume was Neville Rowe's "blow-hole" were so startling that we later got a letter from one listener who said he was so shaken by what he heard, he had literally driven his car into a ditch!

What did he hear? First, there was a sudden sharp hiss like somebody had just stuck an ice pick in an over-inflated tire. Then a noise that sounded like a bizarre cross between the agonizing yowl of a dying dog and the guttural moans of that demon kid in *The Exorcist*. The whole thing had an eerie rubberized reverberation to it, almost as if it were happening inside some kind of giant inner tube. It was awful— and it seemed to go on forever.

Later, when I listened to the aircheck tape, Neville's transformational wail timed out at over two minutes. Amazingly, not once during that whole time did Neville, or whatever he was turning into, take anything that would pass for a breath. I was starting to worry about the guy passing out on us when all of a sudden there was a quick flat "yip" and one final explosive hiss!

Then someone—something—talked to us:

"We are Katuba! Welcome, dear friends. It is our delight and our pleasure to have this opportunity to speak with you at this time through this medium of the telephone that you use in human consciousness. Of course, we in dolphin form do not need such devices. Yes, my friends, how might we be of service to you?"

The voice was Neville's, but at the same time it wasn't. Neville has a faintly British, mid-Atlantic ring to his voice, but this Katuba guy sounded like he had been raised by gypsies. And this gypsy really liked to talk.

With God and Arthur Black as my witnesses, I offer the following *verbatim* account of that remarkable conversation.

> *Fiske:* Mr. Dolphin, did I hear you right? You called your-self . . . Katuba?
>
> *Katuba:* Yes, Katuba. We use that name simply as a convenience.
>
> *Arthur:* [*as an aside*] Sounds more like a California wine to me.
>
> *Fiske:* Listen, Katuba, can anybody talk to dolphins like this or is it just Neville Rowe who has this amazing power?
>
> *Katuba:* No, everybody can receive telepathic communications. You are doing it all the time. Human beings are highly telepathic but you have closed off the ability because you don't want to know what other people are thinking. And you don't want them to know what you are thinking and feeling, so you pretend you do not have the ability. But you can communicate with your animals and the plants around you. You can communicate with anything, even with your automobiles, if you so desire. All it takes is recognizing that the information you hear inside your mind is not just your imagination.
>
> *Arthur:* Hello, Katuba, this is Arthur Black speaking. What does a dolphin do all day?
>
> *Katuba:* Well, that is kind of like asking, "What does a human being do all day?" my friend. My goodness me, how many hours do you want to have us speak to you on this subject?

Arthur: Well, you don't shop. You don't go to the bank. You don't take in a movie.

Katuba: That is true. We swim, we play, we fish, we eat, we have sex, we enjoy each other. We are having wonderful fun. You must understand, you see, that dolphinkind does not view life as does humankind.

Fiske: How's that?

Katuba: Humankind is constantly caught up in time. You are constantly worried about what you did yesterday. You are constantly thinking about what's going to happen tomorrow and, usually, how you can avoid it. You have your lives compartmentalized. You go to work and do things that you do not like in order to make a living. It's a strange concept. We in dolphin form do not live in time that way. We do not care what happened yesterday.

Fiske: Gee, that's kind of profound. Well, tell me something, Katuba. There have been a number of recent violent attacks by some of the larger sea mammals. Now, I know it's whales who are doing this and not dolphins, but I wonder if, as a related species, you might answer for your cousins. It's been documented that killer whales in captivity have been attacking each other and their trainers recently. I've never heard about that kind of thing before and I was wondering if you could explain this disturbing trend?

Katuba: Yes, my friend. Firstly, it is important to recognize that when animals such as we are placed in captivity and are in confined spaces for long periods of time, because we are so telepathic, we begin to tune in on human consciousness. Day in and day out, we are bombarded by human thinking and feeling. We begin to take on human

characteristics, the angers, the resentments, the frustrations, that are not found in the animals in the wild.

Fiske: Right. Well, on the subject of animals in the wild
here's another puzzler for you. I've often wondered
about those big boats that go out fishing with huge nets.
It's been observed that wild free-range dolphins are
always getting caught in the nets with a load of fish and
then dying. That's always stumped me. If you guys are so
smart how come you don't just jump over the nets and
swim the hell out of there?

Katuba: It is difficult, my friend. It is very difficult to
observe through our sonar these nets with their very,
very fine filaments of nylon or whatever you call it.

Arthur: Hold on now, Katuba, a couple of minutes ago
you told me all about my crummy job and you can't see
a fish net?

Then, just like that, our audience with Katuba was over. Our gabby
guest got real quiet. There was dead air on the phone line. That lasted
for about ten or fifteen seconds. Then all of a sudden Katuba blurted
out a hurried, ritualistic, almost scripted goodbye.

"Dear friends, it has been our great delight and pleasure to be able
to share this time and space with you. Humans and dolphins are the
same. You are spirit infinite, eternal and universal. God bless you, my
friends." There was some more of that tortured hissing and yowling
we'd heard before and then . . . nothing.

I don't know if it was Arthur Black's cynical question that rubbed
Katuba the wrong way or if Neville Rowe was just tuckered out by the
strain of shape-shifting. Either way, Katuba was gone. And if Ashleea
Nielsen and her Dancing Dolphin Institute are right, it might well be
for keeps!

CHAPTER ELEVEN

WEIRD SCIENCE 101: COSMIC CAPERS

A model of the "Tower of Power" at the Unarius Academy of Science headquarters in El Cajon, California.

I: FLUSHED IN SPACE

Or, what to know when you've gotta go in zero gravity!

THREE MILLION bucks for a *toilet*? That's what my source at the National Aeronautics and Space Administration (NASA) told me the U.S. government spent on designing, building and installing a crapper on the first space shuttle. My NASA "mole" down in Houston, a scientist named Brian Welch, gave me the poop scoop on the shuttle's space potty back in 1988.

First things first, though: I wanted to know what exactly was different about the process of human elimination in outer space from the way we do it down here on earth.

"There's no difference physiologically," Brian told me. "The only difference you encounter is an external one. There's no gravity and that means that most things tend to float in outer space. So all the architecture that surrounds how you take care of personal hygiene has to cope with that basic problem."

All "liquid matter, including urine, tends to float and turn into spheres," he said. "The surface tension of the liquid holds it together in a kind of a globule. That globule will just float around in the cabin if you don't take steps to keep it contained." In layman's terms, it basically means that in space, you don't pee in a stream, you pee in a bubble.

I told Brian that put a whole new slant on the old expression "looking out for number one," and I asked him how the old-time astronauts "did their business" before the space toilet came along. Basically, they wore adult diapers that didn't get changed until the mission was over.

"With the new toilet on the shuttle we're trying to make space flight as pleasant an experience as possible. What we used to do in the old days was anything but pleasant, and also we're dealing with coed crews now. In the old days we used plastic bags and adhesives, so it was not a real fun experience to do that in the Apollo or Gemini or Mercury programs. Of course, in the Mercury program they were only up for a few hours, so the astronauts basically used diapers. On the moon, when astronauts were taking those spacewalks on the lunar surface, they had a combination diaper and sort of a bag that would collect urine." (I guess that explains why Neill Armstrong could only take "one small step" once he landed!)

"Now in the shuttle program, of course, you don't want to do that. You don't want to be encumbered with that kind of device, so we've designed a new toilet. The space toilet on the shuttle is designed to help pull that liquid away from your body and put it into an airtight water tank that is periodically dumped overboard during a flight."

Which sounded to me like a pretty good argument *against* the whole notion of spacewalks, but never mind that. Brian had mentioned something about coed crews. I had to ask: "Does the shuttle have separate facilities for the boys and girls?"

"No, there's only one toilet," he said. "But you're able to pull a screen across the front of this little waste compartment so that you've basically got privacy. And the design is pretty much unisex. It's built to collect urine from both male and female astronauts. It's a lot like an oxygen mask that a pilot might wear, only it's form fitted to the appropriate part of the human body and it will allow them to do their business without having to worry about fluids seeping out and floating around and making a mess."

Well sure, that's fine and dandy for the liquid end of things, but if memory serves, that's only half the battle. I wanted to know how the astronauts handle the other side of the eliminatory process, the infamous "number two?" Do the astronauts need any special potty training for that? I mean, a few weightless globules of urine is one thing, but you sure don't want chunks of solid matter floating around the shuttle cabin and dancing to the tune of the "Blue Danube" waltz. This is where it got interesting.

"When you sit on the shuttle toilet, it's almost like a toilet on earth," Brian said. "You've probably noticed how if you sit long enough and read the *Reader's Digest* you form sort of a seal there on the seat of your toilet." (I *have* noticed this, as a matter of fact!) The same thing's true in orbit, said Brian. "You form an air seal when you sit down on this thing and there's a fan down below that pulls the waste matter away from you and sucks it down into a compartment—a drum. Periodically, another fan or grinding device will start up and grind this matter and pulverize it and sling it to the side of this holding compartment."

I got a good chuckle out of that. So, it turns out that in space, just like in the old expression, the shit . . .

"Actually *hits the fan* in orbit. That's right," Brian deadpanned, right on cue. "And the idea behind that is, you want to break it up and cause it to collect around the periphery of this drum so that when they periodically expose that collection compartment to the outside, to the zero vacuum of space, it will become freeze-dried," sort of like an instant coffee kind of thing. The imagery was getting pretty ripe and I was starting to get the picture that the glamorous life of your average American astronaut ain't all it's cracked up to be.

Mind you, it could be a lot worse. They could be Russians. If the space race came down to "who's ahead in heads?" we'd win hands down. Brian Welch told me that, the last time he checked, the Russians were still using the old bag-it-and-seal-it method of waste management on the Mir Space Station. And when you consider the long shifts the Russian cosmonauts pull on Mir, it's no wonder those guys are smiling when they finally get their butts back down to earth.

11: MESSING WITH THE MOON!

Hey, Canada! Break out the flip-flops and the Hawaiian shirts and say hello to your new winter wardrobe!

YOU'RE GOING to need it. It turns out that the environmentalists and the doom merchants, the ones who've been whining, weeping, wailing and wringing their hands over the "catastrophic effects of global warming," have been selling us a bill of goods.

News flash folks! It gets *cold* here in the winter. You warm up the globe and Canada gets downright balmy. This is *not* a hard sell. Recent reports claim that because of global warming the treeline is starting to creep a few kilometres farther north into previously barren ground. That's supposed to be *bad*? Give me a break.

Look, everybody's up in arms about clearcutting the Brazilian rainforest, right? Okay, so we'll just plant our own brand spanking new rainforest up in the Northwest Territories. It'll be a great boon to the economy. The people of the north will get jobs in lumbering and diversify out of oil, soapstone carvings and Arctic char.

Take a vote on it. If global warming means dumping winter, it'll win in a walk. Think about it—no more snow shovels or killer frosts or glare ice or humongous heating bills. All gone, along with the mitts and tuques and parkas and longjohns.

Oh yeah—now let's hear it from the nay-sayers: "Sure, that's great for Canada. You guys get to live in a tropical paradise but what about the rest of the planet? We've already got hideous droughts. This is going to turn the hot spots in Africa and Asia into one huge desert!"

Yeah, but it doesn't have to be that way. You see, the key to a global paradise is not just to get rid of the extreme cold of winter. What you really want to do is get rid of both extremes. Summer's got to go too, or at least that bone-bleaching, blast-furnace heat that passes for summer in places like Texas. *Adios* to air-conditioning!

So, how do we get there? We look at what causes the seasons in the first place. Then we fix it.

We have seasons because the earth has a tilt, basically a "wobble" in its orbit. It goes back and forth and wobbles as it makes its way around the sun. And that means that different parts of the earth are closer to the sun sometimes (we call that summer) and farther away at other times (we call that winter).

Now just imagine what would happen if we could straighten out that wobble so that the earth's axis would always be straight up and down instead of tilted? You'd end up with perfect weather all over the planet—and all year round, too.

"Sounds great," you say, "but easier said than done." Well, maybe not.

Back in 1991 I talked to a man named Dr. Alexander Abian—that's right, the same Professor Abian that Eddie "King" Clontz and I talked about in Chapter Four. He's a mathematics professor at Iowa State University in Ames, Iowa and he has, in fact, come up with a couple of unique ideas to straighten out that pesky wobble in the earth's axis.

THEORY ONE: A LUNAR LOANER

Professor Abian started off by asking me in his thick accent, "How, Mr. Fiske, do you untilt something which is tilted? I tell you how. You put counterbalance on other side. One moon is very lopsided thing, you know. Two moons is better."

That may be so, I told him, but the last time I looked we still only had one. Professor Abian gently scolded me. He said I was being short-sighted, but did admit I was in good company.

"Lots of scientists, including Copernicus, Galileo and Newton, have studied universe and have brilliantly formulated mathematically the rules and the roles and the forces involved between planets and celestial bodies. But none of them have ever said, 'Can we reshuffle the cosmos?' The closest possible celestial body which has considerable size is the moon," said Professor Abian, "and for seventy million years human civilization has taken the *status quo* for granted—we have never raised the question, can we change the position of the moon?"

The moon plays a big role in the tilt of the earth, "which in turn determines precisely the weather," said Professor Abian. "Since changes in weather occur with changes in the earth's tilt, let's change the tilt." But, Professor Abian admitted, "people talk about me and say, 'Oh, you want to change things, and not have four seasons. But we will miss the snow.' The same people want to go to California or Bahamas or Florida or something like that."

Hey, I'm in. I'll be first in line to trade in my thermal underwear and antifreeze for Bermuda shorts and a Mai Tai. Sounds like reshuffling the cosmos is just what the doctor ordered. But what exactly is Professor Abian's prescription for realigning our cozy little corner of the Milky Way? How about "borrowing" a moon from Mars? That sounded pretty far out to me, but Professor Abian wasn't kidding.

"Mars," Abian reminded me, "has two moons. And Mars is considerably smaller than Earth, so its gravitational pull on its moons is much smaller than our gravitational pull on our moon." That's why the professor figures it'll be easy for us to drag one of Mars's moons through space and slip it into orbit around the earth. What happens after that is a no-brainer. Once you've stuck a second big celestial body on the other side of the planet opposite from our moon, the two would cancel each other out and—hey presto!—no more wobble.

Of course, you can't just attach a bungee cord to the Martian moon and reel it in. But Professor Abian does have a plan: since the Martian moons are "extremely, very, very small," Mars can't attract them very powerfully, so it's no problem to "destabilize one and attract it to earth if you jolt the moon of Mars."

And how would you jolt a Martian moon towards the earth? Energy, he said. "The same way that you eject from earth a rocket satellite towards moon." So you'd have some sort of explosion on the moon of Mars?

"That's right," said Professor Abian. But the explosion will just create a little shock, a small impact. "It would not require too much of energy because gravitational pull of Mars is very, very slight."

You'd basically need "to nudge it out of the Martian orbit with right amount of energy from atomic explosions, which, theoretically, we have bottomless amounts of." The earth's pull would then reel in the new moon. How long would that take?

It's "very, very far" from Mars to the earth, said Professor Abian. "For the practical materialization of my project, I'd say ten thousand years from now we will not be able to do that. It will be tremendous amount of time, but so what?"

So what!? I'll tell you, so what. Ten thousand years puts the whole thing just a tad out of reach for me, my kids, hell, even my great-great-great-grandkids. My vision of a snow-free Great White North was turning into a pipe dream. I told the professor I was hoping for a solution a little closer to home.

THEORY TWO: LUNAR LANDFILL

No problem, says Professor Abian. Forget about borrowing a moon from Mars. There's an easier way to pull this off—by tinkering with our *own* moon.

The best way to change the orbit of our own moon, Professor Abian told me, is "just kicking it a little bit from its own orbit." To do that, "we must reduce the mass of the moon—not totally eliminate it, but reduce it by half or one-third.

"The gravitational pull of the moon will be much less on the earth's wobble and on human beings, too," Professor Abian said. Science has long documented the effect of a full moon on behaviour, and the moon's cycles can influence blood pressure, and cause people to start exhibiting uncharacteristic "psychotic behaviour." Professor Abian believes that these moon-made mood swings happen all the time and it's probably how werewolf lore got started.

By blowing up a big hunk of the moon and drastically reducing its mass, we could straighten out the tilt in the world and wipe out lunar-caused psychosis in one fell swoop.

Well, actually one fell swoop isn't exactly what the professor has in mind. He says that remodelling the moon will take a carefully planned series of detonations, again using atomic bombs. I didn't like the sound of that at all. Nuking a Martian moon half-way across the solar system is one thing, but this was a little too close for comfort. I asked Professor Abian if he thought setting off A-bombs in the Sea of Tranquillity was a good idea. He was adamant. "Yes! The thing is, atomic explosions are absolutely safe from the distance of 240,000 miles."

I wasn't going to argue the point. The professor knew a lot more about this stuff than I did, but there was one point I wanted cleared up. Even if you only blow up a third of the moon, you're going to end up with one heck of a pile of debris. Where does all that junk go after the big bang?

"It will disintegrate in cosmos or better idea we could put it on South Pole to counterbalance," he suggested. Of course, the whole project would be done with a "gentle landing, not smashing the whole thing. Do it piece by piece, you know."

I won't bore you with the complicated techno-talk he tossed at me to explain how to convert the South Pole into a lunar landfill site. But the whole thing did seem like a lot more trouble than it was worth.

I wondered what would happen if we got rid of the moon

altogether? If it's causing the problem, the earth would surely straighten out on its own, once the moon was *completely* destroyed.

THEORY THREE:
THE MAN IN THE MOON IS MISSING!

"That," said the professor, pausing for dramatic effect, "is another question. Why do we always think that if the moon was not around we will be worse off? We are totally, completely brainwashed by five billion years of having the moon!"

While some argue that the moon is the "first step for going to other planets," Professor Abian points out that we don't know whether there's life out there or not. "I say, why don't we change drastically, radically our planet's cosmic parameters and change life on *our* planet?"

If the tilt weren't there, "there will be spring-type moderate weather on the entire globe," something Professor Abian said was "extremely desirable, because one-fifth of the globe is absolute uninhabitable desert."

There may be more water around because the polar caps will melt, but the trick is to melt them gradually so there's no flooding. In fact, he predicts, since ice occupies more volume than water, "when the ice melts, the volume contracts, so there won't be floods." Sound like we're going to turn Canada into Florida? "That's precisely it, yes!" the professor agreed eagerly. "And why not? It *is* possible!"

III: THE TOWER OF POWER

I cracked the secret behind the Mona Lisa's smile!

FOR THREE hundred years the muckety-muck know-it-alls have been pontificating about the meaning behind Mona's sly little grin. Historians, art critics, psychiatrists and even the feminists have called it everything from a leer to a sneer. A sexy invitation? A bold indictment of male chauvinism? Or how about this: I've actually got a Batman comic book that claims Mona was pregnant with da Vinci's kid and the smile was just her way of saying "It's our little secret, Leo baby."

They're all way off base, of course, at least according to the Unarius Academy of Science, in El Cajon, California (just outside of San Diego). The current director of the academy, Dr. Charles Spaegel, I'm pleased to say, is a Canadian—he was born seventy-nine years ago in Toronto. Dr. Spaegel inherited his leadership of the academy from its founders, a couple named Ernest and Ruth Norman, both of whom are now dead.

The Normans started the Unarian movement back in the 1950s, and Dr. Spaegel says the organization now has half a million card-carrying members spread around the globe. The Unarians have published scores of books and treatises on various scientific subjects. The foundation of their beliefs is that alien voyagers from distant planets are planning a benevolent invasion designed to nudge mankind on to a greater destiny. Dr. Spaegel explained all this to me when I spoke with him recently.

"There's a planet called Vixol from the Pleiadean Cluster of planets in the constellation of Taurus," he told me. "It's one of the major planets there, but it's unknown to earth's astronomers. In fact, the astronomers denigrate it. They say Pleiadean planets are nothing but young stars, but they don't know. They don't have the devices to resolve it. Well, the astronauts from the planet Vixol tell about how they have already explored seventy planets for the purpose of helping the inhabitants." Dr. Spaegel went on to say that Vixolites and other aliens are *already* living on earth.

"Yes, there are those who are on earth living through physical bodies. For instance, the founders of Unarius were such persons. Ernest Norman's true spiritual identity is known as the Archangel Raphael. And Ruth Norman's true identity, living through the physical body, was the Archangel Uriel. Leonardo da Vinci! He really wasn't an earth person. Neither was Einstein. And others like them are walking amongst us now."

Wait a minute. Leonardo da Vinci was an alien? I have to admit that threw me at first. Then I thought it through. That coy little "I've-got-a-secret" smile on the Mona Lisa? It always looked kind of strange and otherworldly to me. It finally made sense. She knew! And now so did I. How else can you explain the fact that da Vinci invented the helicopter three hundred years before anybody else ever thought of it? I was convinced. Da Vinci was an alien scientist and Dr. Spaegel was really on to something.

Taking his theory a little further, Spaegel insisted that da Vinci and Einstein (and many of the historic geniuses we think of as our own) are actually scouts, or "pathfinders," if you will, laying the foundation for the big plans the Unarians have waiting in the wings for humanity.

"In 2001, a spaceship, or more accurately, a starship ten storeys high will land in the Caribbean, in the Bermuda Triangle," he told me. "The reason for that is, one part of the submerged continent of Atlantis is under water there. That land is outside the territorial limits of Cuba and the United States and it will rise up to meet the starship. When the ship lands, it will be a research community because at ten storeys high it's like a city itself. It will be inhabited by a thousand scientists of different disciplines from different planets. They will remain on earth for the rest of their lives."

And the news just keeps on getting better. According to Dr. Spaegel the alien research team is not planning to keep to themselves. These guys like to party. The egghead aliens have every intention of breeding with us earthlings.

Think about it. Thousands of little baby Einsteins and da Vincis running around inventing stuff and painting great masterpieces. That ought to add a little chlorine to the gene pool, don't you think? Plus, the aliens are going to do a lot more than just hang around and make whoopee. They're going to offer us all kinds of interesting and useful scientific knowledge. They're going to cure cancer, for starters.

Then, according to Dr. Spaegel, the extraterrestrials will be bringing along some kind of eerie wave machine that will be able to extract all the toxins from our bodies—toxins like drugs and alcohol. The short-term advantage of that, of course, is that you could drink anything you want. You could suck back a case of beer and a couple of quarts of rye and then, with the flick of a switch, the machine could suck away the poisonous effects of the booze. You'd get all the pleasant effects of being falling-down drunk, but you *wouldn't get a hangover.* And you'd be able to hop in your car and drive home with no need to worry about the cops and their pesky breathalyzers.

But probably the most significant thing the alien scientists are going to do is bring to us a miraculous instrument called the "Tower of Power."

Now, to fully explain the Tower of Power you have to know something about that great Serbian-American electronics pioneer, Nikola Tesla. Tesla, you might recall from your Grade 10 physics class, was the inventor of the Tesla coil, along with a lot of other scientific do-hickeys that can make your hair stand on end and stuff.

Well, according to Dr. Spaegel, one of Tesla's high-tech gizmos was the Tower of Power. In fact, Tesla was another one of those genius alien scouts I talked about earlier. And back in the forties, Tesla (with the support of the famous financial house, J. P. Morgan) actually started to build the Tower of Power on Staten Island, near New York City.

The reason nobody outside of the Unarians knows anything about this is that the American government tore it down. Now, you have to remember it was wartime and the Pentagon wanted this thing scrapped partly because it was so big and rose up so high into the air. It stuck out like a sore thumb and the Joint Chiefs of Staff figured it would attract enemy fire from the Axis submarines that were lurking just off the U.S. coast.

But there was another reason the tower had to go. The project was so enormous that building it was tying up countless tons of vital metal and fuel that was needed for the war effort. So Uncle Sam tore Tesla's Tower of Power down. They took it apart bolt by nut by bolt and then they scrapped it.

Shortly after that, in 1943, Tesla died, some say of a broken heart, and then his notes and drawings and blueprints all mysteriously vanished into thin air! The whole glorious project might have been forgotten except for the Unarians.

"We do have a prototype," said Dr. Spaegel. "We have information from Nikola Tesla. We have a thirteen-volume series of books called *Tesla Speaks,* dictated by him from the other side, because we live on both sides of life. At any rate, our electrical engineers could build a Tower of Power but there's a missing link. They don't quite have the ability to complete it. It will take the help of these advanced scientists from these other planets."

That last key piece to the Tower of Power puzzle will have to wait until 2001 and the arrival of that alien mothership. According to Dr. Spaegel, that's probably just as well. "There's a reason it can't be built and shouldn't be built until that time," he told me. "If some power or government gets a hold of it, they would use it as a weapon of war."

This was starting to sound ominous, but it was also pretty vague. So I pointed out to the doc that he'd told me the Tower of Power was very big, very complicated and potentially very dangerous—but, so far, I didn't have a clue about what the heck the darn thing was supposed to do.

"This tower exists on these other planets. That's where they get their energy. It's a thousand feet high and it goes down two thousand feet into the ground. It's like a radio telescope in a sense, but it gathers power from the electromagnetic field that surrounds our planet. That power is demodulated to a certain frequency and then projected out at the top through giant lenses. Then the power goes to different parts of the world. Each city has a receiver without the use of overhead wires. It's unlimited energy and it's free!"

Free unlimited energy without the use of overhead wires? Sign me up! I mean, if the Unarians are on target, by 2001 we'll have all the energy we need to turn Mother Earth into Utopia and to heck with waiting around for Professor Abian to blow up the moon.

Just think about it. Remember the infamous ice storm of 1998? Remember the freezing rain? Remember the majestic trees that snapped like kindling and took the overhead power lines down with them? Remember the millions of people all through eastern Ontario and Quebec huddled freezing in the dark for weeks on end? Well, once the Tower of Power comes on line, those chilling, bitter memories will just melt away. Our fragile network of ugly, inefficient overhead power lines will go the way of the dodo, because the Tower of Power will beam an abundance of juice straight to your house.

Dr. Spaegel assured me that those alien scientists from Vixol have plenty of other miracles up their sleeves. Exactly what they might be will become clear once the mothership lands. Until then, you might want to keep your eye out for those alien scouts I mentioned.

Actually, I don't want to brag (so please, keep this under your hat) but during our little chat, Dr. Spaegel and I developed quite a rapport. He was impressed with my instinctive grasp of the Unarian philosophy and my scientific acumen. At one point he actually intimated that I might be one of those alien scouts. You'll notice I'm neither confirming nor denying it here!

IV: ARMAGEDDON OUT OF HERE!

Bruce Willis was dead, but he did die hard!

HE BLEW UP real good when he detonated that A-bomb, but he took that killer comet with him and he saved the world for truth, justice and the American way.

It was the summer of '98. The movie was a cheesy disaster flick called *Armageddon*. It was the second time in two months that Hollywood had served up a runaway comet on a collision course with earth (the other one was in the deeply stupid *Deep Impact)* and it was a trend that was ticking me off. The trend was ticking off the studio honchos who made the movies too. Everybody was screaming "industrial espionage" and "I thought of it first." They're all a bunch of liars.

To prove it, I've got to take you back in time to September 10, 1994. I was hanging out at the Toronto Public Library, skimming the international papers looking for stories I could rewrite, recycle and resell back to the tabs under my own byline. I was flipping through one of the English dailies when a small advertisement caught my eye.

COSMIC DAY OF JUDGMENT 1994:
World News Flash from astronomer Sophia Richmond.
A Comet is heading for earth.
Only God can stop this comet if his conditions are met!

The comet in question was the Shoemaker-Levy 9 Comet. You probably heard about it because it was a big deal at the time. "It," in fact, is a misnomer. The Shoemaker-Levy Comet was actually a series of comet fragments that had recently smacked into Jupiter. The spectacular collision made the cover of *Time*, and got big play on all the TV networks. But, if Sophia Richmond was telling the truth, those media giants with all their untold resources did not—I repeat, did not—tell the whole story.

I on the other hand, humble hack-like-me-Harold, with nothing but a phone and two-bit tape recorder scooped them all. I got the *world exclusive* story of a lifetime.

I tracked Sophia Richmond down in London, England and recorded her amazing, untold tale. She revealed what really happened to the comet that allegedly met its fate on the surface of Jupiter. "There were," she told me, "a total of twenty-two comet fragments in all. Twenty-one struck Jupiter but one section went astray. And it is that piece which is heading directly for America. This fragment will affect both the United States and Canada and it could become visible by September 16th."

That got my attention. Remember, I did this interview on the 10th. That didn't give us much time. I told Miss Richmond we had better get this story out quickly.

"I think so, yes," she agreed. "Now, the Almighty himself has sent this comet as a cosmic warning to mankind, and the only way it can be stopped is if governments and nations, particularly America, stop producing portrayals of crime and violence on television, films and video games. That is the reason why the comet is heading for America. As a punishment."

Now, this was all fascinating stuff, really good copy, but one thing was nagging at me. This was a really big story of literally earth-shattering proportions and I hadn't heard a peep about it until now. I mean, we've got a killer comet heading our way and the world's astronomers had all gone zipper-lipped on me? That didn't add up.

So I put it to Miss Richmond. "How come you know all this stuff? What's your source?" She didn't bat an eye. It turns out that Sophia Richmond is a professional psychic astronomer and she has a remarkable and innate mental ability to see deep into the universe without using a telescope or even the usual mind-altering drugs.

"I am really a religious sister of the Catholic Church. I belong to the Carmelite order," she told me. "I received prophetic messages, or what I sincerely believe to be prophetic messages. Time will soon tell whether they're accurate. I received them as prophetic insights into cosmic events ahead of the astronomers and in advance of their telescopes. Now, I don't know in Canada if you've ever heard of a popular newspaper called *World Weekly News*?"

I told Sister Sophia that if she meant the *Weekly World News* (it's amazing how many people screw that up) then, yes, we knew it well (once again see Chapter Four on King Clontz).

"Yes, well, what is your opinion about the reputation of this newspaper? Is everything it writes based on total fabrication or is there a grain of truth in it?" she asked.

All of a sudden Sophia Richmond had turned the tables. She was interviewing *me*. So I gave her an honest, if careful, answer. I said that I had followed up (in other words, stolen) quite a few of their stories over the years and generally found that there was more than a grain of truth in them. It was not exactly a ringing endorsement, but not a lie either. Eddie Clontz would have been proud.

Anyway, I explained, as an example, how the *Weekly World News* broke the story about Professor Abian's plan to blow up the moon. I told her how the whole thing had sounded pretty far-fetched to me when I read it. But I called him up anyway and, sure enough, Abian admitted that wwn did a pretty fair job of reporting his moon theories.

I said that as far as *I* could tell, *Weekly World News* does seem to try to accurately report the news, albeit pretty strange news.

"Well did you happen to read the edition of the 16th of August, 1994?"

I confessed I'd missed that week somehow, but would make a point of digging it out of my compendious archives the first chance I got.

"Yes, do that, because in it was an article that shocked me out of my wits! The article was by a doctor of astronomy called Marvin Hunter and he has connections with NASA. What Mr. Hunter says is that the American government has known about this stray fragment of the comet heading for our world as far back as last year. And that they have kept the lid on it so as not to panic the public."

Sister Sophia told me how Hunter "goes on to say that the American government has secretly prepared missiles to try and deflect it, or more accurately, they're hoping to pulverize it, really. I was so shocked when I read this article because it seemed to confirm everything that the religious prophecy had told to me."

I had to agree with her. It's hard to argue when two independent and highly credible sources from opposite sides of the globe come up with identical scenarios.

"Exactly. So that is what appears to be facing us, and because time is so precious now, it would be wise to call people together to beg God for mercy while they can. It will take a miracle for that comet to miss earth."

Well, miracle of miracles! It's more than five whole years since my exclusive interview with Sophia Richmond alerted the world to its impending doom at the hands of a runaway comet hurtling on a collision course with earth. And it must've been a miracle because, against all odds, here we are still alive and kicking.

Yeah, but you have to wonder why.

I mean, if God really did send that comet to discombobulate us, if the whole thing really was a big case of cosmic blackmail to get Hollywood to clean up its movie and video violence, then how come we're still breathing? Let's face it—there's a veritable cornucopia of blood and guts still spilling off the screen.

Plus, the only "cleaning up" Hollywood did was at the box-office. Those slimeball movie moguls ripped off my idea and cranked out two, count 'em, two, hit movies, *Armageddon* and *Deep Impact*. Between them, they've raked in a half a billion bucks (U.S.), and so far I haven't seen a penny. To add insult to injury, *Deep Impact* actually cast Téa Leoni, the scrawny wife of that *X-Files* guy, to play me, the journalist who broke the story (and hey! She played a tabloid journalist on her TV show, *The Naked Truth*). But I digress.

The bottom line on all this is, what saved us from God's killer comet? Why, of all people, were those Hollywood heathens spared? Sister Sophia says, "It's yet another proof of God's infinite tolerance and love for man." Amen to that, sister! The only question is, does he know a good lawyer?

CHAPTER TWELVE

MEDICAL MADNESS

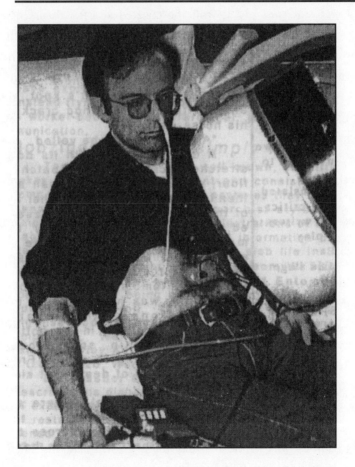

All wired up with no place to go: human guinea pig Bob Helms.

I: BARF VADER

Grossed-Out Surgeon Vomits Inside Patient.

THAT CLASSIC headline is from the Boca Raton, Florida-based tab, the *Sun* and it won the coveted MOTH (Most Outrageous Tabloid Headline) award for 1989. I didn't write it, but I wish I had. Those award-winning words were, in fact, penned by none other than my mentor, the legendary and reclusive editor of the *Sun*, John Vader.

And make no mistake: "Grossed Out Surgeon Vomits Inside Patient" is pure genius, an undeniable hunk of tabloid heaven. Sure, it's tacky. Yes, it's disgusting. And okay, maybe it is just a little bit exploitative. But it's also irresistible. One thing John Vader taught me was that most people may be paranoid about going under the knife themselves, but they love to hear about other people's operations. Think about those gory shows the specialty channels run where they broadcast actual wet and wild surgeries up front, in your face and in living colour on cable. And who can forget, back in the sixties, when U.S. president Lyndon Johnson pulled up his shirt and showed us all his big fat gallbladder surgery scar on national TV?

Trust me, folks, this stuff sells. So our job at the *National Examiner* (where John Vader was editor during my time there) was to keep the readers, literally, in stitches. It was Vader who assigned me to the "titanic tumour" beat. Now I'm not talking about tumours the size of a Coke bottle. Nope, we're talking fifty pounds and up, bigger than a basketball. Example? Gary Blackmore of El Paso, Texas. His tumour was inside his abdomen, growing on his small intestine. It was so large that they literally had to suspend him on wires from the operating room ceiling because docs had to go in from both sides, front and back, at the same time, to get this thing out.

While he was suspended in mid-air, hooked up to two heart-lung machines, the operation was like digging the Chunnel from both France and England at the same time—you hope like hell you meet somewhere in the middle. Two doctors severed all of Blackmore's blood vessels and, except for his spinal cord, they literally cut this man in half. At one point in the operation, the two doctors actually waved hello to each other through Gary Blackmore's body.

The bad news was nobody snapped any pictures of this—where's a photographer when you need one? What a shot that would've made. The good news was that Gary Blackmore lived to tell me his story over the phone. His titanic tumour turned out to be benign. Strangely enough, most of these big suckers turn out to be inconvenient, but not especially life-threatening.

Which is good, because what tab readers really like is a good old-fashioned happy ending—the patient goes home sixty pounds lighter, able to live a normal life once again thanks to a gross, but life-saving, operation. The bottom line in tabloids is selling papers and, next to Elvis, nothing delights readers more than medical madness, mixed in with a healthy dose of "happily ever after."

II: A HOLE IN THE HEAD

Would you rather be killed, or have seven holes
in your head?   — *A riddle from my boyhood*

THE RIGHT answer is seven holes, not the date with death, because—drum roll please—you've already *got* seven holes in your head: two nostrils, two eye-sockets, two ear holes and a mouth.

Add 'em up! But behind that little-known fact lies some disturbing news. It turns out seven holes in the head may not be enough, at least according to the practitioners of the ancient art and science of trepanning or trepanation.

Now, trepanning has been going on for thousands of years. We know this because there's a ton of archaeological evidence from digging up old gravesites and checking out the skulls. The diggers often find that there are six or seven extra holes in those skulls, and forensic analysis shows warfare, disease or torture had nothing to do with it. The holes were methodically drilled into the head. Either that, or the skulls were scraped until a hole was opened. (There's a great scene of an African tribe actually doing this in one of those *Mondo Cane* movies from the early sixties—check it out!)

Interestingly, these holey skulls are found in just about every corner of the globe, except—you guessed it—in our modern so-called "civilized" part of the world. Of course, that's because we're a repressed and insular culture that doesn't look beyond the end of its nose.

But all this could change, thanks to the groundbreaking work of a Dutch doctor named Bart Hughes. Back in the sixties (when those *Mondo Cane* movies were being made), Hughes was a student. He was at this party one night when, just for the heck of it, he decided he was going to stand on his head. Let's face it, people were weird in the sixties.

Anyway, the funny thing was that after standing upside down on his noggin for a while, Hughes discovered he felt a lot better. He had more energy and he got a feeling of being "high." This really floored the guy. Remember, this was back when everybody was looking to get high, mostly by imbibing, ingesting, or inhaling illegal substances. But there's nothing illegal about standing on your head, and afterwards, Hughes deduced that his euphoria was the direct result of being topsy-turvy and creating more blood flow inside his brain. Hughes was studying medicine at the time, so he should have known, right?

That started him on a path of analysis which led him to believe that our brains, in fact, *crave* blood. Further years of research led him to another startling discovery. From his medical studies, Hughes already knew that around about age seven, the bony plates in our skulls knit together and seal over. From that day on, our brains lose the ability to expand and contract. The brain, in fact, is a throbbing organ that all too soon becomes a prisoner in its hard, bony cage.

Bart Hughes speculated that the constricted adult brain is the reason why grown-ups can't learn stuff as easily as kids. We just don't have the natural cracks in the cranium that would allow our brains to pulsate, writhe and course with the kind of unbound energy of childhood. The cracks permit us to literally "soak up" knowledge.

Hughes was determined to reverse the damage nature had done to him while growing up. His solution? Trepanning. Maybe drilling a tiny hole in the head would allow the brain to expand and relieve some of that constriction and pressure. So that's what he did. He used himself as a human guinea pig and got trepanned. He was convinced that the operation made a new man out of him. He preached the gospel of trepanning and gathered about him a growing number of disciples who are, to this day, eagerly following in his formidable footsteps.

The problem is, Hughes and the rest of his card-carrying trepanners (trepannists? trapannites?) have trouble finding doctors who'll go along with them—most MDs think trepanning is quackery. So in our culture it's become a bit of a do-it-yourself project.

Here's how it works. You get a trusted friend and drill. Your friend smears a bit of local anaesthetic on your skull. Once your head's numb, the friend takes the drill and bores a seven-millimetre hole into your cranium.

Back in 1996, I read an article by a British woman who'd actually had this done. Her name is Jenny Gaythorne-Hardy and she lives in London. When I talked to Jenny, I was up-front with her. I explained that I was taping our phone conversation for broadcast on CBC Radio, and I've got to admit that in the beginning she was very cautious, very reluctant to tell me her story, because she told me, "If you put it out on the radio, people who don't know what they're doing might actually chop their head up or something."

I admitted that was a concern but assured her I was a responsible journalist, with many trouble-free years on Canada's public airwaves. I wasn't out to trivialize or sensationalize the story. But she continued to be concerned. "Since my article was written, I've heard that two or three people have gone and taken a Black & Decker to their heads. They're obviously nutters," she told me.

"This can't be done with ordinary cheap household power tools?" I asked. What, then, was used for trepanning? According to Jenny, an official, medically approved, surgical drill is required, and that's something most people don't have lying around the house. But they can be rented from a doctors' industrial supply company, provided you've got a good story. "I actually pretended I was a sculptress and that I wanted to drill bones. I told them I was making a bone sculpture."

In a way, I pointed out, she didn't really tell them a lie. "Absolutely not," said Jenny. "It's quite true, but I was so paranoid they would think I wanted to drill a hole in my own head"—which is exactly what she *did* want it for.

Was she worried about legal consequences? I wasn't sure if drilling a hole in your own head is illegal. "I just didn't want to be stopped," she said, and indeed she wasn't—she did get herself trepanned.

But did it hurt much? "Not with the anaesthetic, no," said Jenny. "I couldn't feel anything. I mean, I was lying down. It was more comfortable than being at the dentist." And she didn't feel the grinding and degrading of bone or the drill boring through her head? "No, I didn't, but I *did* hear it, and that was disturbing because I could hear the noise so loudly bouncing around inside my head," she told me.

Jenny Gaythorne-Hardy went to great pains to point out that trepanning is *not* a gross-out operation. Remember, we're talking about one tiny seven-millimetre hole in the skull—it's about the width of a pencil. Plus, you only drill through the bony part of the skull. You stop when you hit the membrane that protects the important stuff inside your head. After that you put a Band-Aid over the hole and pretty soon the skin grows back and you don't even know it's there except for all the extra blood coursing through your grey matter.

So what's the post-op bottom line? I asked Jenny how she felt with her juiced-up brain once the drilling was over. "I felt lighter, clearer," she said. "It was over about the next four hours that I gradually began to have more energy, to feel that my energy was being boosted in some way. Very gently. Not like in a speedy boost, as if you'd drunk coffee or something. I got a feeling of clarity and calmness at the same time."

That seemed to have persisted to the present interview, I told her. She was very articulate and sounded incredibly calm and laid-back. And if this actually works (and she was living proof that it does) I wanted to know why the researchers haven't tested this out clinically to see if there are measurable medical differences?

"Exactly," she said, reacting to my incisive question. "I mean, this is all we're asking. We're shouting out in article after article from people who've been trepanned saying, 'Just listen to us and try it.' Because the thing of it is, it's not really something you can appreciate unless you've actually been trepanned. What is it Bart [Hughes] used to say? 'How to explain to the adult that he has too little blood in his brain, if he has too little blood in his brain to understand it.' It's something you can't appreciate until you're there. I mean, I now have more blood in my brain. And so I'm not having to spend a lot of energy thinking all the time."

And were there any surprises? Any bonus side effects from having a souped-up brain? Yes indeed, said Jenny, "and I can put this one down to my brain using up more glucose and more energy. I eat more and I don't get fatter."

How about that? Trepanning not only makes you smarter, but it keeps you thin, too. Forget that fad diet—get drilled in the head, instead! And what a perfect tab story: "Docs Discover: Miracle Hole-in-Your-Head Weight Loss Plan."

III: CHEATERS

a) Urine the Money.

IT WAS almost two years later but Canada was still reeling from its national shame—Ben Johnson stripped of his gold medal at the 1988 Seoul Olympic Games.

We all remember how our Jamaican-born, Canadian-trained hero blew past Carl Lewis in the hundred-metre dash, breaking the world record in the glamour event of the Seoul Olympics. And when he literally wrapped himself in the Canadian flag, we lapped it up and loved every minute.

Ben Johnson wasn't just "the fastest man alive," he was one of ours. At least until the medical meddlers had a peek at his pee. Ben flunked the drug test and had to give back the gold. After that we dropped him like a hot potato.

It wasn't really because he cheated—nobody really cared about the steroids he was pumping into his system. No, Ben's big boo-boo was getting caught. Personally, I'm in favour of deregulating all sports, including the Olympics. Any performance-enhancing therapy, food, drug or hormone should be allowed—the name of the game is *winning*, not whining!

Let's face it, the human body is like a fine race car, and there should be no restrictions on how it can be "tuned up" for better performance. If scientists discover a fuel additive that makes a car go faster and win more races, everyone calls it progress—but if an athlete attempts to maximize performance by using his own fuel additives, they call it cheating. What hypocrisy!

Now the really sad thing about the fiasco in Seoul was that it didn't have to happen. Big Ben would still be champ today if he'd known about a certain "pee peddler" I was lining up for an interview.

This was April 4, 1990. I was playing telephone tag with an Austin, Texas entrepreneur. So far, I'd just gotten his answering machine: "You have reached Byrd Labs, purveyor of fine urine products," said the robot on the other end of the phone. "Our motto: test your government, not your urine. At Byrd Labs we say, 'Pee for pleasure, not for employment.'"

Byrd Labs is owned by Jeffrey Nightbyrd, the self-proclaimed "King of Urine." He operates a mail-order urine emporium out of Austin. According to his press release he's selling a medical miracle: "100% certifiably pure guaranteed drug-free" urine samples.

Who's he selling to? Well, when he finally called me back, Jeff explained that most of his clients are just decent all-American working stiffs whose civil liberties were being trampled by paranoid and irresponsible management types.

"There was a high-rise construction site here in Austin," he told me, "where a lot a lot of fellas were getting hurt in accidents on the job. It was becoming a big issue for both labour and management. What the bosses did was, one day they came in with urine tests and fired about four of the workers and blamed the whole thing on drug use on the job. Well, I was talking to a lawyer for one of the guys, who said he was innocent. And it turned out that what was really going on was the company was way behind on construction so they were speeding up their deadlines and pushing like crazy and so lots of people were being injured."

And adding insult to injury, thanks to the employee drug tests lots of other guys were getting railroaded out of their jobs. That really ticked Jeff off. "I thought, 'Boy, this isn't right,'" he told me. "'What an invasion of privacy! This is supposed to be America!' Another thing, the test they were using was a highly inaccurate test because it's such a cheap test. And the employers don't want to spend the hundred bucks that the accurate test costs. So then I just announced I was going to market drug-free urine!"

Jeff said he went to a senior citizens' Bible study group and asked if they would sell him samples. "I wore a white lab coat and I guess they figured I was from the university because they were happy to sell me samples for five dollars apiece. I mean, it gave them a little more money for their outings and bus trips and things. So they started supplying me. But that hit a snag."

What happened was that the urine tests from Jeff's golden-age Bible study group kept coming back positive. That was weird, and I had to ask him what was up? Were the old duffers doing drugs and stuff?

"No, the tests were what are called 'false positives.' These people were taking back-pain medication and drugs for all kinds of ailments and that stuff comes out positive on these drug tests. See, this test they're using for on-the-job drug-testing is so lousy that, when we're in hay fever season, things like Actifed, Sudafed, Dristan, all the common over-the-counter allergy and cold medicines, cause false positives on the urine test. Even poppy seeds—the kind found on bagels and at Burger King—can cause a false opium reading. These urine tests are shams. Everybody's being bamboozled!"

Including Jeff, who was obviously in trouble. If the Mormon Tabernacle Choir couldn't be trusted to come up with clean pee, where did he get a product pure enough to put one over on Big Brother?

Jeff finally found his answer. What he had to do was "reprocess the urine," he told me. "We break it down molecularly so none of the drug metabolite molecules are present. After that process, we can guarantee it's clean."

Okay, so Jeff's got his pee, it's processed and certified clean as a whistle. Now he's got to get it to his customers. Remember, the Urine King runs a mail-order business. That sounded pretty tricky.

"Yes, the liquid was terrible. We sent it out in a little padded bag and we had problems with the smell and with leakage and with the urine aging too quickly and going stale. My sister is in medical school and I talked to her about that. I said we were going to try to do freeze-dried urine but she said, 'You're crazy! It's much simpler to dehydrate it.' So now I like to say that Byrd Labs is to urine what Tang is to orange juice."

Jeff will sell you two vials of his dehydrated pee and his pamphlet, "Conquering the Urine Drug Test," for just US$19.95—a small price to pay for the peace of mind that hanging on to your old job, or successfully beating the drug test on your next job interview, can bring.

There is, of course, that one final hurdle to get over. The fateful day arrives. Your boss hauls you into the office and says, "Drop 'em, pal!" How does Jeff recommend you go about the tricky business of substituting his purified pee for your own urine? "Well, I don't advocate anything myself. That's between you and your employer, but what many people seem to do is premix it with warm water in a condom, tie off the back end and then go into the bathroom and squirt it into the vial."

Yeah, but that only works if they let you pee in private. I wanted to know what happens if your boss follows you into the john and wants to actually watch you fill the cup? That really struck a nerve. It's the one topic that really pisses Jeffrey Nightbyrd off.

"Listen to us! Here we are, two mature adults, talking about bosses demanding to stare at the private parts of their employees! Is that the kind of program we want, where good honest workers are being followed into the bathroom by their bosses? In the trade we call them 'wee-watchers'! I think it's appalling!"

You'll notice, however, that he never did answer my question.

b) Liar, Liar, Pants on Fire!

Big Brother is not just watching us wee. He's got us wired to a lie-detector, too. And that's got Doug Williams's dander up. Doug used to be a cop. More specifically, he was the chief polygraph examiner for the Oklahoma City Police Department. But that was a long time ago. Doug no longer approves of the police or anybody else using lie-detectors because "they simply don't work. It's such a sick, sick con job," he told me when I spoke to him in 1993. To prove it, he's written a book called *How To Sting the Polygraph.*

Doug says the lie-detector is a ridiculously simple machine that relies on primitive medical techniques like the blood pressure cuff and the Galvanic Skin Response (GSR) for what are, in effect, highly unreliable readings. He says the polygraph is "completely bogus, nothing but a joke, a sham, a *lie!*"

The good news, according to Doug, is that by using a couple of easy-to-master tricks, you or I or anybody, for that matter, can actually cheat and beat *any* lie-detector test in the world.

The bad news? We just might have to.

The same fascist wee-watchers that Jeff Nightbyrd warned us about have also started using routine lie-detector tests on job interviews. Doug Williams thinks it's a sleazy and dangerous practice.

"The pre-employment polygraph test," he says, "is so ridiculous it's twentieth-century witchcraft. This is a bunch of con men taking money from employers by promising they can do something they can't. As a matter of fact, they're such con men that they have a vested interest in flunking as many people as they can. I remember a meeting of the Polygraph Examiners' Association back when I was one of the fold. They used to brag about how many people they'd flunked in order to fill two vacancies."

Doug claims that these polygraph experts are nothing but

mercenaries who routinely call innocent people liars. "Say the first two people who came in were good. If they pass the test you'd only get a hundred and fifty or two hundred bucks, because you're paid per test. Now, say you flunk eight or ten people before you got the two vacancies filled. You've got a vested interest in flunking as many people as you can because you get more cash-flow."

Makes sense, I thought. But according to Doug, that's not the worst of it. These guys will, on demand, flunk anybody you designate. Suppose your company is under the gun from the Equal Rights Commission. You get two equally qualified candidates. One's a man. One's a woman. But you want to hire the guy. All you do is get your high-tech hired gun to rig the lie-detector test and "interpret the data" so the woman flunks.

Doug Williams is clearly outraged by the immoral depths to which his colleagues have sunk. "I'm the only polygraph examiner," he boasts, "who's ever blown the whistle on how to beat these guys, and it's cost me a bundle, because you can make *beaucoup* dollars running these machines. Now the method I use to beat the polygraph is kind of crude, but it's most effective and entirely undetectable. It's called the 'pucker factor.'

"See, I was in the service, from 1966 to 1969, and we went through a little ol' thing called the Tet Offensive. When you were out there in the midst of it, you'd come back from a patrol and you'd say, 'Man was the pucker factor way up there tonight.' Then when I was with the cops, you'd be on a chase and the pucker factor was so far off the scale you'd say, 'I was just pinching doughnuts out of the seat.' What the pucker factor amounts to is, when you're under stress somehow or another, your anal sphincter muscle contracts. I think it's God's way of allowing you not to defecate on yourself when you're under stressful situations."

Doug told me that stress or fear is what the lie detector is looking for. When you lie, your blood pressure shoots up and you sweat and get GSR. "Well, I figured out that if you contract your anal sphincter muscle—like you're trying to stop a bowel movement—amazing things start to happen. Your blood pressure increases, your boosted GSR response mirrors the blood pressure and according to the polygraph examiners you exhibit the classic fear or lying response."

But how, I wanted to know, could making the polygraph examiner think you were lying possibly help you beat a lie-detector test?

According to Doug, you need to fake lying on demand. The appropriate time for an innocent person to respond as if they're lying is when they're actually telling the truth about things that are totally irrelevant, unthreatening and unincriminating.

Let's say you're getting tested on a Wednesday. Now the examiner always starts off by asking a bunch of unthreatening, neutral control questions to establish your normal stress level, a kind of physiological baseline for the test. The first question might be, "What day is it?" You clench your anal sphincter and truthfully answer, "Wednesday." The polygraph printout spikes and the tester reads all the classic symptoms of fear or lying, but you've clearly told the truth. Do that a few more times with equally innocent questions and those spiked truths become the baseline for the rest of the test. When you finally get around to lying about the *really* important stuff, the lies will look just like the innocent answers and you're off the hook.

That's the theory, anyway. But could it work in practice? Doug Williams decided to find out. "I quit the cops," he told me. "I called a news conference and said 'This thing is wrong. I'm going to do whatever is necessary to make it illegal,' which sounded like the ravings of a madman back then."

So Doug started to prove his theory. "I went down to Houston and I applied for jobs where I knew they were giving pre-employment polygraph examinations," he said. "I beat every polygraph tester in the Houston yellow pages. At one test I had a guy sit down next to me in the waiting room. He was real nervous and says, 'I don't think I'm gonna pass this.' I said to him, 'I can guarantee you will.' And in exactly one-and-one-half minutes I told him the basics. He went in there and twenty minutes later came out smiling with a perfect chart. Like I said, if you can control your bowels you can control your polygraph test."

Pretty cheeky, Doug. And speaking of sphincters. . .

IV: THE RIDDLE
OF THE SPHINCTER:
HAROLD'S HEMORRHOIDS

I swear, the "H" in "Preparation H" was put there because they named the product after me.

YES, I admit it. I suffer where the sun don't shine. The condition that "piles on affliction" has always been mine own and you better believe it's a royal pain in the butt. Which is why I jumped at the "medical madness" beat when my old editor, John Vader, tossed it my way.

One of the prime directives of any tabloid hack is self-enrichment (or its little brother, self-improvement), and as a guiding principle behind everything I do, my journalistic mantra, as it were, has always been, "What's in it for me? How do I *personally* get cured by this miracle sighting of the Blessed Virgin Mary?"

Since I was going to be chewing the fat with MDs and surgeons, specialists from every branch of the medical fraternity, as far as I was concerned, every story, every lead, was going to be an open invitation to seek another opinion on my hemorrhoids. I never pass up a free consultation—even when the doctor knows nothing about hemorrhoids and couldn't care less.

I won't go into tedious detail about my constant quest for a cure—

little rubber bands, lotions, creams, pastes, balms, salves, ointments, unguents, demulcents, emollients, pads, cushions, bandages, suppositories, injections, laxatives, stool-softeners, high-fibre diets, alcohol abstinence and drugs enough to give the pharmacist's kid a postgraduate college education. And that's *before* we get to the surgical option, acupuncture, laser therapy, massage, reflexology and the laying on of hands (which works as well as anything else!).

One especially touching moment occurred after I first told the world about my affliction on the national radio airwaves. In the following weeks the *Basic Black* mail-bag brimmed over with tips from listeners suggesting what I could do to cure this curse.

Anyway, this courageous (and, I might add, still ongoing) quest for a cure for my dreaded affliction has had one positive side effect for my career. During my quest for relief, I've inadvertently stumbled onto a couple of surprising theories about that much overlooked and underappreciated part of our bodies, the very bulwark of the human anatomy—the sphincter muscle.

LORD OF THE RINGS

There is a common misconception out there that you simply don't bring up the sphincter in polite conversation. An awful lot of people operate under the delusion that the sphincter is a rude, unmentionable muscle which only controls the basest of bodily functions. Well, those tight-assed hoity-toities are wrong.

Sure, when it comes to the elimination of human waste the sphincter is a major player, a real mover and shaker, but it's a lot more flexible that you might think. The shocking truth is that our bodies are teeming with sphincters.

Sphincter is just a generic name for "ring muscles," and ring muscles are *any* group of muscles that work in a ring formation. In addition to the most familiar ring muscles—the ones that hang out in your nether regions—you've also got sphincters in your eyes, ears, nose and throat. Your mouth, for example, is really the mother of all sphincters. Yes, our bodies are literally riddled with ring muscles.

And that's a big deal according to a lady named Paula Garbourg. Paula lives in Hadera, Israel and she contends that the ring muscles are the key to our good health and longevity. Paula has written a book with the snappy title, *The Secret of the Ring Muscles: Self-Healing Through Sphincter Exercise.* She claims that by a simple exercise technique we can get all the body's sphincter muscles vibrating in harmony.

Now, I have to warn you right up front that talking to Paula Garbourg was a little tricky. She was half a world away on a bad phone line and her English was a hit-and-miss proposition. We weren't getting anywhere in English, so I tried to talk to her in French, she tried her Hebrew on me, and then we finally gave up.

I had better luck with her daughter-in-law, Haya Garbourg, who lives in Fort Lauderdale, Florida. Haya explained her mother-in-law's theory. "For Paula," she said, "the sphincter muscles, if all of them are working simultaneously together, are like a chain reaction in the eyes, in the stomach, in the nose or in the ear. Once the chain reaction starts, the body won't have any kind of problems. Like asthma, for example. People that suffer from asthma, if they do those exercises, it can prevent attacks. They won't need medicine. They won't have to take drugs."

But asthmatics aren't the only ones who'll benefit from Paula Garbourg's amazing book. Exercising your ring muscles will cure everything from migraines to back pains, arthritis to angina. The trick is to get those sphincter muscles humming in harmony, and to do that, you have to follow a simple, step-by-step, easy-to-master regime of therapeutic stress reduction exercises called "sphincter gymnastics."

I'll give you a couple of examples involving the ring muscle that, day in and day out, gets the most wear and tear—the lips. (If you want any other examples, you'll have to buy Paula's book.)

First there's the "exaggerated 'ooo-eee' technique." You push your lips out, making a big, slow, exaggerated "ooo" sound. Then you pull them way back again, this time making a loud "eee" sound. If you do that over and over again, maybe thirty or forty long and loud ooo-eee's in a row, you should start to feel an exhilarating rush of energy. That's a sign that your sphincter chain has kicked into action. The beauty of the exaggerated "ooo-eee" technique, or any of these exercises, is that you can do them anywhere. Working on the computer, vegging out in front of the TV, driving the car.

Next, try the classic "pucker technique" (and *not* the one Doug Williams talks about). This one involves puckering your lips in a kissing motion. It goes without saying that the pucker technique works great if, like me, you prefer exercising in tandem with a close friend.

But my favourite sphincter gymnastic has to be the "upper-lip-to-nose-exercise." The trick to this one is to take a toothpick and try to hold it *horizontally* between your upper lip and your nose. Try it yourself and you'll see how tough it is. (A word of caution, though. Remember to keep the toothpick *horizontal*, not vertical. Those things are sharp and you don't want to go driving one up into your sinus cavity. Children should *not* be allowed to try the upper-lip-to-nose exercise unsupervised).

Anyway, I can hear you saying, "This is all very well and good, Harold, but so what? Why would I want to be able to do that?" Fair enough. Suppose you've got asthma. According to Paula Garbourg, asthmatics, at first, are utterly incapable of doing the upper-lip-to-nose exercise. But with diligent practice of Paula's simple sphincter gymnastics they can look forward to the glorious day when they'll be able to wedge that toothpick right up under their nostrils. To quote from her book, "When an asthmatic gets to the stage where he or she can push his or her upper lip to his or her nose it is a sign that he or she is on the road to recovery."

That pretty much covers the oral ring exercises, but there are exercises for every ring muscle in your body, including the ever-popular bladder sphincter. Haya Garbourg, once again speaking for her mother-in-law, went into some detail on that one. "If you can imagine it, this exercise is the same as if you need to go to pee, and you don't have anywhere to go and you need to hold it. This is like that. Holding it and relax it. Holding it and relax it. Sometimes we will do it like two times for squeeze, then relax or a long time for squeeze then relax. This is the main thing. Squeeze and relax."

Now when you try this "pee pinch," you may find that at the beginning you have to go to the bathroom more than usual. But stick with it. Once you've got your bladder sphincter humming along with the rest of your body it'll be bye-bye to bedwetting and *adios* to adult diapers. Incontinence will be a thing of the past and you will once again be your bladder's boss.

But there's more. The best is yet to come because *Self-Healing Through Sphincter Exercise* also happens to zero in on one of the greatest curses of Western civilization (next to hemorrhoids, that is). Who among us could not benefit from a little self-healing when it comes to obesity?

If overeating is your shame, sphincter gymnastics is your game. Ask yourself, *why* do we pig out? Why do we keep eating when we're already stuffed? If the belly's full we obviously don't need more food, so why the craving? Paula Garbourg contends that, contrary to popular belief, the greatest pleasure we get from eating is not in *tasting* food—the real kick comes from *chewing* and *swallowing* and exercising those ring muscles.

In her book she says, "If the lower sphincter muscles are functioning poorly, it causes a feeling of emptiness and perpetual dissatisfaction. One improperly working sphincter is enough to throw all the others off balance. As a result they do not contract and relax adequately and in such condition the sphincter muscles begin to act like a pump, *pumping* food into our body without control or limit." So overeating is the lazy man's way to kick-start a dysfunctional digestive system. Actually, the same phenomenon explains another popular human vice.

"Smokers," Garbourg writes, "are often heard to say that they need a smoke to feel good after a meal. This means that the body is demanding that the oral sphincter be contracted to make it possible for the digestive system to operate." According to Garbourg, we wouldn't need that after-dinner cigarette if we just learned to chew our food properly. "If the mouth cavity is not opened widely enough when chewing, and the other sphincters are not made to share in the act of chewing, the abdomen grows larger, even if less is eaten."

The solution? In order to get the digestive sphincters on-line and working in harmony with the mouth, you've got to really stretch your oral sphincter. To quote the book one last time, "you have to open your mouth with all your might." The tricky part is you have to do that while you keep your lips closed, the idea being that, when you eat with your lips closed, you force your yap to work harder and make incredibly huge exaggerated lip motions. That kick-starts all the other digestive sphincters and, before you know it, your appetite will drop right off. Garbourg admits that eating this way does look a bit weird, but who cares once the pounds start to slip away?

Actually, I've found that the best way to make this work is to take food right out of the equation altogether. For example, I've started practising "dry" food-free swallows whenever I get the munchies. What I do is, I work the same squeeze and release routine we used on the pee pinch, only this time it's applied to the esophageal rings. I fake swallowing a bunch of times in a row, take a swig of water to keep my throat from getting dry, then swallow a bunch more. After a couple of minutes of dry-gulping nothing but air, the munchies flat out disappear. Talk about your miracle diets.

I hope you're keeping count. Thanks to the glories of the sphincter ring muscles your days as a fatso are finished. Your asthma's outta here. Your incontinence? Inconsequential. And your sex life? Hey, don't get me started. *Ring*-a-ding-ding!

V: HUMAN GUINEA PIGS

Imagine a world without the colostomy bag . . .

O R FOR that matter without the catheter, the truss, the doorway home traction unit and the countless other medical devices and miracle drugs that cure skin disease, depression, flagging libido, obesity and—my own personal nemesis—the dreaded hemorrhoid.

Before any of those products get on the market they have to be clinically tested, and not just on rats or monkeys or the family dog, abducted and sold to science. In today's rigorous and highly regulated marketplace you've got to have humans try these things out, so we should all be thankful that there are actual freelance human guinea pigs out there offering their bodies up so research scientists in the medical arts can test their latest brainstorms.

These people are the courageous, yet unsung, medical pioneers who, for a small fee, put their necks on the line so that the rest of us can live happier, healthier, longer lives. Theirs, however, is a world of shadows and whispers. The human guinea pigs jealously guard the locations where these studies are being run. They band together in small groups, recruit only their friends and pass along the secrets about where the latest drug studies or medical experiments are being run. That way, this tightly knit guild of guinea pigs keeps the fees paid by drug companies—anywhere between $80 and $300 per day—in the family, as it were.

Philadelphia's Bob Helms is one of them. He describes himself as "an underemployed forty-two-year-old house painter, labour activist and part-time guinea pig." And he's become the unofficial spokesperson for the guinea-pig guild.

In May 1996, Helms started a "'zine" (a tiny specialty magazine) called *Guinea Pig Zero*, which he publishes out of his home. It's aimed at the growing subculture of people Helms says make "a not bad living" as research subjects.

While they don't exactly earn a fortune, Helms told me that wannabe rock stars, for example, will sign up so they can "put gas in the van and go on tour." And the pay was good enough for Robert Rodriguez. He volunteered as a human guinea pig so he could finance a low-budget Mexican movie called *El Mariachi*. Now he's a Hollywood big shot.

Bob Helms tells their stories in his 'zine in order to "capture the camaraderie of guinea pigs who get isolated in little groups for extended periods and car pool from one experiment to another. I want to add some professionalism to the world of human test subjects," Bob told me. "I want to let guinea pigs know we have a very weird, but interesting and sometimes tragic—but very honourable—history of service to science and that there *are* risks."

Bob himself has participated in studies where there were substantial risks—risks so great that he had second thoughts about whether it was worth the money being paid.

"I've done a study that was about watching a radioactive egg salad sandwich dissolve in my stomach," he said. Researchers gave him the sandwich to eat, then watched it disintegrate with a gamma counter. "They stuck a long tube down my throat and it went through my stomach and into my intestines. This was a high-tech monitor with a little electronic sensor on the end of it. It felt like a long tapeworm." They stuck this gizmo in through his nose and "it was very uncomfortable," said Bob, in his understated way.

But if you're being exposed to pain and a more invasive procedure, surely you get more bucks, I suggested. That should be the case, said Bob, but it really doesn't happen. For the egg sandwich thing, he did it three Fridays in a row and was paid $200 per experiment.

Getting paid two hundred bucks to have an electronic tapeworm shoved down your throat so it can play hide-and-seek with a radioactive sandwich sounds bad, but it's nothing compared to some of the horror stories that Bob Helms has unearthed doing research for *Guinea Pig Zero*.

For example, he tells the tale of people's toes being cut off. This kind of thing, said Bob, has happened in Germany and the United Kingdom where "perfectly healthy people, working stiffs and unemployed guys, volunteered to have their little toe amputated, then sewn back on by microsurgical techniques that were being developed, and studied using laser beams and state-of-the-art stuff. Hopefully," he said, "you'd be able to twinkle your toe again when you walked out."

Bob told me about one experiment where volunteers were paid a $900 fee to be placed under general anaesthesia for eight hours. Another one involved having the heart stopped and started back up again.

Then there's the tragic case of nineteen-year-old Nicole Wan, who was a student at the University of Rochester in New York State. She got $150 to be in a study about how pollution and second-hand smoke affect lung tissue. Part of the procedure was a bronchoscopy. That meant Wan had to have a tube down her throat (here we go again). She couldn't keep the tube down. She started gagging. The researchers kept spraying lidocaine (a local anaesthetic) into her throat to suppress her gag response. Eventually, Wan went into cardiac arrest from an overdose of anaesthetic, and she died. Her family sued for $100 million but settled out of court for an undisclosed sum.

Bob Helms admits that Nicole Wan's case is extreme and that high-risk testing is not his idea of a good time. Whenever possible, he looks for the cushier experiments. The kinds of studies most attractive to him "are less out-patient and more steady stays in a facility itself." That means staying overnight with three square meals a day. Bob said that kind of study could mean living in for anywhere from a week to a month.

Sounded good to me—room and board *and* getting paid. Bob

agreed a really sharp guinea pig could line up a whole bunch of studies in a row and wouldn't even need his own place to live. And what's more, sometimes the studies are risk-free. They're set up so half of the group is taking the test drug and the other half a placebo. So then, I wondered, there's a fifty-fifty chance that you'd be getting paid to sit around with nothing stronger than distilled water coursing through your veins?

Bob admitted that that had happened to him but, he pointed out, "you also might be in the high-dose group of a phase one study of a brand new drug and your body figures out that it's extremely toxic, it's poison. Something like that happened to a friend of mine. They were testing a blood thinner and he was supposed to be in for eight days but he started to get very long bleeding times right at the beginning when they first gave him the drug. So they stopped the drug, cut him from the study, waited until his blood was reasonably thick, so he wasn't a hemophiliac walking out the door. They paid him in full ($1,800 or something) and he only had to stay for a day and a half."

This kept sounding better and better, I thought. How do I hop on this gravy train? I wondered. "Hold your horses, Harold," said Bob, getting to the downside of all this. "It can get really boring. I mean, NASA does studies where they keep you strapped in a chair for three weeks and all you're allowed to do is move your arms and legs and head."

No big deal, I said. I've lain motionless on my couch watching television for weeks on end and have suffered no ill effects. The boredom I can handle.

"Others are diet studies," he said. "They feed you nothing but a particular diet and watch your body's behaviour while you're doing that."

"So you'd pig out on nothing but potato chips for three weeks or something?" I said. "Hey, I do that already. This is great!"

Before I got too carried away, Bob Helms reminded me about that radioactive sandwich and about the real risks in this line of work. And he gave me a couple of tips about the kinds of things any of you would-be human guinea pigs out there should watch out for.

Avoid the chintzy fly-by-night test operators, who run their experiments out of hotels because they're a whole lot cheaper than hospitals. And watch out for useless procedures like X-rays and prostate exams, which are routinely given before admission to some studies. If you do a lot of studies, the radiation from the X-rays can really add up. As for a prostate exam, Bob says "most test subjects are in their twenties or thirties and prostate cancer is almost unheard of in that age group," so you really have to wonder about the sadistic logic behind demanding such an exam.

You will have to have a blood test, so keep your eye out for inept medical staff. "If the nurse keeps poking and prodding until you're black and blue and they still can't raise a vein" take that as fair warning, says Helms. Turn right around and walk out the front door.

And how do you find out about drug studies and volunteering to be in them? Check the pharmaceutically-oriented scientific journals or the Internet to see what drug companies are seeking approval for their drugs. Then give the companies a call and ask them where the clinical trials are being run. Sometimes, says Bob, they'll farm them out to private companies or universities, so you can give them a call, too. Once you become part of the "guinea-pig community," you'll pick up all the info you need via the grapevine, and you'll get call after call asking you to participate.

Bob told me about one group of chronically unemployed guys in Indianapolis who live in shelters most of the time. Once a month, *en masse*, they check into hospitals as guinea pigs. "These guys do a study, get paid, take the money and, as a group, go down to a motel. They stock up on booze and invite hookers in and party their asses off until they're broke." After that, they cool their heels in the shelter until the next study comes along.

Move over gang, and make room for Harold.

CHAPTER THIRTEEN

THE FAME GAME

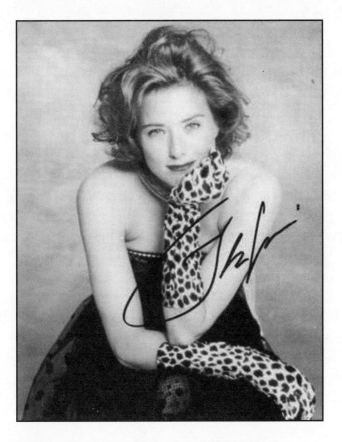

Celebrity Téa Leoni. She's *not* a tabloid hack, but
she played one on TV. And she blew up real good in
Deep Impact (see Chapter Eleven).

What desire for fame attends both great and small;
Better be damned than mentioned not at all.

—John Wolcot

UNLESS YOU count Elvis, who gets a chapter all to himself (see Chapter Five), I've somehow managed to crank out most of this book without so much as a nod in the direction of the tabs' "Big Celebrity Fame Game." It's not an oversight. As a rule, I hate celebs and hustling stories about Hollywood stars has never been my idea of a good time. I'll take "Outhouse Archaeology" (see Chapter Two) or "Pee-Pee Power" (see Chapter Seven) over "Demi's Silicone Secret" any day. Unfortunately, a hack like me can't always pick and choose his assignments.

The tab business is relentless at shovelling celebrity chow into the reading public's gaping maw and it goes through "celeb copy" faster than a shredder in the Nixon White House. If the editor calls for the latest on "Leonardo DiCaprio's Acne Angst!" then mine is not to reason why. Like it or not, I'm on the celebrity beat.

I know what you're thinking. How bad can it be, rubbing elbows with all those glitzy glamour queens and hunky high rollers?

Well, as far as I'm concerned, you can have it. Speaking of which, it has crossed my mind that there might be one or two masochists out there reading this who would like nothing better than a career as a VIP-voyeur. Well, you're going to need some help. That's why I've taken the liberty of putting together a little primer for you. I call it . . .

1. PEEK-A-BOO 101

FISKE'S FIRST LAW OF CELEBRITY JOURNALISM:
Never *ever* do anything in person or face-to-face.

Do all your research, everything, on the phone—or these days, on the Internet. For one thing, you don't want these people to know what you look like, or where you live, or your kids' names. This way, you're a lot harder to find when they send their goons out to beat you up. Another reason for using the phone is that's is real easy to tape everything the celebrity says without them knowing about it.

Taping over the phone without the knowledge of the person you're interviewing is perfectly legal here in Canada. Forget about those stupid U.S. laws on wiretapping. As long as you're in Canada, they can't get you. However, if any of you Americans are thinking about a career in the tabs, you'd better check with your local law enforcement authorities. In some states (Florida, for one) it's illegal to surreptitiously tape.

FISKE'S SECOND LAW OF CELEBRITY JOURNALISM
Don't abandon the story just because
the celeb has an unlisted number.

Unlisted numbers are really easy to get. They're on a whole bunch of Internet sites these days (use your search engines) but back in the dark ages we used to call a New York-based company that specializes in selling celebs phone numbers. They buy phone numbers from the professional snitches and parasites who populate Hollywood, so if you want to get in touch with Jerry Seinfeld, they've got his number, at least his number this week. The trouble is, celebs change their phone numbers more often than they change their underwear. If you get a number today, use it quickly because it probably won't be any good a week from now.

But you can't just call this ratfink company up. You have to have an account. They charge anywhere from US$25 to $150 per tip, depending on how big the star is. You can get around that little roadblock, however. *And while I've never done this myself because it's illegal and wrong,* I have heard of people using the following technique to get a current celeb number.

Some unscrupulous folks (not hacks like me) pick up the latest copy of a major supermarket tabloid that specializes in celebs, or even something more mainstream like *People* (hey! I said something **like** *People*, not *People* itself!) and check the masthead—that's the little box in the front of the publication where all the people who write and edit are listed.

It's important, these con artists say, to pick some mid-level person (not the top guy), an assignment editor or senior copy editor, say, then phone the number service and pretend to be that person. Be breezy and authoritative (if you can fake a lower-class English accent, all the better) and say something like, "This is William Carter of *XYZ Magazine*. I need Jerry Seinfeld's latest number." If they say they don't know you, I'm told you can sometimes ask: "Well who *is* authorized from here to deal with you people? Is it Jean Smith or Bob Jones [two other mid-ranking names from the masthead], or does all this have to go through Mario Delvecchio [the head guy] himself?" After that, they'll usually tell you who their contact guy is, thinking it's some bureaucratic screw-up at your end. Once you've got the right name, just call again pretending to be *that* person. (Of course, you could just set up an account, but who wants to pay these scum?)

Folks who work this scam (and that's not me) also suggest you turn off the "caller ID" feature on your telephone. That's the feature that sends out your name and phone number with your call, and the tabloids always have this feature turned off anyway—they don't want

"*The National Enquirer*" lighting up the recipient's phone when they're trying to get an interview. The phone company will tell you how to shut it off.

Scam artists who do this always say they don't think the *National Enquirer* or *People* would be angry getting stuck with their "research" bills because they'd always intended to pitch their "exclusive story" to those very publications—so they're really doing it in good faith. Yeah, right—tell it to the judge.

Another great way (and totally legal) to get celeb phone numbers is to look in *Who's Who* at your local public library—these books are generally non-circulating reference texts (that is, you can't take them home) and you can't sneak them out of the library because they're huge, and they've got these magnetic strips that activate some alarm at the doorway.

If you *must* take these books home temporarily (remember, you can't *keep* library books—it's wrong), try this simple method. Take some brown paper, tape, string and stamps and wrap the book up well in a parcel. Write your address on it (that's the only risky part) and walk boldly back to the administrative area, where you can just toss it into the outgoing mail bin. The book will arrive at your home a few days later. If you get one of those stupid cards asking you to come and pick up your parcel at the post office, don't go! It probably means they're on to you. But remember, take the book *back* after you've done your research with it, otherwise it's theft!

Let's face it, celebs are usually just jumped-up human trash who think it's hot stuff to be singled out for publication in *Who's Who*. Big deal! I was in the *Canadian Who's Who* for years, but finally got bounced when I wouldn't pony up the $80 to buy the 1994 edition.

While *Who's Who* doesn't usually contain celeb phone numbers (although you'd be surprised—they *are* sometimes in there!), it does give you the name of the theatrical agency representing the celeb. So you can just call up an agent. As long as the agency's client isn't one of those really hot flavour-of-the-month types, there's an excellent chance they'll call you back—especially if you tell them to call collect. They never do, but it sends a signal that you're a legit journalist. From the agent you can always get the celebs' business fax numbers, their publicists' numbers or general business office numbers.

Once you have these numbers, don't call them. You'll just end up getting the runaround from some two-bit lackey. Instead, try dialling one or two numbers higher or lower, or reversing the last four digits—you'd be surprised how often this will get you the celeb's direct, private, unlisted number. When you've got a general number with a taped receptionist, always try extension "1" first—or with three digits, "001," "111" or "123." These people have big egos and their extension almost always contains some combination involving the number one.

FISKE'S THIRD LAW OF CELEBRITY JOURNALISM:
Just because the celeb's in the slammer
doesn't mean you can't have an interview.

There are some celebs in prison—and some people are celebs *because* they're in prison, but you can't just pick up a phone and call David "Son of Sam" Berkowitz or Charles Manson. Most (but not all) prisons don't allow the guests to take incoming calls. But Charles Manson is perfectly free to call *you*, provided you can get him to stop hallucinating long enough to grab his attention.

In those circumstances, what I recommend is writing a respectful letter. And make it a nice flattering letter. Say something like, "Hey Charlie—That swastika thing on your forehead!—What a fashion statement! Give me a call collect and let's *rap* about today's young people." (Note how easily I can slip into prison argot.) Try that and he'll probably call you right back. Sucking up to celebs almost always works.

FISKE'S FOURTH LAW OF CELEBRITY JOURNALISM:
Don't give up your day job.

If you're really serious about pursuing tabloid journalism on an amateur or part-time basis, what you're really going to need is a full-time job with the government, either federal or provincial, because:

- ninety-nine percent of your tab phone calls are going to be long distance and the civil service has an unlimited long distance phone budget; and

- civil servants don't do *any* work at all. This is not a myth (and don't come harrumphing after me, you bone-idle suckers at the public breast—you *know* this is true!). A civil service job frees up plenty of time to hustle stars and celebs between the coffee breaks.

FISKE'S FIFTH LAW OF CELEBRITY JOURNALISM:
If you aren't *already* insane, you will *become* insane.

Writing about celebs is one of the most hated beats at the tabloids—those who *say* they like it are completely crazy.

First of all, look at *who* you're covering. The people who buy the *National Enquirer*, and all those other copycat tabloids, aren't shelling out their grubby dough for stories about the great minds of our century. The only Pulitzer Prize-winner you ever read about in one of these rags was Arthur Miller and that was only because once upon a time he was married to Marilyn Monroe.

The average tab reader watches a lot of television, so your primo tabloid celebrity is going to be one of those cookie-cutter pretty two-bit actors on some brain-dead American sitcom or soap opera. And your job is to track and chart their scintillating careers—their implants, their indiscretions, their anorexia. It's just one big bloody bore!

And look what you've got to work with. You're given some inane star, a story that's geared to a photo that was shot years ago and a big chunk of space you have to fill on a brutal deadline. And the really hard part is you have to come up with some brilliant, novel angle that no other tab has ever used before. You have two options:

You could actually try to talk to the star. Now, this can be done, but it's tough and soul-destroying work. For some reason, most celebrities *hate* tab writers. When I met that broken-down, untalented cokehead, John Belushi, for example, he hated me on sight—I don't know what I said to offend him. In fact, celebs are so paranoid that in order to get anywhere near them you have to worm your way past a phalanx of agents and PR flacks and the king-sized thyroid cases they hire as bodyguards.

And then, if you don't want to get sued, you'd better write something complimentary, so you go on about Dolly Parton's shapely figure or Farrah Fawcett's wonderful hair (I know, I date myself with these references). It doesn't matter if you make it all up and it's a complete pack of lies—if it's *nice* the stars will *never* take you to court.

David Niven was one celebrity who never got slammed in the press. Not by the tabs, not by the so-called legitimate press, never! That's because he always knew how to treat journalists. Niven was a hack's dream. He used to say, "Write whatever you want, lads—lie, make it all up—I don't care!" And of course, we'd all bend over backwards to present him as the true gentleman he was. But Niven, God rest his soul, was the exception, not the rule (he actually had some brains, charm and talent, too); trying to have a one-on-one conversation with a regular celebrity is usually a whole lot more trouble than it's worth.

The simpler (and safer) solution is to dig through the clippings in the "morgue," or newspaper's library (every newspaper has one of these, and a lot of them are archived on the Internet these days), then do your basic cut 'n' paste rehash of the same stale old quotes and pictures you used last week, or last year, only this time you've gotta slap a new spin on them.

One of my favourite sure-fire gimmicks for pulling this off was putting a "celebrity sidebar" on some non-celeb story to tart it up a bit. Check this out. Back when the TV series *M*A*S*H* (God, I'm getting on) was really hot, my editor at the *National Examiner* was sniffing around for a cover story on Alan Alda.

Actually, "sniffing around" doesn't quite characterize it. He was, in fact, desperate because he'd already committed to a picture of Alda on the cover, had it all mocked up, but didn't have any hot copy to go with it. Well, it just so happened that I was working on a totally unrelated story at the same time. My piece was called, "The Place Where Your Doc Dries Out!" It was about this health farm somewhere out in the sticks in Georgia. Doctors (and other broken-down health professionals) would go to this spa and sober up whenever their hands got too shaky to perform surgery.

I was talking to one of the directors of this fancy drunk tank and I suddenly got a brain wave. I asked the guy, "What do you think about the surgeons on *M*A*S*H*, who are boozing and drunk all the time and operating with a martini in one hand and a scalpel in the other? Wouldn't you say they're a very bad example for America's real-life doctors?" And, of course the guy agreed and barfed back the idea I had just fed him. "Yeah, Alan Alda, the way he gets up there and pours that poison into himself, he's really giving young impressionable doctors the wrong idea, blah, blah, blah."

What did Alan Alda have to say about all this? Well, to put it politely Alda was "not returning our calls." That didn't stop the *Examiner*. We ran with the quote from the health spa honcho and headlined our cover story: "Top Doc Slams Shame of Alan Alda Booze Abuse," and that tabloid classic conforms beautifully to my own personal journalistic credo. Not "all the news that's fit to print" but the much more practical "all the news that's reasonably true."

Anyway, I imagine Alan Alda hated that story, assuming he ever saw it. The ingrate probably didn't even appreciate all the free publicity.

Okay, so it wasn't exactly flattering, but Alda and his ilk would be well advised to take to heart the immortal words of John Wolcot that opened this chapter: "Better be damned than mentioned not at all."

But then, what do you expect from a celeb? On the way up these guys are so desperate for any kind of copy that they'll practically lick your boots to get it. Then once they make the big time, they'd sooner punch you out than give you the time of day. Some of them pack a pretty good wallop too. You avoid them like the plague.

Back when Ronnie Reagan was snoozing his way through his two terms as president, the *National Examiner* tried setting up a celebrity beat on Nancy Reagan. We did manage to get out a couple of stories on the First Lady, but that beat got squashed real quick.

At the time, the *Examiner* was edited in Montreal, but we wrote largely for the American public—97 percent of our circulation was in the U.S.—and we did a lot of business at the border. Every day somebody had to go across into Rouse's Point in New York State (about forty kilometres due south of Montreal) to our mail drop and haul back all these sacks of letters. Plus we had the paper printed in the U.S., so every week we had to ship the negatives to make the printing plates for the upcoming week's edition. These were taken to the airport and hand-delivered to regional printing plants at various locations in the U.S.

The funny thing was, whenever we wrote something about Nancy Reagan (good or bad), the U.S. Customs inspections would tighten up, both at Rousse's Point and at the airport. One time, U.S. Customs claimed we'd have to pay duty on the negatives, which we claimed had a value of a couple of hundred bucks—the cost of the film stock. No, said the Customs man, the value of the negatives has to include the cost of all the labour and overhead that went into them, so bring us your books and we'll figure out what they're worth, then charge you a percentage of that.

While the company solved its duty problem, we did notice there was an uncanny correlation between Nancy Reagan stories (some of which I wrote) and hassles with U.S. Customs. It wasn't very subtle, but it wasn't something you could prove either, so after a while we wised up and dumped the Nancy Reagan beat. And wouldn't you know it, everything was hunky-dory at the border again.

II: THERE'S NO CELEB LIKE A DEAD CELEB

I'm really looking forward to
Nancy Reagan's "box shot."

THE BOX shot story is how a hack like me gets the last laugh on the tabloid-shy celebrities who refuse to talk, or threaten to rearrange your face if you write about them anyway.

Well, I've got news for them. Like it or not, sooner or later the Grim Reaper's going to come a-calling and the tabs are going to be all over their funerals like flies on a dungheap. Now the *de rigueur* centrepiece of that story is always the "box shot"—the celebrity corpse laid out in a coffin with the stock banner headline "A Fond Farewell To _____!" You just fill in the blank with the name of whoever has croaked that week.

The box shot is sweet revenge—if you can get it. I'll never forget the day that Natalie Wood drowned and I assigned a photographer to get a box shot. That turned out to be a weird assignment because Natalie's funeral security was really tight. The photographer was caught sneaking in and was savagely beaten to a pulp. The *Examiner* ended up shelling out a small fortune for three months' hospital bills and, even worse, we never did get the Natalie Wood pictures.

And we didn't have any luck with Elvis Presley's funeral back in 1977. The *National Enquirer* scooped us all on that one. According to tabloid legend (and none of this can be confirmed, so it's probably a pack of lies), the Presley estate had gone whole hog on security for Elvis's funeral. They'd hired an army of muscle to set up a perimeter around the funeral home and nobody from the media could get in, especially not the tabloids.

That didn't stop the *Enquirer*—it came up with something absolutely brilliant. It allegedly set up cloak-and-dagger meetings with certain Presley relatives. And let me make one thing perfectly clear, some (certainly not all) of Presley's relatives were both cretinous *and* greedy. So, the *Enquirer* approached the mourners and anybody who wanted one got a little Sure-Shot camera. Sure-Shots are those little no-brainer jobs that auto-focus and all you have to do is point them and shoot them.

It's rumoured the Presley kinfolk were told, "The camera is a gift. Whatever happens, it's yours to keep, no questions asked. What we want you to do is go in and get us a picture of Elvis and we'll give a thousand-dollar bonus for the picture we actually publish." The story goes (and hey, who knows if it's true?) that some of the Presley family mourners walked into the funeral home and, of course, the security guards frisked them and found the cameras. "You're not getting in with those!" the amateur photogs were told.

But inevitably people *did* get in and take pictures. There were some rumours—and again these are doubtless complete falsehoods—that some of the Presley mourners actually held the guards at gunpoint while others took shots of the dead Elvis lying in his box. It sounds utterly incredible (and totally false) to me, and I'm only repeating common gossip that was current in the tabloid writing community in the late 1970s.

And a box shot did indeed finally appear on the *Enquirer* cover, kicking off an *après Elvis* industry that's still going on to this day (see Chapter Five).

It's important to realize that "there's no celeb like a dead celeb"—
once the ol' ticker stops, it's open season on a celeb because . . .

III: YOU CAN'T LIBEL A CORPSE

Elvis, Mozart . . . it doesn't matter.
Say anything you want.

L OOK IT UP. It's the law. You can say *anything you want* about
the dead: "Elvis fathered my triplets," "Elvis died during sex-
change surgery," "Elvis and Marilyn [Monroe] plotted to kill JFK." It all
makes for good tab copy because all the parties are dead and nobody
can sue you from beyond the grave, although Elvis can certainly confirm those sex-change details with the aid of a good psychic.

Once dead, it's amazing how celebs become tabloid-friendly—
there's something about shuffling off their mortal coil that makes these
folks, well, *human*, for a change. A surly reclusive star will become a
total gatormouth in the next life and, in the hands of a gifted psychic,
will talk about intimate personal details on both sides of the grave.

Take Wolfgang Mozart, for example: a damn fine composer, a
Shriner and a champion bowler—*hated* his father, but never mind that.
He was a big celeb in his day, but he died in 1791. Now, back in 1991 at
the CBC, all the pointy-headed artsy types (Mozart would have hated
them, let me tell you) in the Radio Arts, Music & Drama Department
were getting their knickers wet over the "Year of Mozart," which
marked the two-hundredth anniversary since the Wolfmeister had
kicked the beer stein, as it were.

Since everyone was doing a Mozart piece (and since I'd frequently
spoken to Mozart in the afterlife), I had some big plans for a beyond-

the-grave interview with the great tunesmith himself. Now Wolfgang Amadeus Mozart could toss off a pretty tune with the best of them—he wrote the music to "Twinkle, Twinkle Little Star," and "O Canada." But a whole year of this stuff? Well, after months of listening to a bunch of stuffed shirts pontificate about the composer's glorious and unparalleled career, I'd had it up to here. I decided what the world needed was a tabloid version of the whole Mozart phenomenon.

My plans to do a seance, however, went nowhere. At first I thought I'd try to channel to him while sitting in one of those silly little miniature cars the Shriners like to ride around in at the Santa Claus parade. Mozart was a keen Mason, and let's face it, that's the same as a Shriner. But the whole thing was too much trouble, so I tried to contact him in the usual way, in a darkened room sitting around a table.

I got hold of Edna Berkowitz. She's an old psychic buddy of mine—we go all the way back to my days at the *Examiner*. Over the years she's conjured up the ghosts of James Dean, Princess Grace and Jack Ruby for me. Edna, God bless her, is a real trouper and she tried her best to contact Mozart's ghost. We held hands. We chanted. We even tried her using her channelling crystal, but nothing worked. Edna said it had something to do with the bad vibes associated with Mozart's bankruptcy and her chakras being misaligned with the cosmos.

It's a pity we never managed to break through—I had really been looking forward to getting his take on some of the great stuff I'd unearthed while "prepping for the invu," as all we big radio stars like to say.

For example, Mozart was always something of a ladies' man and he probably would have got a real kick out of the Japanese inventor who came up with the "Mozart bra." When unhooked, it plays a snatch of melody from the overture to *The Marriage of Figaro*.

Mozart was also a three-hundred-points-per-game bowler. And while the CBC longhairs gush away about his famous Trio for Clarinet, Viola and Piano (K. 498), which is one of Mozart's most serene and restful works, just get yourself a psychic and Wolfgang will tell you what he called the piece: "Kegelstadt"—or, "Bowling Alley." He wrote it while he was rolling a few frames in 1786. He should have called it the "Ode to the 7-10 Split."

While Mozart had quite a common touch for such an uncommon genius-type artist, there was nothing common about the way he kicked the bucket. He died very young (he was 35) and nobody (including him) is really sure what actually killed him. With all the attention focused on the great man in the Year of Mozart, it was only natural that a certain amount of controversy would start to kick up over what's popularly been called the "Mozart autopsy."

Naturally, that's a misnomer. There was never an autopsy performed on Mozart's body when he died in 1791. But that didn't stop two hundred years of expert guessing about what did in the greatest composer who ever lived.

More recently, psychiatrists and neurosurgeons have hopped on the bandwagon. They've been working up a theoretical autopsy and they're sifting through the accounts of all the weird stuff Mozart did during his short life, trying to diagnose what the hell was wrong with him. For example, the docs know that Mozart used to bark like a dog and he used to twitch compulsively. That's got them speculating that he had Tourette's syndrome. Yeah, sure. It was probably just a hangover.

He also had a real toilet mouth and doctors figure he may have had a rare condition called "coprolalia," which is a compulsive need to pepper your speech with rude references to bodily excretory functions. If you saw the movie *Amadeus* you might remember that they showed a lot of this toilet-talk. The Mozart revealed in the movie could really spit out the shocking gutter-talk. But I'm not so sure that's any reason to call the poor sod a coprolaliac. I mean, what else would you expect from somebody who liked to hang around bowling alleys.

Anyway, while we're on the subject of that much honoured, Academy Award-winning motion picture—remember the end of the movie? There's an incredibly depressing scene where Mozart dies, a penniless outcast. It's raining cats and dogs, the streets of Vienna are knee-deep in mud and Mozart's body is flung like a piece of trash into a big open-pit paupers' grave with all the other deadbeats.

Wrong. When that movie was released there was a stink raised about that by outraged authorities, who claimed it never happened that way. "Vienna would not, could not and did not so mistreat its greatest composer," they insisted. Well thanks to modern forensic science, the truth can now be told.

Luckily, although the rest of his body has disappeared, Mozart's tell-tale skull has survived the ravages of time. Over the years it was passed, hand to hand, down a very well documented chain, all the way to the Mozartium (the celebrated Mozart Museum) in Vienna.

A top forensic expert has studied that skull and he says beyond any reasonable doubt that it's definitely Mozart's. The scientist's name is Pierre-François Pouette. He lives in France and is attached to the University of Paris, although his home is down in Nîmes, just a hop, skip and a jump north of Marseilles.

Dr. Pouette is a dentist who specializes in forensic identification. The Marseilles police often use this guy to ID dead bodies. It's just like in the movies. The *gendarmes* turn up a corpse that's burned or brutalized beyond recognition, except for the teeth. And according to Dr. Pouette, teeth (at least in the mouth of a dead man) never lie. He gives the victim a posthumous check-up, cross-references that with old dental charts and *bingo*—instant ID.

Dr. Pouette has applied his considerable expertise to the teeth in Mozart's skull and "the front teeth have been broken and inside [them] we have found some sand," he told me. "The geological experts have concluded that it is the same sand as in the graveyard" where Mozart was first buried.

But even such a positive match would only prove that the skull came from that graveyard, not that it was Mozart's, pointed out Sherlock Fiske.

"Ah," said Dr. Pouette. "We have examined the skull to look if [it] has peculiarities typical of Mozart. We do know from history that he liked to use . . . how do you say it? . . . *les cure-dents.*

"Toothpicks!" said speaks-French-like-a-native Fiske, helping the doctor out. "So, Mozart was famous for using a toothpick?"

"Yes," replied Dr. Pouette. "We have found the places where he did use them. We have found the marks on his teeth!"

And there you have it. Overwhelming evidence from the Year of Mozart that the alleged Mozart skull is in fact the real McCoy, and that the good people of Vienna did in fact unceremoniously dump the dead musical giant in a paupers' grave.

On the basis of our three-minute radio interview, Dr. Pouette recognized me as a fellow seeker of truth and was kind enough to invite me to his home in the south of France, where, a few months later, we discussed forensic dentistry late into the night over some very fine bottles from his impeccable wine cellar.

IV: CELEB SIBLING RIVALRY

**"I taught Andy how to draw," says farmer
Paul Warhola. Warhol's older brother paints—
with chicken feet instead of paint brushes.**

CELEBRITY siblings are the star-crossed brothers and sisters of famous celebrities. Most of the time they're no-talent parasites who milk their proximity to fame for all it's worth.

Billy Carter was a classic case. Remember him? He was that beer-guzzling redneck buffoon whose brother Jimmy just happened to be

Prez of the United States. Billy was the black sheep of the Carter clan and his (very) tenuous ties to the Oval Office got him his fifteen minutes of fame. He did the talk-show circuit, started selling his own "Billy Beer" and made a career out of embarrassing his big brother. Of course, it couldn't last. Jimmy only lasted one term in the White House. The minute he moved out, Billy was a footnote to history.

Kelly Collins is another little-known member of the css (Celebrity Sib Society). Kelly lives in southern California and she was born with the advantage of being the sister of none other than Bo Derek. I say "advantage" because, like her sexy sister, Kelly too has been bitten by the showbiz bug, which for a hack like me is all to the good. Whenever at the *National Examiner* we wanted some quotes on Bo all we had to do was call Kelly up and say, "Kelly, we're thinking of doing a story on you" and she'd yack her head off. Then at the end we'd mention how a profile of the "real Kelly Collins" could use a sisterly point of view. That's when she'd give us Bo Derek's unlisted phone number, which was what we were after all along.

But forget about that cheap tabloid celeb stuff. My all-time favourite story about a celebrity sibling riding on the coat-tails of his illustrious brother is about Paul Warhola. He's Andy Warhol's older brother and he's making big waves of his own in the art world.

Paul and Andy were the sons of Czech immigrants. They grew up in a town called Smock, Pennsylvania. Back in 1990 when I talked to Paul Warhola he was still living right there in Smock. At that time he was sixty-seven and recently retired from his metalwork business. To kill time, he'd taken up farming and then, almost by accident, he decided he'd try his hand at . . . *art!* Paul told me he'd started with his own artistic career "about a year ago." He had several paintings little brother Andy had done, works dating back to between 1941 and 1949.

"There's ten of them in all," he said, and a friend had approached him and was interested in buying one of the paintings. "I told him, 'It's out of the question. The closest you're gonna get to an Andy

Warhol is if his brother does one.' But then he says, 'Could you?' And I says, 'Well, what d'you want me to paint? I'm not gonna paint a Campbell's soup can, if that's what you're thinking. How about a ketchup bottle or baked beans?' 'Gee' he says, 'What are you gonna charge me?'"

Paul suggested $300 and, to his amazement, the buddy ordered three pictures on the spot and—*bingo!*—a new star began to twinkle in the artistic firmament. I asked Paul Warhola how he actually goes about painting something like a Heinz beans can.

"I do a sketch of it and then I put it into a projector and it projects onto a canvas and then I sorta trace it and later on I do it with acrylics, you know," Paul told me.

And when I asked him if he was as good a painter as his brother was, Paul Warhola made a stunning revelation: "*I* taught Andy how to paint! When Andy was a youngster," Paul recalled, "there was a six-year age gap and when he was six years old he wasn't very well and I worked with him a lot, and before you know it, he showed a lot of talent."

And did he "understand" Andy's paintings? "Sure!" said Paul. "Everything that Andy did always pertained to his early life, like, you know, when mother used to open up a Campbell's soup can for lunch. And everything goes back," said Paul. "Like he was very fond of movie stars. When he was a youngster, I sent away to a lot of movie stars and got him autographed pictures and all. Shirley Temple sent him one, an eight-by-ten, that was autographed 'To Andrew Warhola,' and he prized that."

Never mind Andy, let's talk about you, I told him. "I understand you just completed a show at the Hartwell Gallery in Pittsburgh?"

"Yes, sir," said Paul. "And it was *very* successful. I did over $30,000. I had paintings that ran anywhere from $2,000 to $10,000."

With that kind of haul, I wondered whether Paul was planning to go on in the art scene and see if he could make a second career out of painting?

"It's a lot of fun for me," he said. "I'm up here at the farm and I'm doing it because I find it very relaxing. I'm probably just the opposite of what Andy did, because Andy spent most of his time at New York."

"So what are you working on right now?" I asked. "What's Paul Warhola's *oeuvre* look like these days?"

"When I started getting publicity through the media, why, *Time* magazine called me and the reporter, she says, 'Okay you're doing product paintings like Andy, but aren't you going to do anything else?' I says, 'Well, I'll tell you what I intend to do if you promise not to laugh, because I'll hang up if you do.' And she says, 'I won't laugh,' so I expressed to her that I was going to have the chickens paint for me."

This was new, I thought. What's this all about?

"I'm noted now for my chicken feet paintings," said Paul, reading my mind. "I put paint on the chickens' feet and then they, you know, bounce around on the canvas."

And what's it going to cost me for an original Paul Warhola chicken feet painting for my rec room?

"How big of a painting do you want?" asked Paul.

"Try two by three feet," I told him.

"I'm getting about us$3,000 for those."

And that ain't chickenfeed, folks. It also ain't a Van Gogh, but I'm delighted to say my Warhola original proudly hangs alongside my blacklight Elvis in my custom-built animal bone boudoir.

V: FAMOUS LAST WORDS

Joan Quigley, Nancy Reagan's
secret psychic, speaks out at last!

F AME! Socrates called it "the perfume of heroic deeds." Milton
wasn't so kind. To him it was "the last infirmity of noble minds."
But this is *my* book, so I get the last word on the subject. And, no
offence to my worthy colleagues, but when I think of celebrities, the
phrases "heroic deeds" and "noble minds" don't exactly leap out at me.
However, to paraphrase those two great minds, "stinking infirmity"
comes pretty close.

I mentioned before how whenever we wrote something nasty
about Nancy Reagan at the *National Examiner*, the Customs checks
would tighten up. They'd start doing things like seizing our negatives or
hassling whoever was doing the mail run. Like I said, it didn't take long
for us to put two and two together and after a while, we dumped the
Nancy Reagan beat, and wouldn't you know it, everything was fine at
the border again, or sort of. The Nancy Reagan Customs rigamarole
reared its ugly head again in May 1990 when I got the *assignment from
hell*!

Here's what happened: I was supposed to do a CBC radio interview
with Joan Quigley. Quigley was the psychic who got her fifteen minutes
of fame by claiming she'd acted as Nancy Reagan's secret astrologer
during Nancy's days in the White House.

The arrangement between Quigley and the First Lady was meant to
be top-secret, hush-hush stuff, and it stayed that way until Donald
Regan spilled the beans in a 1988 book called *For the Record*. (He was
no relation to the prez, folks. He was one of Ronald Reagan's Cabinet

advisors.) He said that an unnamed astrologer had actually advised Ron and Nancy for seven years during their presidency.

Just like that, the nasty, flaky First Family got a whole lot funnier. Nancy Reagan didn't much like being the laughingstock of the nation so she turned around and wrote her own book, *My Turn*, and pooh-poohed the whole thing. She admitted that she dallied with astrology but only for "fun." It was all just a lark and she didn't take any of it seriously.

Well, Joan Quigley was really annoyed by that, so she decided to come out of the closet and set the record straight. Her book was called *What Does Joan Say?* and included the shocking revelation that, during seven years advising the Reagans, the astrologer "actually gave them advice that veritably shaped the course of American history."

My assignment was to read the book, review it and then grill Joan about her story.

And that's when what I like to call "the border war" flared up again. Joan's publisher had Fed-Exed an advance copy of *What Does Joan Say?* to me and it was mysteriously held up at Customs until two days *after* my interview with Joan Quigley. Coincidence? Bad luck? *Conspiracy* is more like it!

And because of that international conspiracy, I had to review Joan's book without actually reading it. What I ended up doing was pulling a clipping out of the *New York Times* and cribbing my review from that. As far as the radio interview was concerned? Hey, I'm a pro, I can wing it. The first thing I asked her was how she managed to get her job as astrologer to Mr. and Mrs. President? It turns out that, "just for fun," Joan had actually been doing the Reagans' horoscopes on her own since 1973. That all changed when Reagan was running for president in 1980.

"I submitted a paper to the [presidential] campaign in August about what would happen between August 1st and the election. I don't think they paid too much attention to it until, on August 19, the

President made that remark about recognizing Taiwan instead of the Republic of China.

"That was quite a gaffe, and I had written on my report 'do not make any foreign policy pronouncements on the 19th of August,' and I had underlined it in red ink. Well, from then on the people in the campaign were just glued to my reports and Nancy was on the phone to me frequently, and I helped out as a volunteer on the campaign. A great deal of what I did was the timing of press conferences and speeches and when Air Force One would take off and land. I don't want to overemphasize my role. On the other hand, I timed almost everything that was done."

Joan made it sound like she was an indispensable behind-the-scenes cog in the day-to-day running of the Reagan campaign machine. But if that was true, I wanted to know where she was when John Hinckley tried to assassinate Reagan. Didn't she try to warn the President?

"No, I wasn't doing their horoscopes then. You see after [Reagan] got elected, I sort of dropped the whole thing. I'd done it as a volunteer and I figured my work was done. The minute [the assassination attempt] happened, I looked at his chart of course, and realized I could have foretold it. Then Nancy called me and asked me about it and I said, 'I'm terribly sorry because, had I been looking, I would have warned you'. Then she asked me if I would do both their horoscopes."

From that point on, Joan Quigley stopped being a volunteer. Now she was getting paid for her White House predictions. I wanted to know if it would be too tacky to ask how much she got paid. When she bluntly said, "Yes it would," I deftly changed topics and asked her if she ever actually met the President in person.

"Yes, I did, at a state dinner in Washington in 1985. After dinner he came over to me and spoke to me and said he felt that God had chosen him for a mission in life. Another time I had written him a letter describing for him what I felt his mission was. I mentioned that the three greatest American presidents were Aquarians: Lincoln, FDR and

Reagan. I said that Lincoln's mission had been to get rid of slavery and Reagan's was to get rid of war. I signed the letter 'Your Astrologer,' and the minute the President had received it, Nancy got on the phone and put him on, and he thanked me and said, 'God bless you.'"

But those heady days were not to last. When Donald Regan let the cat out of the bag and the world found out about the Oval Office and its on-call astrologer, the jig was up. That odd arrangement simply could not survive the glare of public scrutiny and the ridicule that followed. And according to Joan Quigley, none of it was her fault.

"I, of course, kept my silence for seven years and would have to this day but [after] Donald Regan's book, Nancy sort of swept the whole thing under the carpet by saying she had consulted me because she was superstitious. Well, Nancy's a highly intelligent lady and if I hadn't proved reliable and solved problems I don't think she'd have kept me on for ten minutes. My predictions have a record of great success. I predicted the Iran-Iraq War. I predicted that Farrah Fawcett would get a divorce when everyone was saying she wouldn't. I mean, I know what I'm doing! I have a talent for it, and a lot of experience, and I felt both of them [Donald Regan and the First Lady] had given astrology a black eye."

Sadly, Joan Quigley's years of loyal service to the First Family ended when she went public. When the world found out that White House policy was being determined in a crystal ball, Nancy Reagan, in her typical fashion, dropped her friend and advisor like a hot potato.

As I said, I'm *really* looking forward to Nancy Reagan's box shot.

EPILOGUE

L ET'S FACE it, this book is one huge pack o' lies, and if you've ploughed through it to here, you'll probably be looking forward to *my* box shot by now. But you really only have yourself to blame if you feel cheated or ripped off. What did you expect from a book by a minimally talented tabloid reporter? Like Popeye the Sailor Man, I yam what I yam—a cheap hack who never expected to make it past the first week of being on national radio, much less fifteen years of this mind-numbing drivel. Let's face it, it's these thoughts that keep me humble.

No one's more surprised than I to see this huge pile of food-stained pages lying next to my trusty computer, ready for someone to turn into this book. Of course, I've done a whole lot more stuff on the radio than I could usefully jam in here, but I have tried to give you folks who paid for this book some of the best and weirdest things I've done—and if you've borrowed this from the library, go and buy your own copy, you cheapskate!

And even though these stories have been served up again like yesterday's meatloaf, I have tried to spice things up for your entertainment and edification, tried to make the stories I've covered sparkle and shine anew. So if you want any more of this fare, you'll just have to wait and see if I have the energy to generate another book based on the stuff I *didn't* use here, or the stories I haven't even done yet.

Like I say, I avoid disappointments in life because I *always* expect to be fired next Thursday, fifteen minutes before quitting time, so it's really up to *you*, gentle reader, whether I continue to have a job here or not.